THE
UFOBIAN

KCBRYANT

for Nelda

too far away to touch
but still, so very close

excerpt dialog – Selby interrogation – July 17, 1967

"It was a thing, I dunno, a giant thing that come crawlin' up outta the desert. Like one a them big whales trying to climb up outta water, see? Or a submarine, yeah, that's what it was like, a submarine. Coming right up outta the ground. A land submarine!"

(long pause)

"I ain't crazy."

The UFOBIAN

The UFOBIAN

Chapters page 2

1 The Grotto Ingling

Spylgyn was running on all four appendages. Though it was not a natural movement to the Ingling, it gave him speed and he was anxious to get to his final destination overlooking the black runway that stretched across the desert. Only rarely did he stop for reconnaissance, since the orb did that work for him. The device traveled directly over Spylgyn, usually kept a distance of 25 feet high but sometimes would dip or elevate when an unknown entity needed clarification to assess danger or intent. Data and images were not constantly relayed to the Ingling since it was rare to encounter any hazard that would need his immediate attention. However, the orb suddenly sent a declarant – stop motion, assess situation. Spylgyn quickly dropped to the ground, curled into a ball and became motionless. In this defensive position, he hoped that he would be mistaken as a simple rock embedded in the soil and of no interest or concern to anything that passed close by.

Spylgyn absorbed the images sent by the orb and waited for further information. The orb produced a pictoric scan of the desert with a sound byte of a peculiar scratchy noise that was probable movements by the threat that had been located. Spylgyn relayed an order to disengage and proceed for closer inspection of the cause. As the orb rapidly moved in an easterly direction, telepathic images began to lose clarity and definition caused by the abrupt speed and distance of the tracker. In only seconds, the orb had flown 1.27 km and initiated a suspended hover a short distance from the reptile that allowed a clear view for Spylgn to assess.

Monster was the first thought that popped into Spylgyn's head. It was a lizard-like crawler with an ugly snout and a rough and bumpy external. Its black shape stood out well in contrast from the light-colored dirt that it stood upon. Like the cavernite still crouched in the gully, the reptile had also become very still, most likely because it had seen the orb hovering above the desert. Most creatures usually did not see the recon device with its reflective surface but as the orb circled around, the monster's eyes clearly followed the slow movement of the intruder but did not appear combative, just curious or wary. The orb silently altered station to allow multiple angles. Images were then sent to Spylgyn for viewing. Without warning, the lizard suddenly attacked, displaying a definite aggressive nature. The orb retreated easily to a safe distance. Then, it reduced itself to the size of a baseball and, with a speed that made it almost invisible, shot forward and rammed into the monster's snout. The creature reacted with shock and quickly scurried away into the shelter of a small outcrop of stones.

The orb remained watching for 2.9 minutes, then sent the assessment results

- Identify – surface reptile
- Size – 56.27 cm
- Weight – 2.18 kg
- Threat assessment – extreme danger
- Solution – avoid, change direction, 11.7° oblique →

Spylgn knew that a confrontation with such a clawed creature could cause serious damage in a conflict. Spylgyn sprang up and began running in the suggested direction. It would take him a bit longer to reach his destination but safety took priority. Battle with any desert creature was never a good idea and, in fact, avoidance was one of the prime directives of cavern law.

The orb resumed position over Spylgyn and soon indicated that the danger had been reduced to 0.0. Apparently, the monster had decided to go in a different direction as well but the Ingling kept a fast pace anyway. The orb reported that three flying creatures were in the quad but not assessed as threats yet. A large cactus was near and Spylgyn altered direction to hide in its shadow.

The shade was comforting for Spylgyn because he didn't feel so exposed like he did on open desert. The sun was not yet high in the sky but it was going to get much hotter before he reached destination. Direct exposure for too long would be enough to cause severe burn to exposed skin if he did not shelter in shade occasionally.

He took this rest period to check his small supply of provisions. Consumption had been minimal since jump. Water volume was still at 88 percent and food source was untouched. Although Spylgyn wasn't hungry, he knew that he should eat now while resting. There may not be an opportunity later.

He had not seen either of his crew since they separated and began to wonder about their journey to the black runway. G'Thorp was experienced and would probably be at location before him. No problem there. But, Spylgyn had some concerns about Neela. This was her first day-outing and she just seemed too confident and dismissive of the dangers. Of course, the other orbs would have relayed any threats to his own companion if any had been encountered by them. And they had probably been notified of his proximity to the clawed reptile and eventual escape to safety.

Spylgyn queried the orb, "Location request – Neela".

"Direction – 7.21°, distance 1.1 km," replied the orb.

"She was ahead of him! How could that be? She's not being cautious," he reasoned.

Safety was always a factor on expeditions and Spylgyn was determined that the orb should disengage with him and provide added surveillance for Neela who was being reckless. It was unusual for the primary orb to break contact with the team leader but Spylgyn gave the command for the orb to reposition directly over Neela and provide assistance to her until Spylgn could overtake her.

He swallowed a mouthful of feed, took another sip of water then he began to run again.

2 The Lost Gas Station

"Dust debil," whispered Alice. She had tried not to say it but the words just popped out. Her brother said nothing in response, so maybe he hadn't heard her. "That would be good," she thought. The last time he had spoken, she heard his angry voice, low and growly, which meant to leave him alone.

Alice understood that he no longer wanted to play the counting games but there just wasn't anything else to do. Her backseat domain had lost all charm and had become quite boring miles and miles ago. She had been staring out the window for the longest time, it seemed. She couldn't count the billboards anymore because they had vanished. "Lots and lots of cactus," she thought, "but way too many to count."

She decided to name the dust devil 'Oh Fred Behave' but didn't say the name out loud. She could keep secrets just like her irritating brother.

"Mommy, can you turn air con on now? I'm hot again," Alice blurted out.

Jenny was hot too... and scared. She didn't want to look at the temp gauge again, as if that would somehow keep the needle from edging toward the red.

"Weren't they any damned gas stations along this stretch of road? Or a house... anything?" she wondered.

Jenny would stop anywhere now, even honk at a passing car if there was one and knew that desperation was again grabbing hold of her as it often had in the past few months. She knew that if she took a hand away from the steering wheel, it would be shaking, just like her left leg had done some miles back. More frequently than she would admit, Jenny had begun to shift her body slightly in an attempt to stifle the panic that coiled within her.

"Just a little farther, baby, then we'll be okay," she replied to her daughter.

She glanced over at Bobby to see if he had heard the tremble in her voice but he was still looking at the map and hadn't seemed to notice or, if he did, was keeping it to himself.

"I don't hafta go, Mommy, I'm holdin' it," Alice said.

Jenny glanced in the rearview mirror but saw no cars behind her, just that damned U–Haul trailer following like some wraith chasing them across the desert. That was a mistake, she knew that now. One of many choices that turned out to be wrong. She should have left everything behind, just put themselves on a bus and be gone, away from it all.

"Just junk anyway," she said.

Her fingers were at her lips now, as if they could take back the words that she had so quietly uttered. She was very surprised that she hadn't screamed.

"I need to go. Is that alright with you guys?" Jenny remarked. "Isn't there anything up ahead, Bobby? I mean this road has got to have something, a gas station somewhere, doesn't it?"

Now, Bobby was looking at her. She tried to smile at him but only felt her lips oddly twitching in response.

"What, honey?" she asked.

"There's some kinda road ahead, I think. Shouldn't be too far. On the right," Bobby replied.

"About time," Jenny said with relief. "I was beginning to think this road would never..." She took a deep breath, felt the tears coming and only just managed to keep them from spilling onto her cheeks.

"I shouldn't have left the Interstate," Jenny whispered. Then, in the distance she saw a shape rising upward out of the flat desert.

It had been a gas station at one time but now it was just an abandoned structure, silently surrounded by miles and miles of sand, cactus and scrub brush. How many years ago, Jenny didn't care. Just the fact that someone had built it, and now it existed, overwhelmed her. She turned the car into the entrance and coasted underneath the triangular roof that jutted away from the building. She pressed the brake too hard as they entered the shade, jolting all of them just a little bit.

"Sorry," Jenny said, then switched the key off. "Thank goodness, we don't need gas."

The gas pumps obviously had been useful to someone, because they were gone.

"Honk the horn," Alice cheerfully offered.

Bobby didn't look at her but replied, "there's nobody here, ug-butt."

"Don't call me that. You're so nasty." Alice made an ugly face at him but not before she knew her brother wasn't looking.

"We'll just let the engine cool off a little bit," Jenny said, not moving, "then, we'll go on."

Bobby was the first to get out of the car. Pausing only briefly to stretch away the irritable kinks of confinement, he walked over to the building to look inside. A shaft of sunlight pierced through a broken window near the battered door and Bobby could see a flurry of dust particles floating in the radiance inside. The service counter with shelves below still held cans of oil and other car supplies as if the owner had just decided to walk away one day and leave everything behind. There was a calendar on the wall behind the counter with a picture of a bikini girl holding a mechanic's tool and smiling at him.

"Bobby, don't go in there," his mother cautioned.

"I'm just looking," he shouted in reply, though he had been about to step inside, curious about what was left behind. He knew there were things in there that needed to be discovered. Reluctantly, Bobby turned around and walked away.

Jenny had the hood up and was looking forlornly at the tired old engine. "You've seen better days, I know," she said softly, "but I need you to make your last best effort to get us to Inyo."

"Did you say something?" asked Bobby as he walked up beside her.

"Just talking to myself," Jenny replied, hoping he hadn't heard the plea.

"That engine is cooked," Bobby said as they both stared at the oily, stinking mess.

"Just the radiator," Jenny hoped. "It needs to cool down and then we can go on."

"Probably needs water," her son replied. "There's got to be some around here somewhere."

Jenny turned away from the disappointing engine and planted her butt on the fender.

"This is such a terrible place. So desolate... and sad. Why in the world would anybody build a gas station so far from anywhere at all?" she asked, more to herself than Bobby. He just shrugged his shoulders, 'don't know'.

When Jenny opened the 'Ladies' Room' door of the gas station, she knew that people had been there but how long ago she could not even guess. Not recently anyway. The stench wasn't horribly bad but it did smell of something tainted – an odor of rotten fruit that had been boiled in dirty engine oil, maybe. She looked at the toilet and shook her head. "No way in hell," Jenny thought. She was just going to squat and pee on the tile floor. She removed some tissue from her purse and began to unbuckle her jeans, a queer smile on her face as she realized just what she was about to do. "Don't anybody take a picture," she sighed.

Bobby had already looked in the men's toilet hoping to find a water source but there was none. It was as dry as the desert outside. The back of the building was not promising either. There were some oil drums, a broken ladder, a pile of abandoned tires and lots of other junk – worthless stuff that you would expect to find in a place like this, but no convenient bucket full of water. Whatever moisture fell from the sky as rain was probably sucked up by the brutal sun as quickly as it hit ground, he imagined. Just going to have to go inside the place, maybe there was something in there. It's not like he had any other choice really.

He returned to the bathroom doors to announce his intentions. "Mom, nothing out back. I'm going to look inside the place, see if I can find some water," Bobby said in a not very loud voice. He didn't wait for an answer. Maybe she heard him, maybe she didn't and he quickly walked away before his mother could say no.

Bobby didn't have to risk going in through the broken window with the shards of glass that might cut him up.

With some hefty shoving, the front door opened enough for him to sidle on through. It was darker than he expected inside and Bobby waited patiently for his eyes to adjust. He didn't want to step on a rusty nail or plant his feet in anything nasty. Crude oil was the only odor that he could really smell but there was a dry, dead feeling to the room that made him want to turn around and just forget all about searching the place. The floor was caked with a thick layer of dust and sand, "most likely blown in through the window by desert winds," Bobby thought. And there were so many small tracks in the dust, going this way and that, as if some animal had somehow gotten inside and then couldn't figure out how to get back out. He grabbed a worn out broom that had been left behind just in case he had to fight a trapped animal if it was still in there.

Jenny came out of the women's toilet, hoping that she never had to do that again in her lifetime. She closed the door behind her out of courtesy for the next unfortunate soul that had to use the facilities. She hoped it wouldn't be anytime soon so that the tile floor could have some time to dry out.

As she rounded the corner to the front, Jenny stopped and took a few moments to look at her unfortunate caravan. "If only the car could talk to me, tell me what to do," she thought.

"I hate you for doing this to me, that's what the car would say," Jenny said. "Well, I hate you right back, you goddamn beast! Why are you doing this to us? Just suck it up and do your damn job!" Okay, misery gone. Anger had replaced it.

"Bobby?" she shouted to the desert.

Then, an uncanny feeling suddenly spread through her body and she stiffened not unlike a soldier coming to attention. Jenny had a sudden image invade her mind's eye – the scythe that Death carried with him had just swooshed by her head, missing only by inches. Something was very wrong and she began to panic. But, what was it? She quickly looked around but could see no threat.

"Alice?" she shouted.

She ran to the car and looked inside. No, Alice was not in there. The rear door on the other side of the car was open. Alice had a peculiar habit of not closing doors. Car doors, cabinets, bathroom doors, it didn't matter. Like the kid thought that doors should just automatically close by themselves. Jenny scanned the road first but saw nothing but emptiness. "Where's my daughter, dammit?" she wanted to shout.

"Bobby! Bobby!" Jenny screamed.

As usual, Alice took her carry-all bag with her when she went into the desert. It was empty now because all her stuffed animals and dolls were still asleep on the car seat, except Jim-Jim who was still hiding from her. He had probably crawled under Bobby's seat and was waiting for her to find him. But she didn't have time for that right now because of what she saw in the desert.

Alice had wandered off because she thought she saw a balloon floating above a cactus but it was moving funny, not like a balloon at all. It was sort of round and shiny like the Get Well Soon balloons at the Dollar Store but it seemed to be dancing. The balloon moved slowly at first, then it would swirl away and go on to another cactus, then go high — very, very high until it almost disappeared in the blue sky.

"Almost like it was alive," Alice thought.

What if it's a fairy or lots of fairies dancing and their special glow only made them look like a balloon. It was not far, well maybe far but she wanted to see them up close. So Alice went into the desert, chasing fairies just like any little girl would do if they were fairy-lovers like she was.

The door to the gas station was not open enough for Jenny to squeeze through, so she balled a fist and began banging on it in frustration.

"Bobby!" she screamed. "Where are you?"

And then he was there, just inside the opening.

"What?' he said.

"I can't find Alice. She's just gone!"

Alice could not see the fairies anymore. They were too high in the sky. She was worried that they might have seen her chasing them and flew far away and, if that was so, she might never see them again. Or maybe it was the bird flying away that had scared them. She thought it must be a big bird like an eagle. Its wings were very long and it just looked like a strong bird to Alice. The bird was struggling to stay in the air, though, because it was carrying a big package, almost as big as the bird was. That package must be heavy, she thought. And then without warning, the bird stopped flying and it fell out of the sky. Not fast, though. It was trying to fly but its long wings must have gotten very tired because the bird just kind of floated down in a spiral until it disappeared some distance away. Alice thought that the bird might have been injured by the fall. So she went to rescue it.

"Mom, please calm down," said Bobby. "She can't have gotten that far."

Jenny had been running from one side of the gas station to the other shouting for Alice. Running around in circles like that, Bobby was becoming afraid that his mother would pass out in the desert heat. She was panicked, he understood that but what she was doing was not good, not good at all.

Bobby grabbed her as she passed close to him and held onto her even though she tried to break away from him.

"Mom. Stop," he pleaded with her. And when his mother looked directly into his eyes, Bobby was startled. She had a wide-eyed look on her face like a crazy person would have and that scared him.

"Maybe a car came by and abducted her. I wasn't watching. Somebody took her," Jenny wailed.

"No. No, Mom, that didn't happen." Bobby was trying to calm her down. "She's here, somewhere. We'll find her."

When Alice found the eagle, it was laying on its side but perky. Its head jerked from side to side as the bird watched her with what seemed like curiosity. The bird is probably just tired, Alice thought, and it was resting for a while until its strength came back. It didn't seem afraid of her, only curious about her arrival. As she walked closer, the eagle hopped up, spread its wings and quickly flew off, just like that. Alice watched the bird climb into the sky and continue the journey back to its nest.

At first, she didn't notice the fallen package laying on the ground nearby. It was a sudden movement that got her attention. It wasn't a package at all, she realized. It looked like a big, wet rock buried in the dirt, except the rock had arms and legs and a head.

Bobby stood the broken ladder up and braced it against the rear of the building.

"It will hold me, Mom," Bobby hoped. "It's strong wood and I don't weigh that much."

"You're going to fall and break a bone. Please don't do it," Jenny pleaded.

"I can see much farther if I'm on the roof. Yeah?" Bobby said. "I'll find her."

Jenny nodded. "Go," she said.

Bobby had to be mindful of the missing rungs but he easily climbed the ladder until he could step on the roof of the gas station. He looked down at his mother and waved a hand at her. "See. Easy," he said.

"Can you see anything? Alice?" Jenny asked.

Bobby first went over to the front side of the roof and, shielding his eyes from the bright sun, looked both ways on the roadway but could not see his sister in those directions and nothing past the road in the desert beyond. He stepped carefully around the edges of the roof, mindful that there could be rotten boards beneath his feet. Scanning west, then north, he looked into the bleak desert, hoping for any sign of Alice. He didn't see anything, nothing but sand, cactus and rocks. He went to the last side, to the east and again watched for any movement or color. He couldn't remember what shirt

Alice had on but it had to be pink, red or blue. She always wore bright colorful t-shirts, little girl shirts.

Today, it was bright red. Alice was in a north-easterly direction and she was walking back to the gas station. Bobby waved both of his arms wildly and hollered "Alice!" just as loud as he could. Then, he ran over to the back side and looked down at Jenny. "I see her, Mom." he shouted, "I see her."

Jenny collapsed to her knees and buried her face in her hands, crying.

Alice came out of the desert carrying her foundling and she was very pleased because this one wasn't like her other stuffed animals and dolls — it was still alive! This one would be special because Abernathy (Alice had already named it Abernathy) had flown with a bird high in the sky and might could be a very special gift from the fairies. Maybe they wanted her to find Abernathy and take him away to a safe place where he could stay with Florence, Debby with a y and Mindy-Sue, her other very special dolls.

Bobby looked angry when he came running up to her. Sometimes, she wished she had a better brother, one that wasn't so mean and always saying nasty things to her.

"Alice," he said with the angry voice, "come on." Bobby grabbed her by the arm and started pulling her away with him as they walked a fast pace back to the gas station. And when she got there Mommy hugged her so hard that Alice thought she was going to squash Abernathy who was quietly resting in the carry-all bag.

"Mommy?" said Alice.

"What, baby?" Jenny whispered.

"Too tight," Alice said.

Bobby found some water inside the gas station and filled the radiator up to the top. He was pretty certain that they would talk about this incident later on when his mom wasn't so distraught and so recently scared. But for now, the car was running smooth and there was only another

12 miles to go before they reached their destination – Inyo, Arizona.

3   The Girl on the Bike

Kelly Ablan usually woke up just before the alarm clock was set to go off. She didn't know why. She could go to bed at 9:30 pm or after midnight but she was always awake before the alarm was set to ring. Kelly thought that even in her sleep she might be unconsciously counting each second and every minute until it was time to wake up. Still, she always set the alarm the night before just in case.

She lay quietly still for almost two minutes while she tried to recall any dreams that were still fresh in her mind but there was nothing. Then, she glanced at the notepad that lay on her nightside table to see if it had any curious words or drawings snatched from last night's dreams. There was a scribbling that appeared to be a lop-sided 't' and a backwards 'c' but Kelly had no memory of what these symbols could mean or why she had written them down. Indeed, she could not remember dreaming at all last night which was unusual.

Kelly's nocturnal wanderings had become a source of curiosity to her after an incident of sleep-walking that had, at first, frightened her. She found herself wandering in the courtyard of the trailer park, laughing as if someone had just told her the world's funniest joke. Kelly couldn't recall a dream or leaving her bedroom but it had happened. After that, she was determined to remember any other incidents and document what her subconscious mind was doing to her while she was sleeping. Most of her dreams were lost as happens with most people but she learned that by writing a word or phrase, even a drawing, while still half-asleep that an entire sequence of an elusive dream could be recalled after coming awake. Sometimes this happened during the night but most often just after she woke up, not allowing any awake thoughts to come to her until she could remember a dream.

Frustrated that nothing came to her, she got out of bed, did a quick stretch to get the night kinks out, then some twisties and bed bounce-ups to get her blood pumping. Now, she was awake.

Like most mornings, Kelly had no chores. Summer was about half over so school was not even on her agenda yet. Time enough to worry about clothes and attitude once August had departed.

She picked up the worn socks lying on top of her sneakers and looked at them suspiciously. Yes, they looked stinky and probably smelled awful. She had worn them two days, maybe even three days, she couldn't remember. She wadded them up into a ball and tossed them into the corner where all the other dirty clothes went.

Quickly searching her bureau for socks, she could only find two clean ones, though mismatched – a gray one and a white one. She thought about retrieving the dirty socks so recently dismissed but then thought, "okay, so I'll just make a fashion statement today. People shouldn't be looking at my ankles anyway."

She dressed quickly but efficiently – top over, shorts up, odd socks today, then her old comfortable low riders and she was ready for patrol.

Kelly didn't need to creep out of the trailer. Her mother and Ronny 'the mechanic' were sound sleepers. Only the most god-awful noise would disturb their deep slumber, like that time the lot manager decided one morning to finally chain-saw the dead tree at the back edge of the trailer park. Now that had been a racket that would wake a deaf person.

Her bicycle was still hidden under the trailer behind the wood lattice just where she left it yesterday afternoon. Kelly would have parked it in plain view out front but, ever since the incident with the Bailey boy, she didn't trust anybody to handle her wheels or even know where the bike was stashed.

It seemed like no one was an early riser in the trailer park except her. The morning was still on the dark side as Kelly swooshed down the entry lane approaching county road 73. She sat on the brakes just enough to skid the rear wheel around, throwing stones and dirt onto the asphalt pavement in front of her.

Kelly looked once left and then right, not really expecting to see any cars but always mindful that a speeding car or truck could send her small body flying and she didn't want to be crippled or dead today.

She made the two miles to the railhead in good time and luck was with her. There was no train idle on the tracks while the engineers ran for coffee and biscuits at the diner. Poor guys would have had to stand in line this morning because the place was full up. Rheta didn't wave at Kelly like she usually did. "Too busy today," Kelly thought. Truk must be flipping sausage and eggs like a pro to keep up with that crowd. She shook her head in sympathy for the fat man impatiently waiting for his bacon and biscuits.

"Well, there was always time for coffee later," she thought. No real need to bother Rheta with a take-out order just now.

The police station was dark with no light coming from the side window. That meant Officer Posen was still napping, probably dreaming of high speed chases and bank robbery. "132 and Bush. I've got him at gunpoint," Kelly whispered. Okay, put him down on the calendar for later as well. Kelly passed Ronny's Auto Repair at a fast clip without even looking at the place and headed for the hidden trail that led up to the bluff just east of town.

At that high point, which she called Pete's Overlook, sometimes just Overlook, Kelly could see all that was happening on the desert landscape. And as usual, there was nothing, just the crumbling strip of black-top roadway that shot straight-away into No-Man's Land, running away toward Phoenix. But somewhere out there

24

in that direction 'Recovery', as she named it, happened more than 50 years ago.

Kelly didn't get off the bike and sit at the old sun-baked picnic table; she would have if she had coffee. She sat easy in the bike saddle, leaning forward with her elbows on the handle bars, fists holding her head up, eyes moving side to side as if stalking prey.

Kelly watched the sunrise climbing out of the Inyo desert forcing the dark shadows to seek shelter and hide lest they be burnt by the flames that would soon scorch the land.

She looked over to the pile of stones aimed at 'Recovery'. Shaped like a crude arrow in the dirt, only one stone was out of place but it was probably just a strong burst of desert wind that did that. Although, she reasoned, might have been be a jackrabbit or some other curious animal took offense at the unnatural cairn and attempted to bust it up. No one else came up here as far as she could tell. With a heavy sigh, she set the fallen stone back in its right position and stepped away to admire the structure and form of her organic design. Unconsciously, Kelly smiled in admiration at this small achievement that exposed her silent dedication to 'Recovery'.

"So, what to do now?" she thought. Ideas about how to make the coming day more fun or interesting were not coming to her. She was getting really tired of these sad days with nothing better to do than spit and hope for some kind of excitement to happen. She wanted a discovery, an incident, something of note to enhance the coming day. An unscheduled meeting with the boys at the Bureau might be necessary. "Sure, why not," she said aloud. It was always a good day when she had someone to argue with.

Cruising back toward town, Kelly passed by Uncle's house. It was the medium size U–Haul in the driveway that got her attention. An unexpected arrival might be something that could improve her situation today. She stopped at the edge of the front yard to get a better look at the travelers.

A beat up old Mazda was hitched to the U–Haul trailer. The open doors revealed a partially unloaded cargo but she couldn't see anything of real value inside. Just regular old junk was what she thought.

Uncle had visitors just about every day, always local people who needed the old man to do something for them. Some had building projects that they needed advice on or his involvement if they were really clueless. Quite a few of them just wanted to borrow some of Uncle's tools. Everyone in town knew that he had the knowledge and the tools to construct anything out of wood, concrete or iron, no matter what the job.

But, these new arrivals would likely be strangers and they came with furniture and household items. Kelly couldn't help but wonder at their intentions. Considering that the trailer was being unloaded, it would seem that the strangers might be staying for a while with no urgent plans to hurry on to some other destination anytime soon.

A little girl with brown double-knot ponytails was sitting on the front porch swing and she was scrutinizing Kelly in a peculiar way, like the little girl couldn't decide if Kelly was worth talking to or not.

"What's your name?" Kelly asked, as she pedaled closer to the porch.

"Alice," the little girl said, then "what's yours?"

"My name is Kelly. Do you belong to Uncle?" Kelly asked.

"He's my grand-daddy. My momma is his daughter," Alice offered. "We are just visiting but maybe we'll stay a long, long time. That's what my brother says anyway. But, you should know that he is stupid and very mean to me."

"Well, I am really sorry about that, Alice. Do you want me to beat him up?" Kelly said smiling.

"Can you do that? I can be grateful." Alice smiled and pointed to the front door. "He's inside."

Kelly didn't knock on the screen door, just opened it and went into the house. The aroma of strong coffee hit her nose like a fist and she strode down the long hall to the kitchen without delay.

Uncle was sitting at the small kitchen table with a wispy-haired woman who might be pretty, Kelly thought but it was hard to tell because her eyes were all puffy red like she had been wailing miserably recently. The woman was dressed in a fluffy pink nightrobe with no make-up on and her hair looked like some squirrels had been fighting in it earlier that morning.

"Mornin', Kelly," Uncle said. "Little early in the day to be paying rent, isn't it?"

"Rents not due yet. I came for coffee," Kelly said. "I could smell it all the way out in the street as I was passing by."

Uncle pointed to the pot on the stove. "Oh hell," thought Kelly, "cowboy coffee." She grabbed a large mug from the kitchen shelf, filled it with black coffee, then sat down at the table with Uncle and the distraught woman.

"This is Kelly," Uncle said to Jenny. "And this is my daughter, Jenny." Kelly just nodded amicably, then took a large sip of the hot coffee.

"She and my grandkids have come out here to stay with me for a while," Uncle explained. "You're to keep that under your hat for the time being, Kelly, understand?"

"I don't have a hat," Kelly replied.

"Plenty in the front room, take any one you want on your way out," Uncle challenged her. Kelly and Uncle gave each other the death stare, like two gunfighters sitting across a poker table, each one waiting for the other to slap leather or back down.

Kelly sipped her coffee and waited. Uncle finally said. "How are things down at the spa? All good, no problems?"

"It's all good," Kelly said.

"So, did you just come for coffee?" Uncle asked.

"Actually, I'm here to put a beating on your grandson," Kelly calmly confessed. "I've been charged."

"What?" said Jenny.

"Okay, so the lady has a voice," Kelly thought.

"Beat up my son, what are you talking about?" Jenny blurted out.

"Oh snap," Kelly thought, this woman is gonna start bawling any minute now. Anyone could tell by the shaky voice and wide open wet eyes that stared astonishingly at her and Uncle.

"Little girl out front named Alice, she told me it needed to be done," Kelly admitted.

"You can just set that aside for some other day, Kelly," Uncle said. "I expect you got other trouble you can get into right about now, isn't that right?"

"Uhm, yes," Kelly admitted. "Ma'am, I was just joking about your kid. But you should know that Alice wasn't," Kelly said to Jenny as she got up to leave.

"Is it okay to powder up before I go?" Kelly asked.

"Just remember to flush this time," Uncle said.

"I always flush," muttered Kelly as she walked away.

Kelly heard Uncle say to Jenny, "she can be a bit of a rascal at times, but a good kid all the same," but couldn't make out what came after.

Kelly took the stairs two at a time almost like she was in a hurry. Actually, she didn't need to go to the bathroom. She was hoping to get a look at this boy that she was supposed to fight. She looked in open doors on the upper floor but saw no sign of him. The last door before the bathroom was Uncle's bedroom. The door was closed but she opened it anyway and stepped inside – empty. Maybe the boy had heard the contract between Kelly and Alice and was hiding from her.

Uncle's fish tank was on a riser in the far corner of the bedroom next to the window. She walked over to it, curious to see if Uncle had added any new fish and she really wanted to see the octopus that she only got a glimpse of last time. She wondered why he didn't get any more colorful or playful fish. The tank was huge but there were not enough inhabitants. It just wasn't crowded enough for Kelly. "Too sedate," she thought. Then she noticed an odd movement at the bottom back corner of the tank.

"What is that?" she said aloud.

The shape of the creature seemed to be oddly fluid, somewhat like one of those tiny deep ocean squids but she didn't see any tentacles on it. It was almost invisible as it sat close behind a mound of rocks and plants. It was undulating, floating upward then settling softly back down to the bottom again – almost like it was a liquid blob but much denser than the water in the tank. Then, she noticed that it was spotted with markings that seemed to change shade, texture and color as the creature slowly moved about. Now the spots were orange, then they faded to almost invisible and back again as pale blue.

Kelly edged around the tank to get a closer look. She wedged her body between the wall and the tank and put her face right up to the glass to see better. And the creature suddenly looked back at her, startling green eyes stared at her, got larger and blinked. Though she didn't know it, Kelly's mouth fell open. She gasped as the creature slowly raised an arm toward her as if to say, "Hey it's me, who are you?"

"Who are you?" came a voice from behind her.

Kelly hadn't heard Bobby come into the room. She quickly came out from behind the fish tank, rather awkwardly unfortunately. "Not a good first impression," she thought.

"You shouldn't be wandering around people's houses without permission," Bobby stated with some authority.

"Uncle knows me. He doesn't care if I wander," Kelly responded. "You would be the grandson," all the time thinking, "yeah, I could take him easy."

Bobby was blocking the entry door, staring intently, almost as if he was planning a way to capture the intruder. Kelly strode right up to him, ready for a confrontation. "Bathroom," she said as a challenge. "Do you mind?"

Bobby stepped out of the way and Kelly walked past him without another glance but she knew he was still watching her as she opened the bathroom door and went inside.

Kelly sat on the toilet, lid closed, and pondered her next move. She had to admit the boy was kind of cute but not overly handsome. Maybe he would muscle out as he got older. And he would if he became a boyfriend, she'd make sure of that. Kelly wanted a big man to hold her tight and to be strong just as she was wise. Then, she slowly stood up and looked at her reflection in the mirror.

Kelly knew that she was moderately attractive but, unfortunately, had not made any effort to enhance her appearance today. She wished that she had at least showered, brushed her hair, lip gloss – made herself somewhat presentable for unexpected encounters like this one.

"Not much I can do about that now," she silently complained.

After she flushed, Kelly stepped out to find the hallway deserted. The boy was gone, ran way, she surmised. No guts, that was not a good trait for a guy that she considered might be a potential boyfriend.

Kelly wanted another quick look at the creature in the fish tank before she had to leave. She was going so fast that she didn't notice the puddle of water on the floor just inside Uncle's bedroom door. As soon as her foot hit the wet spot, she slipped and fell so fast and hard that Kelly didn't even have time to scream or grab at the bed or anything to cushion the impact. Her head hit the hardwood floor with a solid thump that rattled her brain. Kelly just lay there, not even struggling. She closed her eyes but that only made the dizziness worse. Feeling the hurt, Kelly rolled onto her side and put a hand to the back of her head where there was a large bump forming. She opened her eyes and focus began to come back slowly. She could see that there was someone near and they seemed to be waving at her. She closed her eyes for a few moments. "Dizzy still," she thought, "but never mind". Kelly opened her eyes wide and looked at the blurry figure under the bed.

It was not a someone, just a tiny creature, standing motionless just a few feet from her hiding in the

30

shadows. And then it hop-stepped closer and reached one arm toward Kelly as if to say, "hey, it's me again. Are you okay?"

Kelly giggled then, because it was so unreal for this to be happening. Then she began to cry because the pain in her head was so intense that she thought she might be dying. Kelly reached out to the creature and it bothered her that her hand was shaking so badly. She didn't want to frighten it away.

"I'm scared," Kelly whispered and then she blacked out.

4   What The Doctor Said

Kelly woke up on the way to the medical clinic. The way her head was turned, she could see Uncle driving his truck. He had such a confused and intense look on his face that Kelly wanted to laugh but then decided not to. He might get mad.

He was talking in a low voice to someone, not her. Kelly tried to twist her head a little to see what was happening but couldn't move much because someone was gripping her head and holding tight. Then, Kelly saw that it was the almost crying lady. She could feel that she was lying down and the lady was cradling Kelly in her lap. The lady, what was her name? Kelly couldn't remember.

The lady was talking to her and smiling. The sound of her voice seemed to be far away, too far to make out what she was saying. But the soft musical tones of her voice was very soothing to Kelly, so she closed her eyes and went back to sleep.

When she woke up next, it was because of the pain. There was a man standing over her and he was grinding his fist into her chest. Kelly wanted to tell him to quit it but couldn't because her teeth were clenched tightly together and she couldn't seem to open her mouth. However, the noises she made, like an angry ape grunting someone told her later, and the distressed look on her face got the man's attention and he stopped almost immediately.

"Stop it," she finally managed to say, "that hurts."

"I'm sorry, honey but I need you to stay awake," he told her.

At first Kelly didn't know where she was. Looking around the room helped. She saw the medical equipment and a nurse standing close behind the doctor. On the other side of the room was Uncle and his daughter.

"Jenny," Kelly said softly and smiled at her.

And of course, Jenny started crying.

"Don't cry, Jenny," Kelly said to her. "Everything is going to be alright."

Uncle came closer and brushed the hair away from Kelly's face. His touch was so tender for such a big, burly man.

"I'm sorry, Uncle," she said. "I fell down."

"Yes, child, you fell down. Gave me a fright, I don't mind tellin' you."

Uncle looked at her with what could only be described as genuine affection. He had never looked at her that way before, like someone who really cared about her.

"I'm okay now," Kelly said. She looked at the doctor. "Really, I'm okay," even though she knew she wasn't. Her head really hurt bad and she couldn't seem to focus.

There was some chatter going on between the doctor, Uncle and the nurse after that. Kelly couldn't follow all of the conversation. She didn't want to admit that she was still a little dizzy and confused but she did hear something about keeping her at the clinic for a few more hours.

"Just for observation," said someone, probably the doctor.

Kelly had a really big bump on the back of her head that hurt when she pushed on it. The doctor was talking again saying things like "concussion, brain scan" and "long term effects, MRI something something."

By the time her mother got to the clinic, Kelly really was feeling much better. Ronny 'the mechanic' was busy repairing cars, she supposed, because he didn't show up but that was okay with Kelly. He wasn't the kind of guy to make a fuss over a bump on the head anyway.

When she was finally released from the clinic, Uncle was standing just outside the exit doors and as Kelly walked out, Uncle came at her. At first, she thought that he might be going to scold her for being so clumsy at his house but then he stopped right in front of her and grabbed Kelly with his big, beefy arms. And that was quite a surprise for her.

"I'll be damned," she thought, "the big guy is hugging me."

That's something that he had never done before either.

Kelly thought that being this close to Uncle, he would smell of stink and sweat but he didn't. He had a peculiar but pleasant, odor that reminded her of his work shed with the earthy wood smells and coffee.

Without realizing it, Kelly had reached around the big man and hugged Uncle back and she didn't want to let go.

As she was riding away with her mother, Kelly looked back at Uncle, standing alone in the parking lot, watching her leave. And then, she realized why. He was waiting for her to go before he went inside to pay the doctor's bill. Whether Uncle had offered or her mother had threatened, Kelly didn't know.

5   Uncle Hunkle

His true name was Jacob Aaron Hunkle but only a few people knew him by that identity now. Most folks just called him Uncle. When he was a young man, he answered to the name of Jake or Hey Hunkle. Some damn fool, probably drunk at the time or thinking it was funny, just called out Uncle to him at a party or a picnic, he couldn't remember where or who but that was of little matter. Somehow, someway, that's what everybody started calling him. He became Inyo's official Uncle.

There were a few people that knew him by other names. Jenny called him Daddy. Bobby preferred Grampa and to little Alice he was Gumpa, though he was fairly certain as she got older that she would choose a more proper name whereby a young lady could address her favorite grandfather. But, he secretly hoped not. It was a funny name, Gumpa, and he didn't want to lose it.

After Kelly's accident, Uncle had come back to the house and went directly to his bedroom. He had noticed when he picked her up from the floor that her clothes had been wet but he didn't know why. There had been just no time to investigate. Uncle thought Kelly might have had a seizure in the truck on the way to the medical clinic but if it had been, it was only a mild one. And the doctor had promised him that Kelly was going to be fine, probably. But Uncle was still a worried man.

Uncle really did care for the teenager, even though they sometimes seemed to have a confrontational relationship. Kelly was smart and witty and he enjoyed her company when she came to pay the rent on the spa and other times if they happened to run into each other. It was with some regret that he didn't see her more often because he liked sparring with her on matters of importance or no importance at all. She could tell a good joke, too, when she was in a playful mood.

No matter how hard he looked, Uncle could find no evidence at all in the bedroom, not a single wet spot and no water dripping from a crack in the fish tank. Bobby had told him that Kelly had been looking at the fish when he discovered her 'wandering around the house' as he put it.

He would have liked to send the girl to Phoenix for a proper study of her head injury but Mrs. Ablan absolutely refused.

"Just a bump on the head," she said in a sharp tone when he suggested it.

Uncle didn't like Mrs. Ablan very much, now that he thought about it. He hadn't had occasion to be in her company very often but, It seemed that every time he did see her, the woman was angry, upset or complaining about something. And that made it really quite amazing that Kelly managed to develop such a marvelous spirit under the guidance of a person like that.

"Daddy, are you okay?" Jenny asked.

Uncle didn't know how long Jenny had been standing at the doorway looking at him. He hoped he didn't look too forlorn, even though that was how he was feeling at the moment.

"Just thinkin', hon," and he smiled at her.

"Pops, it was an accident. She slipped and fell. Nobody's fault," she added.

"Pops?" he said to her. "I haven't heard that one since you were a teenager."

And he went on to explain. "I've just been thinking about all the names that people have called me over the years. It's a bunch." He got up from the bed and walked up to her and quite unexpectedly hugged her. Then he pulled away and looked her in the eye.

"I set aside 'asshole'. I'm trying to forget that one," he told her.

"I was an angry child, Daddy," Jenny smiled sheepishly at her father. "It didn't mean nothin'."

"You're my babe," he replied. "Don't forget that."

"Never," she promised.

Later that afternoon, Uncle was doing a tune-up on Kelly's bicycle. It really didn't need much work; she kept it in fairly decent shape. It was just that he wanted to do something for the girl and this was the only thing he could think of. The tires were in good condition with more than adequate tread, proper air pressure and all. He did find a few loose spokes and tightened them up. There was a small dent in the chain guard, so he took that off and gave it a few soft hits with the hammer and managed to straighten it out without losing any paint. He oiled the chain before he put the guard back on. Uncle knew that Kelly wouldn't take kindly to much more than that. She was independent and usually declined any favors from him.

When she came to him and wanted to rent the old abandoned spa, he said that she could use it for free. But no, Kelly insisted that there must be some kind of rent payment or she would find some other place for club meetings. After much haggling, Uncle stated that the price was $125 a month, utilities included, take it or leave it. Kelly shook her head as if ready to turn down the offer but then she smiled at him and said, "eh, okay." She had never been late with rent since she and the gang had moved in and Uncle was content to be an absentee landlord.

Uncle sat down on the work bench and he thought about his life before today, so many things that had happened to him over the years. With all the good and bad of it, he likened that he didn't really regret too much and was remarkably happy about most of it. He caught himself smiling once or twice about pleasant memories that amused him but there was always some sadness in a person's life, too. As one remembrance led him into another, time seemed to fade away. Uncle might have slid into a light slumber for a while. That had been happening more often recently and, before he knew it, he was sitting in near dark with deep shadows crowding the corners of the work shed. The afternoon was gone and he sat up straighter, wondering how it had gotten to be so late.

"Damn," he cursed himself. He needed to be inside the house with Jenny and the kids. They were going through a tough time right now, what with the move and all and he felt like he was being a neglectful old fool.

As he walked across the back lawn to the house, Uncle could smell the aroma of hot food drifting on the wind. Jenny was cooking supper and it could only be fried chicken, biscuits and gravy. Uncle then realized how so very hungry he was and he quickened his pace. If he had been a dog, he would have been drooling.

6 Albino Dreams

Kelly dreamed that night after the accident but when she first woke up, she sensed the dream fading away fast as she lay in bed waiting for the alarm. Remaining still, she closed her eyes and willed herself to find the dream. And it did come back to her – just a short clip though. It played out like an old-time silent movie. There were even frame jumps and scratches on the film as if it was old stock that was worn out from being seen too many times.

Kelly was standing in a damp locker room with concrete floors and dirty shower tiles on the walls. She was being forced to listen to an old hag of a teacher scolding her, stomping away, then coming back so close that Kelly could see her crooked teeth and the prickly hairs on her chin. She didn't know why the woman was so angry; maybe Kelly had forgotten her homework that day or came in late to class. The bitter matron was pointing a ruler at Kelly's face and she thought that the teacher was going to smack her with it eventually.

The teacher's mouth was opening and closing as if she was talking to her but there were no sounds coming out. Kelly wanted to go away to find someone else that could tell her what was happening but her shoes seemed to be glued to the floor and she couldn't move her feet.

And, that was all she could recall. "Well, that's not much of a dream," Kelly thought as she opened her eyes again. She was not even going to try to untangle the threads of that one. There just wasn't anything interesting enough about it.

Kelly sat up and dangled her feet over the edge of the bed. She felt for the bump at the back of her head. It was still there, maybe not as big this morning. It still hurt to push on it though.

Then, Kelly remembered the note pad that sat on her dresser by the bed. Kelly didn't remember waking up during the night to write any thoughts but there was a single word written on the page and some squiggles below that she couldn't make out. The one word snapped the dream zone in her brain and she recalled with some clarity what had been, just moments before, lost. The word was 'albino'.

Kelly was in the desert just walking down an old deserted roadway. It was a blistering hot day and she was searching for some shade where she could sit down and rest out of the heat. Then, she saw a man walking toward her in the distance. He was waving his arms up and down as if he were trying to attempt to fly. His skin was white as flour, every inch of it. She knew because he didn't have any clothes on.

They were walking toward each other but the distance seemed to remain the same like neither of them were making any progress on the road. Kelly had a sense that the man wanted to tell her something and it was important. So, she began to run. It only took moments for her to close the distance that set them apart and she stood right in front of the albino man. He was making movements with his mouth just like the teacher but again she could hear no sounds. Then, she looked at his eyes and could see that he was blind. So, how did he know she was there with him?

The albino man began to move his arms again and Kelly realized that he wasn't trying to fly. He was drowning and his arms were pumping up and down, splashing as if he was desperately trying to keep his head out of water. Kelly wanted to help him but didn't know exactly what to do. There wasn't any water, so he couldn't be drowning.

"How can a person drown in the desert?" she wondered.

Albino Man stopped the arm movements and looked down at Kelly with his empty, blind eyes. Now silent, not trying to say anything to her, he slowly shook his head from side to side and there was a sad smile on his ghostly white face. Albino Man looked away from Kelly and stared into the arid and desolate Inyo desert, so like a predator lying in wait for its prey. The strange man left her on the roadway there. He just calmly walked away into the desert and Kelly was distraught that he was leaving her. She felt like the man had abandoned her.

Kelly wanted to run after him, make him to stop but she had a terrible feeling that if she left the roadway, she might never find her way back again. Her body would blister and burn from the brutal heat and she would die in the wasteland without anyone knowing where she was. Dream Kelly could feel the sun's rays burning into her skin, stinging like her body was being attacked by a swarm of wasps.

She didn't recall waking up from that nightmare but she must have. How else could the word be there on the pad? She must have written it while still in a somewhat unconscious state, then rolled over and went back to sleep.

"Strange dream," she thought. The dream would stay with her now but she would write the story down later. That way, Kelly could add thoughts and impressions to help understand the dream and its hidden meanings.

Now, to the other words. Kelly wondered if they were part of the albino man dream or something else that she had scribbled later during the night. They looked like elongated snakes twisting on the page and not really legible as anything. Kelly examined the scrawls for a time trying to grab some hint but just could not make out even a single letter. She assumed it was two words because there was a definite space between the scribbles.

Kelly tore the page off and set the pad on the nightstand. Martin had explained auto-writing at one of the club meetings. She didn't really think she was psychic but what could it hurt to try? She put the pencil in her hand and stared intently at the snakes on the page. Kelly didn't look at the hand that would be writing but concentrated only on the snakes. Time became blurry as she stared.

Kelly didn't feel her writing hand move at first and later, she would not admit if the writing was involuntary or just her imagination playing tricks with her.

When Kelly came out of the trance, there were two words written on the new page and she stared at them, both surprised and fascinated. The words she had written were "save me".

7   The Inyo Spa and Health Resort

Kelly wasn't looking forward to the long walk into town. Time was most always a factor in her life; she didn't like to waste any of it for no good reason. She was going to miss the sun rising out of the desert this morning, that was sure.

So, Kelly had already decided to take coffee with Rheta at the diner when she got there. The waitress did sometimes have pertinent information about what has been happening in the town. People tended to chatter while having breakfast and Rheta had ears that absorbed facts and details like a thirsty sponge.

Kelly had found out about the burglary at Dwayne Holliman's house from Rheta, not Officer Posen. He hadn't even written up the incident report until the next day, 24 hours after it had happened. The man was just lazy and near to incompetent.

That was another appointment on Kelly's agenda today. She had not been able to get to the police station yesterday. Kelly would have to look at incident reports and the daily logs for the past two days, not that she really expected to find any relevant circumstances that required an investigation. However, she didn't want any probable occurrence to slip away from scrutiny, like the five 25 pound bags of salt that just disappeared from Stormy's place.

When Kelly stepped out of the trailer into an unexpected cool and misty morning, she didn't feel as rushed as she had been while getting dressed for the day. Her bike was there in the front yard resting on the kick stand, ready to go. Uncle must have brought it over sometime last night, probably after she had gone to sleep. And, she had a feeling that things had been done to it but, she didn't mind.

Uncle was a mentor to Kelly, although he probably didn't know that. She admired the skills he had with tools, the way he could work a few simple pine boards into something useful and worthwhile. She could only wonder what kind of valuable knowledge that he had, being such an old man as he was with so many experiences. But he was not a chatterbox, at least not around Kelly, and that needed to change.

Kelly had projects that she wanted Uncle to do for her, too but all of them were still just pencil drawings on paper with a few simple instructions for design. She wouldn't ask Uncle to do anything for her unless she had some way to repay him, whether in trade or by payment. Kelly didn't take favors from anyone, not even Uncle.

Rheta had a coffee already on the counter for Kelly when she opened the door of the diner and walked inside, like the woman knew Kelly was coming in for a sit-down today.

Rheta did have plenty of facts and rumors to share that morning but all of it was out of the realm of interest for Kelly. She was only mildly curious about Mrs. Phillips and how she got a black eye and a split lip last Tuesday night. Her husband, Stan, was a long haul trucker and had been on the road when his wife suffered injury so his alibi was rock solid.

Kelly didn't feel like going to Overlook after she left the diner. If rocks were out of place, they could wait until tomorrow. She was pretty sure the desert would be still and quiet even though Kelly was not there to make certain of it.

The chalk board fastened to the front of the Inyo Desert Spa and Health Resort was blank, so no new alerts from any of the members in 'The UFO Bureau of Inyo, Arizona'. Kelly unlocked the door and went inside.

A poster was tacked on the wall to greet anyone coming in and it gave her a chuckle. Done in the style of a sideshow carnival canvas, 'Zontar, The Magnificent' was a monstrous squid-like alien with one bulging eye, showing off its uncanny magic skills by capturing tiny terrified humans in its tentacles that had miraculously appeared out of a top hat, like rabbits.

Dan the Man was good when it came to layout and art that was needed for the website and some of his posters were great sellers on the internet that brought in substantial monies for funding projects.

The front entry room was empty except for the poster and the solid wood frame chair that was uncomfortable to sit in for any length of time. One of the team had called it a 'witness chair' and everyone thought that was an appropriate term to use for it.

The tactical room, just past entry, was much larger but completely filled with comfortable chairs, file cabinets, tables and computers. The largest object in the room, however, was the landscape table that took up most of the space that was left over. It was 8 feet long and 4 feet wide with a side board encasement and six 2x4 legs to hold the weight. On top of that table was a scaled-down panorama of the town of Inyo, Arizona with roads, trees, houses, all manner of structures and zones that were determined to be important enough to be included.

Of course, not everything was present. "How could it be?" thought Kelly as she looked down at the tiny quiet town. Even after all this time, it was still a work-in-progress.

The landscape was, for the most part, flat. Pete's Overlook was at a higher level, mainly because Kelly insisted on that. There was only a small section of land beyond the bluff showing; there just wasn't enough room on the table to put the majestic Inyo Desert.

There were only three yellow flags that were targets or points of interest but those had been there far too long without any resolution. Kelly considered removing them all but then thought, "no tomorrow, maybe. Or next year."

With a sigh, she turned away from the table and went to a small gray file cabinet. There was a cigar box on top and she reached in and selected a tiny red flag, returned to the table and stuck the banner in the front yard of Uncle's house.

On her way out, Kelly stood at the chalk board on the front of the spa. She used a red piece of chalk to draw and color in a red star design, then with white chalk she wrote in large numbers and letters '1 pm.'

That should give her plenty of time to talk to the new guy, Bobby, about becoming an initiate into the Bureau.

"And, he had better not refuse," Kelly silently warned him, "or there would be trouble!"

8   The Mentor

When Kelly got to Uncle's house, she saw that the Mazda and the U–Haul were gone, For a brief moment, she panicked, thinking that Jenny and her kids decided to leave after all. But no, Uncle said they were here to stay for a while. Probably, Jenny was returning the U–Haul after it had been unloaded and had gone to get her deposit back. Or maybe they were shopping, or gone to the dentist or barber shop. Any number of things that the family could be doing right now. No, they were not gone.

Kelly set her bike against the banister and walked onto the front porch. She listened but could hear no activity. She didn't want to knock on the off chance that Uncle decided to sleep late today. She sat on the front porch swing. "Comfortable," she thought, with pillows and arm cushions. That was Nelda's touch, Uncle's wife. She had been gone now... well, Kelly couldn't remember how long ago, a long time anyway.

Kelly began humming a tune without knowing what the song was. Her feet pushed off from the porch deck and she began a slow, smooth swing. "This is nice," she thought, a real house with lots of room and comforts, too. Not like the split-trailer that she and her mother lived in. Kelly's room there was small, tiny even, with barely enough room to swing a bat or hula hoop.

That was probably why she loved the spa so much. It was huge with so many large rooms, solid floors and high ceilings. It was quiet too. There were no arguments, yelling or curses. There was only one UFObian that got combative every so often but she knew how to handle Martin easy enough. Kick his butt out for the day. When he came back, in time, he would be calm and relaxed for a long good while. He didn't say, "I quit!" anymore. He finally figured out that ploy was not workable. Nobody was going to beg him to come back into the fold.

Kelly heard the saw wind up from around back. Uncle was in the work shed, of course. She hadn't even thought of that until now. Even so, she was reluctant to leave the porch swing right away, it was so pleasant.

Uncle was using the big saw to trim ends off from some boards. He had his back to Kelly and since Uncle didn't know she was there, she just watched him for a while. Uncle reminded her of that old film star, the one that limped all the time but she couldn't remember his name. He always played a side-kick buddy of the big star and was usually dead at the end of the western. It always pissed her off when the big shots killed off a good character like that. All movies should have happy endings with everyone getting all that they wanted out of life. After all, movies were fantasy, right?

"What'cha doin', Kelly?" asked Uncle.

Somehow, Uncle had snuck up on Kelly and was standing right in front of her.

"Hey, Uncle," replied Kelly. "I didn't want to distract you while you were on the big saw. Fingers are important, don't wanna lose any of them big boys."

"You think I got big fingers?" he asked her.

Kelly held up her small hand as a comparison. Uncle's hand was a lot bigger than hers, he supposed.

"Where are them people that were here yesterday?" Kelly said.

"My family (he emphasized family) is on people errands," he explained. "I wasn't informed of all they intend to do. Why do you ask? You still set on kickin' Bobby's butt?"

"No, Uncle. I really was just kidding about that," she said. "I might even ask him to join the club if he has a better attitude today."

"Well, that's just fine, alright," he told her. "I imagine he'd get a kick out of that."

Kelly followed Uncle into the work shed where he resumed working on a cabinet.

"Whereabouts did the new arrivals come from," Kelly asked.

"All the way from Texas," replied the old man.

"So, they came in on old 49?" asked Kelly.

"Mmm, yeah 49," Uncle said. He was looking at the fitting of the cabinet backboard and was not really mindful of the interrogation that was happening.

"Anything unusual happen out there?" Kelly asked while examining the many hand tools on the work table. When Uncle didn't answer, Kelly looked at him feigning complete and utter innocence, "in the desert?"

"Can I see your badge, Kelly?" he asked in a casual way.

"Huh," replied the girl.

"I got a peculiar feeling that there is an ongoing investigation. Do I need a lawyer?" he asked.

"The Bureau, me, we have an interest in the Inyo Desert. Strange things sometimes happen out there. You know about that, don't you?" Kelly explained.

She picked up an unfamiliar tool and held it out to him.

"What does this do?" she asked him.

"That is a curved blade chisel," Uncle told her.

Kelly waited, still holding the tool for him to look at.

"For digging out chunks of wood that shouldn't be there," he explained, "for carving shapes," and he pointed to a squirrel totem on a wall shelf. There was also an owl and a turtle.

"You did those?" she asked him.

"I did" was all he said.

Kelly put the chisel down and picked up another tool and held it out for Uncle to see.

"Block plane," he said, "for shaving wood."

Kelly put the tool down and was just about ready to select another one when Uncle said,

"are you alright, Kelly?"

"I have a bump on my head," she said, "but I am still the same Kelly that I was last week."

"Can I look at it?" Uncle asked.

Kelly turned around and used both hands to pull her hair away from the injury on the back of her head.

"Hurt much?" he asked her.

"Only when people push on it," Kelly responded. She waited while he examined her head, then asked again,"something strange did happen out there, didn't it?"

When she turned around to face him, Uncle was walking away.

"What are you building?" she asked.

"Alice, my grand-daughter, she needs a doll cabinet to fit on the wall, to hold all her dolls," he said.

Uncle looked at her sideways and Kelly could tell that he was confused but whether it was about the questions or her injury, she just couldn't be sure.

"I'm alright, Uncle," she said softly. "Really."

She wasn't, not that she was going to admit that to anyone. She just didn't want to go to Phoenix for a brain x-ray. Kelly was a big believer in self healing, holistic stuff. Anyway, the dizzy spells were not happening as frequently today but the headache was still an ongoing discomfort. She had taken some Advil that calmed it down some but she would be so grateful if it would just fade away like smoke in the wind.

"Okay, then. There's a coffee making machine over there on that table," and he pointed for her. "Go ahead and make a pot for us."

Kelly did as she was told and went to prepare coffee. As she scooped out the grounds from the canister and was ready to put them in the filter, she all of a sudden turned back to him out of curiosity.

"Why do you have a coffee machine out here but you don't have one in the kitchen?" she asked him.

"Because I am a peculiar man, Kelly," he replied.

"You know a lot of things," Kelly said as she poured water into the coffee-maker..

"I must admit that I do," said Uncle as he measured a board for the cabinet.

"You could teach me," Kelly said softly.

Uncle turned to her and said, "what, didn't quite catch that."

"I said you could teach me things," she said louder. And went on, "I do not have an acceptable male role model in my life and that is a truly sad fact for a person of my age."

"Do you want to learn wood-working?" Uncle asked.

"Not just wood and tools, all things," Kelly said with just a little bit of passion, "I need life tools."

Uncle looked at her with a quizzical expression, as if he could not understand what she was asking.

"I want to be your student. I want you to tell me about life, teach me things, show me how to survive like you have."

Uncle turned back to the work table and went back to measuring the wood.

Neither of them spoke for what seemed like a long time to Kelly. She watched him for a reaction and was expecting the worst.

"I can do that," Uncle said as he finally turned to face her.

Kelly grinned at him and Uncle smiled back at her.

When the coffee was ready, they both sat down on the bench, Uncle taking a break from work and Kelly ready to begin their new relationship as teacher and student. Kelly first wanted to know about Bobby, what kind of person he was, have any hobbies? Got a girl back home? She was concerned that the boy may be wound a little tight for his age. 15! Kelly thought he was 16, so he was big for his age, good. She was older by 4 months and that was good, too. Kelly still wanted to be the alpha of The UFO Bureau and had been concerned that Bobby might challenge her leadership. Time would only tell about that as time went by.

Neither of them wanted to get into more serious discussions about life just yet. This new relationship needed to start slow. Uncle and her could get involved in more adult matters about life later on and Kelly was certain that a good outcome for both of them was inevitable.

Kelly didn't talk about whatever strange event happened in the Inyo Desert to Uncle again. She understood that he was being protective of his family. Didn't matter anyhow. Kelly already knew that something had happened to Jenny and her kids out there and, eventually, she would find out what it was.

9 All The Dolls Are In The House

Jenny still had a lot of things on her mind when they returned to Uncle's house. She had hoped that going shopping might remove those worries or at least diminish them, even just a little bit. "Dammit," she cursed almost silently, then thought, "I need to stop doing that." Sometimes Jenny would blurt out something aloud when she only meant to think it. It was a recent bad habit probably caused by the stress and anxiety that was plaguing her.

The outing had been fun for the kids, at least. Bobby found a couple of books at the thrift store and Alice had a new purse that was shaped like a bunny rabbit.

Jenny knew that she had to stay strong for her children. This had to be a difficult time for them, as well. Alice seemed to be adapting to the move well. Bobby, however, well... she was worried about Bobby. He was angry and she couldn't blame him for that. He might never see his old friends back in Texas ever again. It was a tender time for Bobby, she knew. Adolescence had been a troubling time for her at his age, so tumultuous and confusing. "But, Bobby is stronger than I was," she thought. He's got a good head on his shoulders and she silently thanked God that he was nothing like his father, that no-good rat bastard.

"What, Mom?" said Bobby.

"What?" answered Jenny.

"You were laughing. What's funny?" he asked.

"Just... I don't know, Bobby, thinking. We're in a funny situation is all," because she didn't know what else to say.

Bobby went back to reading his book. Jenny glanced at him once, looked back at the road, then looked at her son again. She adjusted the mirror so that she could see Alice in the back seat. Alice was talking to the bunny rabbit purse, though she was doing it quietly like a mother would when whispering nothings to a newborn baby, probably explaining about the new life the rabbit would have with her other dolls and stuffed animals.

"Quite the odd menagerie for a 6 year old," said Jenny to her son. Bobby just nodded 'yeah' but didn't look up from the book he was reading.

"My kids, these are my kids," she thought, smiling.

It was a wonderment to her that they were such good kids after all she had put them through. I will do whatever it takes to make them safe and happy, she promised herself. She would get a job in town, doing something. Daddy would help her, she knew. And she had to get a better car, something more reliable than this old beater Mazda. Maybe a van to give them more room. Or, a truck. In a few years, she would be teaching Bobby to drive and he would probably enjoy a good, solid truck to impress the girls.

"Mom," said Bobby.

"Yeah, hon," Jenny said.

"You passed Grampa's house," he told her.

"Did I?" she said.

"Well, yeah," he said.

Without saying anything else, Jenny turned the car around and went back to the house. When she pulled into the driveway, Jenny saw the young girl sitting in the porch swing.

"Look, it's your girlfriend," and Jenny smiled at him.

Bobby didn't say anything but there was a definite scowl on his face.

Alice was the first one out of the car and, as usual, she didn't close the passenger door. She ran right up to Kelly as if going to see a good friend that she hadn't seen in a long time and presented the bunny rabbit for her to see.

"Look, it has a pocket for valables," Alice told her.

"Oh, I see. That's cute, Alice," Kelly said showing interest, "do you have a lot of valuables?"

"Oh, I've got plenty," said Alice, "do you want to see?"

Alice didn't wait for an answer, just grabbed Kelly's hand and pulled her toward the front door. They passed quickly by Jenny and Kelly managed a "hey Jenny" to her before being dragged inside into the house. With her arms full of grocery bags, Jenny managed to hold the closing door open with her foot. As she was going inside, she looked back and Bobby was just now coming with more bags. Jenny waited patiently for her son.

"You don't like her?" Jenny asked.

Bobby sort of shrugged his shoulders and stepped past his mother.

"I think she's cute," she said to herself, because Bobby was already gone.

After he helped his mother put the groceries away, Bobby went to his room, tossed the new books aside, then sat down on the edge of the bed. When passing Alice's room, he heard the two girls just chattering away like children at kindergarten fun time. Bobby didn't know if he wanted to be friends with that girl. She had attitude and she was intrusive, just barging in like she lived here all the time. Grampa had told him that she was just a girl that he knew from town and didn't really see her that often.

"So, why was she here now?" he wondered. And why was he so agitated that she hadn't said anything to him yet?

Bobby got up, turned once or twice looking for something to do, could find nothing. He moved over to the door of his bedroom and stood half in and half out into the hall. Bobby couldn't hear them talking from that distance, so he walked down the hall until he was almost to Alice's room.

"Why did you name her Blinky-Stinky," he heard Kelly ask.

"Smell," Alice said. In his mind's eye, Bobby could see Alice putting the doll right up to Kelly's face so that she could smell the stinky doll.

"Okay, yes, she needs a bath," Kelly agreed.

"She will still stink after a bath anyway," Alice declared.

"So many dolls," said Kelly. "How many are there?"

"I don't count them, that would be rude," Alice said.

"Yes, that would be rude," Kelly apologized, "I'm sorry."

"I have one more," claimed Alice, "but you can't see him right now."

"No?" replied Kelly.

"He ran away," Alice said.

"He did? Why did he run away?" Kelly asked.

"I don't know," Alice didn't sound surprised that one of her dolls would run away from her. It sometimes happened.

"Where did he go?" asked Kelly.

Again Alice said, "I don't know," but this time sounding frustrated.

"We could look for him. I'm really good at finding things that are lost," Kelly said to the little girl.

"I have looked and looked," responded Alice.

"Maybe... he's under the bed," said Kelly.

There was a shuffling noise like the girl was actually searching for the doll under the bed, Bobby thought, so he stepped around the door jam and went inside Alice's room.

Sure enough, Kelly was halfway under the bed, just her legs and butt peeping out from the coverlet.

Alice looked at Bobby but said to Kelly, "he's not under the bed. I looked already."

"Uh, what are you doing?" asked Bobby speaking to Kelly's butt.

Kelly quickly slid out from under the bed. She sat up, crossed her legs Indian-style and tried to look innocent. The expression on her face was comical and her tongue looked as if it were stuck to her upper lip.

"I was helping Alice look for her lost doll," Kelly admitted, somewhat embarrassed.

"Not a doll," said Alice softly.

"Under the bed?" Bobby asked.

"If I was a doll and I was going to run away, under the bed would be my first choice," Kelly said with conviction.

Alice quietly played with a raccoon plushy and seemed to have lost all interest in Kelly.

"Alice, do you mind if I talk to your brother a minute?" asked Kelly.

Alice slowly shook her head but didn't say anything. Fun time was always over when her brother was there.

Kelly stood up and walked past Bobby. She stopped at the door and gave him a steely look.

"Come with me," was all she said. It was an order.

Kelly followed Bobby into his room where he took a stance of power at the desk. Kelly went to his bed, sat down, leaned back with her arms for support and positioned her bare legs so that they were dangling over the edge. Bobby tried to keep his eyes focused on her face but her bare legs kept drawing his attention. The cut-off jeans were not helping either.

Kelly crossed her legs and waited for him to get a good look at her wonderfulness.

"What happened out in the desert?" she asked as if it meant nothing.

Bobby stopped looking at legs and stared at Kelly's face. He didn't say anything, so she repeated the question. "What happened out in the Inyo Desert?" Kelly was trying to sound like Lauren Bacall talking to Humphrey Bogart in 'To Have and Have Not'.

"You can whistle, can't you?" she said to him.

"What? What are you talking about?" Bobby said.

"Look, bad first impression, I get it. I was temperamental yesterday. I was being..."

"A bitch," Bobby told her, "that the word you're looking for?"

Kelly smiled and gave him a little nod.

"Arrow to the chest," Kelly said as she placed a fist on her chest, "but, yes," then went on, "today, well... I am in a better mood today, let's say," Kelly explained.

Bobby took some time to respond by pulling out the desk chair and sitting down.

"Okay," he said.

"I want you to join the club," she told him.

"What kind of club?" Bobby asked.

"I can't tell you," Kelly admitted. "It's a secret club."

"Why?" he began but Kelly cut him off quickly.

"Because I want you," as Lauren Bacall would say it, "I want you to join the club. Do it for me."

And, thank you, Lauren Bacall, it was working. She could see the boy go soft, like an ice cream cone melting in summer heat.

"We have a meeting at 2 o'clock. Will you come?" she asked him.

Bobby wasn't going to look at Kelly's bare legs again but met her eyes with the same intensity as she was throwing at him. In that moment, Bobby Bronson knew with certainty that Kelly Alban was going to be a lure that couldn't be avoided for as long as he knew her. But, he had to admit, she wasn't unfriendly to look at. There was that.

10   The Recruit

Kelly got to The UFO Bureau at 1:09 pm, running a bit late but she knew that a few of the other UFObians had a tendency to dismiss time; that was just the nature of youth, being late for one thing or another. Dan the Man, Martin and Andy were standing out in front talking about whatever idle boys talk about. Andy saw her first and waved as Kelly turned the corner and pedaled down the street. She let the bike coast to the curb, jumped it and landed right at the entry door.

"You fellas should get out of the rain," Kelly said and used her key to unlock the door.

"It's not raining," Andy told her.

Kelly held out her hand to see if any raindrops fell into her open palm.

"My mistake," she said, "it won't rain 'til tomorrow."

Only Andy laughed but he laughed at just about everything anybody said that was supposed to be funny, even when it wasn't.

Kelly stationed her bike against the side wall, then she pointed at the new poster Dan had made.

"Good one, Dan. Is it selling?" Kelly asked.

"Sold out already, I've got an order in for more," he replied.

Dan walked over and placed a hand on the alien magician poster in a self-absorbed display of admiration for a well-conceived creation.

"I'll have more ready by next week." he said.

"It's gotta come down," said Kelly.

Dan looked at her, confused and, yes, a little bit shocked by her order.

"We're going to have a guest soon and I don't want any hints about what goes on here," she explained to all of them.

"And we need to dandy up the tactical room, just in case we invite him in there," she went on.

"Who?" asked Martin.

She wanted to say something witty but couldn't think of anything, so just matter of fact said, "a new guy, fresh in town, maybe an initiate."

"Why?" asked Martin, seeming not happy about this interloper to their private clique. Martin always had questions, so his stance was not unusual to Kelly and the others.

"It's just possible that he has intel." Kelly advised them and that was all she needed to say. Dan took down the alien poster, rolled it up into a tube.

"Where is Pegs?" Kelly asked to anyone who could answer.

"I left a message for her but she hasn't gotten back to me yet," said Andy.

Kelly shrugged and the boys all followed her into the next room. They spent the next hour straightening up the tactical room, hiding what shouldn't be seen and setting up a lay-out that would be interesting but puzzling, to a guest. Kelly wanted Bobby to be impressed by their projects but not show any spooky things that might scare him off. The guys had more questions about this new person and Kelly answered most of them but there were some she couldn't.

It was Martin, of course, who brought up the subject of skills, probably concerned that the new guy might be a competitor for him. Kelly didn't know what Bobby's skills were, or even if he had any. But, that could be found out during interrogation, she told them.

Kelly wanted this to happen, so she was compliant and congenial to the guys, which was very unlike her usual role as master sergeant to the team. 'Do what I say and do it now' was her usual posture in a situation like this but Kelly wanted the boys to agree to let Bobby in. And she would do what needed to be done to make that happen, even if she had to be pleasant. That is, until she got what she wanted.

Pegs finally arrived 43 minutes late, not unusual for her. She bounced in, just said "sorry" and was quickly informed by Kelly and Andy about the arrival of a possible new recruit that was expected in seventeen minutes. After that she just wandered around the room while all the others finished off any last touches to get the tactical room ready for an intruder.

As 2 o'clock approached, they all waited out in front of the spa. The boys went back to their interrupted boy talk while Pegs chatted up Kelly about the new boy, wanting to know more details about his appearance and personality. Pegs was at that stage where boys had become important to a young girl and getting a fresh one with unknown qualities was exciting to her. Kelly just gave her the basics, as much as she knew anyway but she didn't want Pegs to smother Bobby like the other boys she went after. Kelly wasn't sure if Bobby was going to be her guy but she had to admit that there were hopes there. But, Kelly knew that Pegs would use all her girly charms on Bobby just because she was Pegs and that's what she does. And, if Bobby caved, then he was not Kelly's guy after all.

Kelly saw Uncle's truck coming down the street. He pulled up right in front of the spa, let Bobby out, waved at Kelly and drove away. Bobby stood in the street while he looked over the group waiting as if deciding if he was going to go in or walk away.

"Let's get this done," Bobby finally said and he stepped onto the sidewalk and without permission went into the spa. Everyone followed him in except Kelly. She waited outside while rampant thoughts ran through her mind. Kelly needed to calm down before she confronted Bobby. Her heart had been pumping like she had been running at track ever since Bobby got out of the truck. It was the way he looked at her like she was a bug that needed to be stepped on.

Kelly stomped on the sidewalk, then did it again. Once more for fortitude and whatever she had been feeling was gone. Now, she would be the Kelly that sometimes startles the timid and vulnerable, any that have the misfortune to confront her. She was 'Kelly the Warrior' ready for battle.

It was Pegs that shoved her head out the door and asked if Kelly was coming in or not.

When Kelly did come in, everyone was silent, watching her, waiting for action. The UFObians would follow her lead because she was the queen bee; they were only drones. Kelly didn't look at Bobby who was seated in the witness chair. She walked to the place where the poster had been hung, as if she was concerned about the many tack holes in the wall.

Facing away from all of them, she said, "what we do here is secret." She let that statement lay a moment, then turned to confront her audience, much like a stage actor would do for drama.

"Some people in town may speculate about what we do," Kelly continued, "but they are unaware of the true nature and scope of our project. We look for the odd, the unusual, the bizarre, any event that is inexplicable... incredible. Anomaly, mystery. Phenomenon," Kelly said looking straight at Bobby. She couldn't tell if he was interested or bored. He didn't even seem to be uncomfortable in the witness chair.

"Do you want to know more?" Kelly asked Bobby.

"Yes, I do," Bobby answered.

"What happens in there," Kelly pointed to the tactical room, "must not be talked about to anyone. Not to your mother or Uncle, your grandfather, anyone. Is that okay with you?" Kelly asked.

"That depends on what's in there," he said. "Is it illegal? Something that may get me in trouble?"

"No," blurted Andy, "well... no."

Andy didn't look at Kelly, didn't want to.

"What we do may be of concern to some people but it is not against the law," Kelly told him. "As a matter of fact, I make regular visits to the police station who are aware of the club's involvement concerning events that happen in town and out in the Inyo Desert."

Bobby looked at Kelly and the others for just a few moments, then stood up and said, "Let's go."

When he first entered the tactical room, anyone could tell that Bobby was impressed. He took a minute to observe all of the room, seeing the large table at the center first of course, then looking at each of the three computers on tables with the puzzling images lighting up the screens. The file cabinets and crates stacked with papers and equipment were passed over as non-interesting to him at this first look but would later have more meaning to him in the scheme of things.

Bobby walked toward the town table but as he was passing one of the computers he stopped to look at the slide show that had been prepared for him. Images were held on the screen for 4 seconds only, so that each one could not be examined closely, being quickly replaced by other startling photos of flying saucers, depictions of aliens and unusual artifacts. There were also desert markings that were obviously taken from a great height by an airplane or satellite, massive designs of animals, humans and abstract objects. Bobby had seen a documentary on the History Channel about these unusual patterns in the desert that were made 'by ancient man or aliens?'

Bobby looked at the club members who were watching him like vultures viewing a not-yet-dead carcass and wondering if it was time to pounce, except Kelly. She was standing at the town table, waiting for him to come and see what she wanted him to see. Bobby looked down on the town almost like floating above it. He saw the roads, the police station, the book store, all manner of unfamiliar buildings and structures. Kelly was standing at the far end and as Bobby moved closer to her, he looked down at his grandfather's house with the tiny red flag stuck on the front lawn. Bobby looked at Kelly who had a peculiar smirk on her face. She might have even cocked an eyebrow at him, just for spite, he thought later.

"That's right, boy," he could imagine her thinking, "you're the phenomenon we're going to investigate today."

But first, there was the story of Pete Selby and what he saw in 1967 somewhere out in the Inyo Desert.

11   What Pete Selby Saw Out In The Desert

Pete Selby was cruising down the road in his truck at a soft 25 miles per hour and that's as fast as he dared go considering the condition that he was in. He had 3, maybe 4, too many beers earlier that night and the effects were not going away quickly. He wanted to find a nice quiet spot along the road to throw up and could only hope that would make him feel better. He didn't want to be drunk anymore, not tonight anyway.

"Damn that Jake Pathay," he grumbled. It was because of Maggie and that Jake fella having such a good time together that made me go over the limit, he thought but at least I was smart enough to get away when I did.

See, Pete figured he was probably going to hell anyway for one thing or another that he had done or would be doing in his poor sad life. But he didn't want his time with Satan to be overly traumatic, you understand.

So, he walked away from the bar without saying a word to Jake or Maggie, though he wanted to say plenty. 'Cause he knew that Jake carried a knife just like he did and if things went too far, one or the other of them was gonna get cut, maybe bad cut... like killed, you know? And Pete didn't want that in his ledger when he was talking to St. Peter about which road to take.

Route 49 was dark as pitch like it always was at 3 am but it was a straight-away and not likely that he would encounter another vehicle unless it was some other fool trying to get home like him. So, Pete was watching out for headlights in the distance 'cause he didn't want to get killed by some damn drunk on the road. He put a hand on his upset belly and could tell that the volcano was about to go and he had less than a minute or two to find the proper spot for the eruption.

Pete eased the truck onto a dirt embankment being real careful not to go into the ditch that ran alongside the road. As he opened the door and stuck one foot outside to get out, Pete abruptly stopped moving. He was looking out the truck window to the south almost like he had suddenly been hypnotized by a magician. His eyes were wide and he had to blink once or twice to be sure that he was actually seeing what he was looking at. "Too drunk," he thought, "just too damn drunk for my own good, that's what."

Pete had never had a drunkard hallucination before but it had to happen sooner or later he reasoned. But, right now, he was rather wishing it was pink elephants and dancing ostriches like in that Disney movie he saw when he was just a kid, though he couldn't remember the name of it. Mickey Mouse was in it, he remembered that.

In the desert, about 400 feet from the road was a really big something blacking out the sky so that no stars could be seen in the distance. Pete first thought that it must be a hill, except there were no hills in this part of the desert – it was all flat land. But, the reason that Pete remained so still and quiet staring at the hill or whatever it was, it was moving. Not with any great speed but moving very slow so that a cluster of stars would appear at the tail and more stars would disappear from the head. Now, he was thinking that it was an elephant, cause that's the biggest land animal he could think of, 'cept it was bigger, like one of them whales! "Now, how did a damn whale get in the desert?" he wondered.

Now, Pete wouldn't have done this sober and much later he wished that he hadn't done it drunk but he felt an overwhelming urge to walk toward it, so that's what he did. It was quiet in the desert with no sound of wind or animals. Just nothing. He couldn't even hear his footsteps as he walked farther from the road. So quiet and still that for a few seconds, Pete thought that he had gone deaf. But he didn't stop and as he got closer, Pete noticed that the giant monolith was an oblong metal disc, sort of like a UFO but not a flying one – a dragging one like it was sick and looking for a place to rest for a while. It's shape was something like a submarine but with treads all around the hull like those on a military tank or bulldozer.

"It was a digging thing," Pete guessed, and was not wrong.

When he stood only 30 or 40 feet away from it, Pete could see that the very top of the land sub was high, maybe as tall as a building that went up 2 or 3 stories. He couldn't see the bottom at all because it was deep in the dirt and had been plowing a furrow like it was corn plantin' time. Pete got to the gash in the desert floor first, well behind the still moving giant machine. He looked into the pit but could see nothing because of the dark but he had a feeling that something was in there, some kind of slime worm or snake that was going to reach out and take him, struggling, back into the pit.

When that didn't happen, he looked off to see what the monolith was doing now. Still moving slow, dragging itself through the dirt. Then, just all of a sudden, it tilted to one side, almost like it lost its balance and stopped. And that unnatural silence was frightening, like the quiet right before a massive explosion happens.

Pete backed away and turned to run, just to get away as fast as he could. That's when he saw all the spinning red and blue lights in the distance. Up above there were two helicopters hovering over his truck with blinding spotlights lighting it up like it was on fire. So strange that it was still quiet, though. He heard no whupping chopper blades and no sirens from the police cars with flashing lights coming fast down the road, though there should have been some kind of noise from all that activity.

Then, over his shoulder, he felt the presence of something moving behind him. Another helicopter, this one dark, was hovering over the fallen monolith. A whole bunch of flares exploded in the sky – those kind with the little parachutes attached and they all slowly floated down to illuminate the giant beast laying quiet like a dead whale in the desert. Now lit up like a fireworks show, Pete could see pod openings, blister bulges and strange markings that were alien and frightening. Suddenly, the monolith began buckling and thrashing like a great beast in the throes of death. It was then that Pete turned and ran. He jumped the ditch and stumbled to the ground next to his truck. There were soldiers looking at him in something like confusion, or maybe awe but one of them was pointing a rifle at him like he was going to shoot.

Two men grabbed onto his arms and forcefully led him to one of the helicopters that had landed nearby. He was abruptly thrown into the open door and strapped in to a seat. The chopper lifted off and that's when Pete was finally able to scream. The soldier next to him turned abruptly and slapped Pete's face hard, then calmly said, "be quiet now, don't want to wake the neighbors," followed by a strained chuckle, like the soldier was just as scared as Pete was but tightly holding onto that fear like a good military man would in a conflict.

The helicopter slowly turned and followed the ditch left by the monolith. Wide-eyed and scared out of his wits, Pete stared at the desert below. That's when he saw the massive hole in the earth – the hole that the monster had crawled out of. So, it wasn't a UFO after all. It was something else, something strange and disturbing that came from beneath the earth. As another helicopter shined a spotlight at the massive hole in the ground, it looked as if there was some kind of movement below. From that distance it was hard to say exactly what was happening but it looked like things were crawling out of the pit, scattering for darkness, like roaches will do when the kitchen light suddenly comes on after dark.

Then Pete's chopper turned away and headed north away from the event.

Pete never knew where they took him and if he remembers what happened during his captivity he has never spoken about it to anyone. If asked, he would only say "don't recall." or "can't say about that," anything to stop any more questions about the incident. When he was finally released after 93 days, he was driven to his house and dropped off without any words from the FBI men that took him. Pete didn't want to talk to them and they certainly did not have any words for him, not even "goodbye, sorry for the inconvenience, pal." And that was just as well as far as he was concerned.

Pete stood in the front yard next to his truck watching the scary guy that had sat next to him in the black car. He smiled at Pete out from the passenger window and gave him a thumbs up sign, like all was well and good with the world. Then with a very stern look, the agent pointed a trigger finger at him and Pete knew what that meant. "Yeah, I promise, FBI guy, I'm gonna keep my damn mouth shut about all of this," he thought, "and I'll never tell a soul. I can only hope to God that some day down the road I'll forget everything – what happened in the desert and what happened in that prison. If all goes right with me, nobody will even know I'm alive."

12   True Is Not the Same as Not False

"And that's what happened one dark summer night in 1967," said Kelly. "And, like he swore, Pete Selby has never told that story to anyone... except one person."

"I don't think he even told it to you. You have a vivid imagination, Kelly, and story-telling is just one of your many attriboots," said Martin.

"Call me a liar again and I'll box your ears until you say UFO abduction," Kelly warned him.

It was a familiar taunt because of Martin's peculiarity of speech. When excited or frustrated, he had a tendency to lose letters in long words so that abduction came out as aduction, probility for probability. It was such a frequent occurrence that nobody even bothered to correct him anymore. They knew what he meant, so why bother?

"How do you know it's true, what he told you?" Bobby asked Kelly.

"I am a walking talking lie detector." replied Kelly. "And my lie-o-meter didn't jerk once while that story was being told to me."

"We take the Inyo Incident as fact," Dan stated, "that's our provenance, the whole reason we started The UFO Bureau.

"Yeah, Roswell may have got more publicity but that was before the FBI put the hush cone over everything that's happened since," Andy kicked in. "Even up to 1972, there were government men in dark suits wandering around town and driving out to the desert. They kept an office in the Bailey building, the whole top floor. It was a restricted area, too. Nobody in town ever went in there until it was closed out."

I think we're still being observed, even today. Satellites," Martin said and pointed to the ceiling. "There are occurrences..."

Martin stopped talking because Kelly had directed her death stare at him.

"Some of their documents, and evidence, was recovered before the files could be destroyed but that information is only available to agents of UFOBIA," Kelly stated.

"Ufobia?" Bobby asked.

"The UFO Bureau of Inyo, Arizona," replied Dan. "U.F.O.B.I.A, get it?"

Bobby didn't say "oh", but he got it.

"Okay, bell-ringing time," Kelly stated. "This is the moment for you to decide, Bobby, and it's your only chance. You can walk out of here a free man. Do you want to be with us or do you want to be ignorant like the rest of the town?"

"What? Do I take an oath? Do I get a membership card or something?" Bobby asked.

"No," Kelly said, all serious like. "All you have to do is spit in your hand and we shake." Kelly spit in her hand and held it out to him.

Bobby looked around the room but all the 'agents' had serious expressions on their faces like this was the common ritual expected from new members.

Bobby looked at Kelly with a little bit of incredulity.

"Well, that's disgusting," he said.

But, he lifted his hand up, spit in it, then held it out to Kelly. She pulled her hand back and wiped her palm on the seat of her shorts.

"I just wanted to see if you'd do it," she said smiling. "You're in."

"Somebody's gonna shake my hand," Bobby said, staring at the blob of saliva on his hand.

They all laughed at that. Andy patted him on the shoulder. Martin punched his arm a little too hard and Pegs gave him kind of a squeeze and hug. Kelly just smiled at him.

Pegs elected herself as tour guide for the new member of the Bureau. She showed Bobby the snack bar, the coffee station and the refrigerator loaded with soda, milk and a few groceries. She took him down the corridor to the bathroom where he noticed the toilet paper holder was empty but there was a ready roll sitting on the edge of the bathtub, just out of reach for anyone sitting on the throne.

"Who's the joker?" Bobby thought and he couldn't help but think that it was Kelly.

Eventually, Pegs lost interest in Bobby when he wasn't noticing how pert and pretty she was. So, she let him go.

Back in the tactical room, Martin told him that each member was assigned a skill based on their personal background and abilities.

"I'm the computer guy," Martin boasted. "I can build one from the ground up, better than any you can buy off the shelf. They're faster and not cluttered up with idiot programs and unnecessary junk. Do you know anything about electronics, computers?" he asked Bobby.

"Eh, just the basics," he replied. "I'm not a gamer but I can get around on the internet okay." Martin wanted to know more so Bobby admitted, "I'm a player, not a technician like you."

"Not a problem," said Martin, "I got all that under control."

He opened the web pages for UFO-Bureau-Inyo-Arizona.net and pointed out all the buttons and whistles for Bobby but admitted that those were just for interlopers on the internet, not anything of importance, really.

"Most of our funding comes from the sales of posters, documents and photos that we push on the web pages," Martin explained. The posters for sale click opened up a page of Dan the Man's display of UFO and alien posters.

"Oh man, those are so cool," Bobby exclaimed.

Hearing that declaration, Dan casually sauntered over to join them at the computer, ready to be praised for his art and graphics work.

"New members get one poster free," Dan told Bobby, "but after that you got to pay just like all the other lurkers."

"Yeah, well, I'm probably gonna want more than one, yeah," Bobby said, "but just to start..."

"The cheerleader," said Dan and Martin almost at the same time.

"Yeah, that's the one," Bobby replied.

"That's our best seller," Dan said. "I can't print enough of that one. We're always back-logged on Cheryl."

"Cheryl?" Bobby asked.

Dan held up a finger in a shush command, leaned in and whispered to him. "That's the name we gave her, for artistic purposes, see?"

Dan and Martin looked across the room, so Bobby turned his head also. Kelly was at the coffee maker with Andy and they were in what might be considered an intense conversation.

Kelly was facing the onlookers across the room, leaning backwards against the table, just slightly turned away, much like the poster image of the captive cheerleader being dragged aboard a UFO by a tentacled monster alien. She was aware that she was being observed by Bobby, Martin and Dan but kept listening to Andy as if the others' attention was not peculiar or odd.

Bobby looked at the close-up of the cheerleader image, as Martin zoomed in on Cheryl's chest and he whispered, "she doesn't know."

"Oh, she knows alright," said Dan. "And that's exactly how Kelly will look, next year, maybe the year after." Dan made a motion with his hands to show how boobs can get bigger.

"What does Pegs do? I mean, what's her assignment?" asked Bobby.

"Ah, she's just fluff now," Martin said. "She used to be active, involved but not so much lately."

"She's still fun to watch, though," Dan said while looking at her.

Pegs was playing an internet game on one of the other computers but she wasn't just sitting in the chair, she was using it. Pegs twisted and bounced like she was actually involved in a fierce volley ball game. She suddenly threw both arms in the air like she had just scored a big volley against the other team.

"Yay, team," she squealed.

Turning around to be congratulated, Pegs noticed that Dan, Martin and Bobby were watching her. She waved to them.

Bobby then noticed that Kelly was watching the voyeurs, maybe a little amused by their observations of the club's tart. She walked across the room, until she stood very close to Bobby and said,"there are some binoculars in the cabinet over there," and tossed her head in that direction. She looked at the computer screen that still had a close-up image of Cheryl's boobs. Martin quickly hit the escape key on the keyboard and feigned a movement like 'what?'

Kelly looked at each of the boys in turn in what can only be described as blatant scorn.

"You getting everything you need from these guys?" she asked Bobby and he nodded.

"Well, that's good" said Kelly, then took a long sip of coffee but never took her eyes off the boys, as if studying them like bugs under a microscope, "that's good."

Eventually, as the afternoon dragged on, the UFObians dispersed to their own individual tasks. Martin needed to do some updates and answer questions from online lurkers in the chat logs. Dan the Man was bent over a long flat table and was showing Pegs his latest artwork in his sketch book. Andy was on another computer searching the internet but Kelly had disappeared.

Bobby sat at the last computer station, curious about the desert image on that screen, the one that looked like a spider drawn in the sand by some giant hand. The petroglyph folder had even more strange photographs of the deserts in Arizona, Nevada and New Mexico. All of them could only be seen from a high altitude, Bobby knew. Dan had told him earlier that he thought the drawings could be alien art or might be directional diagrams, possibly information for off world visitors but admitted that most researchers believed them to be constructed by ancient humans, though for what purpose, they don't know.

Bobby searched through another folder on the computer that had hundreds of photos and videos of UFO encounters; some looked absolutely real, while others were obviously faked. There were dozens of folders in the image sub-category with titles like Odd 'Alien' Artifacts, Tales of Abduction and Unknowns. He was about to enter a new file simply called Restricted when he suddenly realized that Kelly was standing next to him, hovering, probably curious about his interests.

"What are you thinking?" she asked Bobby.

"It's all good," he told her. "You guys, all of you... wow!"

As if Kelly had telepathic powers, and a silent command was given, the other members of the club began coming toward him, each one dragging or rolling a chair. They all gathered close, sat down in a half-circle around Bobby and Kelly as if ready to play a board game.

"It's time to tell us what happened to you in the desert," Kelly told Bobby.

One of the UFObians had brought a chair for Kelly and she sat down so that she was directly in front of Bobby.

"You're going to be disappointed," said Bobby, "it was really nothing."

"Come on, tell it," Martin ordered him and Kelly raised a hand to quiet him but not taking her eyes away from Bobby.

Bobby sighed and nodded 'okay'. "My sister was chasing a balloon in the desert and got lost. I found her."

"A balloon?" asked Pegs seeming to be astonished by Bobby's admission. "What kind of balloon?"

"Well, it was a floating balloon, you know, helium I guess," he explained.

"Describe it," Kelly said, showing unusual interest.

"I didn't see it," Bobby said. "Alice told me about it. It was just a balloon."

Bobby was surprised by all of their attention and couldn't believe their fascination about a balloon.

"You need to give more details, like you're telling a story," said Martin.

"Right, okay," Bobby went on. "Alice told me that there was a balloon. She saw it out in the desert."

"Okay, wait," said Martin. "When did she get out of the car. Were you stopped somewhere?"

"Well, yeah," he explained. "See the car over-heated and my mother stopped in at a gas station to let the engine cool off."

"A gas station," said Dan as though that meant something. Then in a spooky voice he whispered, "an abandoned gas station?"

And Bobby gave him a stare as if to say, "how did you know that?"

"I know the one. It's about 12 miles out on route 49," Dan said with authority.

"Yeah," said Bobby and everyone turned their attention back to him.

"Go on, Bobby, tell the story," Kelly said in a soft pleasing tone.

She was using that calm sensitive voice again, thought Bobby, speaking with low breathy sounds as if she were talking in a quiet room surrounded by insane patients and didn't want to disturb them.

Bobby decided to play along. He put his hands on knees and leaned forward for emphasis. He tried to use a scary voice like a kid would use when around the campfire telling a ghost story but, truthfully, he felt like he was at an 'idiot party'.

"I was looking for water," he said in a hushed tone, "to go in the radiator after it cooled down. I was inside the gas station when I heard my mother shouting. "Alice is gone," she said. "Alice is gone!"

Surprisingly, Bobby saw that the group was enthralled by his performance, so he became Rod Serling as he told the rest of the story.

"Alice was missing, gone, vanished as if she had been taken, abducted by an unknown force. Or maybe just swallowed up by a massive sand pit in the Inyo Desert. Yes, we were frantic. Where, oh where was little Alice, we wailed."

Kelly's expression told him to tone it down a little.

I climbed on the roof of the gas station.

"How?" interrupted Pegs.

"Huh, what?" Bobby looked at her in confusion.

"How did you climb on the roof?" she said.

Bobby quickly got back into character and continued the story.

"Oh, there... there was a ladder," he told her.

Now focused on wide-eyed Pegs, Bobby said "an old ladder at the back of the gas station. It was missing some steps and it was rotten but I didn't have a choice, did I? I had to get a better view of our surroundings, to find my little sister."

"The desert was like an ocean of dry, hot sand with cactus reaching to the barren sky as if praying for rain. And, tumbleweeds tossed by the wind, blown across the desert sands but going nowhere, really."

Bobby looked at Kelly, hoping that she was being entertained. He saw only a smirk on her face, not really a smile but she seemed to be at least slightly amused at his tale.

"I looked to the south, my eyes blinded by the fierce sun but there was no sign of little Alice," Bobby told them while being properly sad. "I ran to the west edge of the roof and again saw nothing, just a warped and burnt road frying in the heat like a piece of over-cooked bacon."

"But wait," he suddenly sounded excited, "there, to the north. Could it be? Yes, sweet little Alice in her red t-shirt with the bright blue pony rearing up. It was the colors, you see? Colors that should not be in the Inyo Desert."

"I rushed down the ladder and ran into the desert to rescue her. And, she fell into my arms, exhausted and afraid. She looked up at me and Alice managed to whisper from her parched lips, "thank you, Bobby, thank you for saving me from the Inyo Desert.""

Bobby leaned back in the chair, an indication that the tale was done. In his own voice he finished by saying, "then, I put some water in the radiator and we drove on to Inyo," but he didn't say 'The End'.

For a moment, the audience just sat there with expressions of awe, skepticism or disbelief.

Martin was the first to stand and walk over to him and Bobby felt like it was appropriate to also stand for some odd reason. Martin grabbed his shoulders, nodded his head in admiration and said, "mad skills, man. Can you write like that? I could use some help on the website."

Bobby didn't know what else to do but nod. Pegs came over then and hugged him real tight and didn't let go for a while. Bobby looked at Dan who gave him a Roman salute, a fist to the chest. Andy just looked at him with an expression of utter awe. Pegs let go after that and looked up at Bobby's face and he was astounded to see that there were tears on her face; she had been crying.

As Pegs wandered off to find a tissue, Bobby turned to Kelly who was still seated in the chair. As she slowly stood up, he noticed that her right hand was balled into a tight fist and had a fleeting idea that she might be getting ready to punch his lights out. Instead, Kelly held out the fist to him and opened it to reveal a shiny black stone laying in the palm of her hand. She indicated that he was supposed to take it.

"What's this for?" he asked her.

"I'll let you know when the time is right," was all Kelly told him, then she walked away.

As the afternoon dragged into evening, the UFObians dispersed, each going back to their miserable and stale normal lives. Only Kelly and Bobby remained in front of the spa. It wasn't an uncomfortable silence but they didn't say anything to each other, just waited. It wasn't until Uncle's truck turned the corner, that Bobby blurted out, "you should come over for supper."

"It's been a long day, Bobby. I need a shower," she told him.

"Oh, yeah, sure," Bobby said.

"I couldn't go like this," and she indicated her casual attire. Then, "maybe tomorrow?"

Bobby smiled and said, "yeah, tomorrow. Tomorrow would be good."

Uncle sliced over the wrong way and the truck coasted right up to the curb.

"I'll dress nice, try to make a good impression, you know?" Kelly said as Bobby walked around the truck to get in.

"My mom already likes you," he told her as he walked over to get into the truck, then from over the truck hood, he made a goofy face at Kelly and said, "she thinks you're cute."

Uncle leaned out from the truck window and asked Kelly, "so, you kids have a good time?"

Kelly looked at Uncle and nodded. "Mm-hmm," she uttered. It was that yes noise that little children sometimes make to adults when the child is not really listening to what's being asked.

"You need a ride home, Kelly?" asked Uncle. "You can toss the bike in the back."

"No," said Kelly. "I want to ride," indicating her bike.

As they drove away, Kelly didn't watch them go. She hopped quickly onto her bike and went in another direction.

While she was pedaling away into the dusky evening, Kelly thought back over the afternoon, all that happened with the UFObians and Bobby. Yes, she admitted to herself, it had been fun, more fun than she had had in a very long time.

And more than that, it had been exciting. Kelly wanted to throw her hands in the air just like Pegs had done but she didn't. Instead, she pedaled faster.

"Zoom!" Kelly shouted as she passed the drug store, startling an old lady that was just coming out.

"Zoom!" she cried again as she turned the corner and suddenly disappeared as if grabbed away by a fortunate alien that had caught her unaware, much like Cheryl the cheerleader.

13   Something Fishy

Jenny didn't knock on Bobby's door, just opened it and walked right in. Bobby was still laying in bed, and as she burst in, he quickly pulled up the blanket to cover his naked body.

"Oh God, Bobby, I'm sorry," Jenny blinked then turned around so that her back was to him. "I should've knocked. I'm so sorry." She was embarrassed just as much as Bobby was.

"Mom, it's okay. I wasn't..." Bobby started but his mother interjected quickly.

"Gram paw's making pancakes for breakfast. I don't want you to sleep late all day. There's plenty to do. Your grandfather could use some help, I imagine. He's building something for Alice. It would be fun, wouldn't it? Just... come down when you're ready."

Jenny left the room closing the door behind her.

"Knock, next time," she silently admonished herself. "I don't want to catch him doing it. I really don't. That would be so awkward."

Jenny thought of Kelly then and was almost certain that the cute town girl was on Bobby's mind as well.

"Does he sleep like that, naked, or...?" Jenny quickly banished that thought out of her head.

Jenny walked quickly to Alice's room but again she didn't knock, just walked right in. The bed covers were on the floor, kicked off in the night or when she got up, Jenny supposed. Alice was gone, and for just a moment, she almost panicked. "Alice is gone!" was her thinking, just like in the desert.

Jenny called for Alice, probably too loud, she thought, so took a deep breath.

"Alice?" she called out again.

"In here, Mommy," came her voice.

Jenny went into the hall, then to her father's room. She found her daughter sitting on a high stool that had been placed at the center of the fish tank. Alice didn't turn around to greet her mother but kept looking into the tank as if searching for hidden treasure.

"What are you doing, hon?" Jenny asked the little girl.

"I'm looking for Abernathy," Alice responded matter of factly.

"Oh, Alice, you didn't put a doll in there, did you?" she said and rushed over to the tank.

"I don't put him in, he jumps in," said Alice.

"No, no! Where Alice? Where is the doll?" as she looked into the tank with Alice.

"I don't think he's in there right now," Alice said glumly. "He 'probly' came out. He doesn't sit in there all day, just sometimes," she said as if her mother should know this already.

"You shouldn't be in here without Gumpa's permission. And you mustn't touch the tank or throw things in it," Jenny warned her daughter. "And for heaven's sake, you don't grab at the fish, do you?"

"No, Mommy, I am polite," said Alice. "I would not just grab him. He needs to come back on his own."

"You shouldn't be sitting on this high stool, either." Jenny took hold of her daughter and lifted her off the stool and put her down on the floor. "How did you get up there anyway?" Jenny asked her.

Alice didn't answer, just ran out of the room on her way to 'Gumpa breakfast'.

Jenny inspected the fish tank one last time to be sure that no dolls were in there. The wrap paper that her father had laid out along the floor and beneath the tank was still dry with no sign of any water leakage. She had helped her father put the paper down yesterday afternoon just as a precaution but he explained to her that there was another tank hidden in the support cabinet below the fish tank that was supposed to catch any water that might leak out.

"Even if the fish tank was broken apart, most of the water would be captured by that reserve drum," he said to her, sounding confused. Jenny knew that her father still blamed himself for Kelly's accident but the cause, it seemed, would remain a mystery to both of them.

When Jenny finally came down to the kitchen, everyone was busy eating flapjacks, bacon and eggs. And there was a pile of fresh hot biscuits that Jenny thought must have been delivered by the biscuit man while she was upstairs. "Just like Mama used to make," Jenny thought and a sadness crept over her because her mother couldn't be there with them. This had been her time of day, breakfast. Jenny could still remember the wonderful odors of her cooking any meal. Mouth-watering was the only way she could think to describe it.

It was a comforting scene, this, all the family seated around the table. Daddy must have told a funny story or a joke, Jenny guessed because Alice was giggling and Bobby had a big smile on his face.

"Sit down, girl, or there won't be any johnny cakes left over," he said to Jenny. "These scoundrels are gobbling them up like bears at a picnic.

Jenny sat down, smiling the big smile, as if she had heard her father's joke as it was being told.

Alice stopped eating and looked at her grandfather.

"What's a scow... scwon..." she tried to ask.

"Scoundrel," Jenny said it for her.

Uncle made a funny face at Jenny, a way of saying he didn't have a definition for that word. Not one that would satisfy a small child, anyway.

"It means a bad guy," said Bobby.

"Well, no," Alice argued. "I'm not a bad person. I just like flapjacks."

And they all laughed at her joke. Alice didn't know why they were laughing, it was the truth.

Bobby did join his grandfather in the work shed, helping him to apply lacquer to Alice's doll cabinet so that it would be all glossy and smooth. It probably wasn't big enough to hold all of Alice's dolls. Uncle didn't know that there were still as yet unopened boxes filled with the 'not important dolls' as Alice would put it. But, once she saw this pretty cabinet, and loved it, Bobby knew those other dolls would appear, brought out of hiding at just the right moment, and they would need a cabinet also.

"Do you know if the junior high school has a baseball team," Bobby asked.

Uncle thought a moment, then said, "no, they've got one at the high school. There's the little league. It's late in the season but they sure do need a good hitter," and shook his head in dismay. "Coach is a friend of mine. I can talk with him if you want me to."

"Yeah," Bobby said, "I want to play."

They worked on in silence for a time, then Uncle asked, "Good time with Kelly yesterday, was it?"

"Yeah, it was fun" he said truthfully, "more fun than I thought it'd be."

"Say now, what goes on down at that spa anyway?" Uncle asked as if it meant nothing. "What are you kids doing in there that's so secretive. Kelly won't tell me a thing."

"Well, Grampa, I'm not supposed to say," he replied. "It's a secret club."

"So, there's no carrying-ons that I should worry about?" he asked Bobby.

"No, nothing," and Bobby shook his head with emphasis, "nothing, just a bunch of us having a laugh."

"Humph, that so?" Uncle said, all the while looking at Bobby as if he had just caught him in a big lie. "I heard it was about aliens. You know, space aliens and UFOs and such."

When Bobby didn't answer, Uncle went on, "you know, there was talk, some years ago, that a flying saucer crashed in the desert just east of here. Don't know if it's true or not. but some say so. 'Course I was just a baby when it happened, maybe happened," Uncle corrected himself. "You believe in those things, Bobby?" Uncle asked him.

"I think maybe I do," Bobby confessed. "Not like in the movies, though," he went on. "I've seen pictures and read some stuff in books. Some of it could be real, I suppose."

"Yeah, could, I guess, can't know for sure, though, that's my thinkin'," Uncle told him.

"I like that Kelly girl," Uncle said and Bobby sure was glad that his grandfather was changing the subject from space aliens.

"Loose lips and all," thought Bobby, scared to think he might spill the beans by accident if they kept talking about it.

"Why, she's just a peach, isn't she?" Bobby said but couldn't remember what movie that was from.

"What?" Uncle asked.

"I mean she's nice," Bobby said. "Mom says she's cute and I guess that's so. I didn't think that at first. She's got some attitude, you know?"

"Comes on strong, yeah, I know that first hand," Uncle admitted.

"She's coming over for supper tonight," Bobby said.

"Is that so?" asked Uncle.

Bobby nodded, "I invited her. Is that okay?"

"It is," Uncle replied, "I like company as much as the next fellow. You might let your mom know, so she can cook up something special. She's pretty much taken over the kitchen from me, just like your grandmother used to."

His voice quietened some when he said that last about Gram-maw. That's what Bobby had called his grandmother. He missed her, too. Bobby had taken an old picture of her and his grandfather a year before she died suddenly of a stroke. His grandmother had been sitting on the back porch steps, Grampa standing next to her with one hand resting on her shoulder. She had been wearing an old-style dress with flowers and bumble bees, a white kitchen apron draped over the front. She had been a tiny woman compared to Uncle's huge frame but they somehow looked right together, big and small as they were.

Uncle had become quiet as the memories of Nelda flooded his thoughts.

"I miss her, Grampa," Bobby said to him.

"Me, too, son," Uncle said. His grandfather reached an arm over to his grandson, resting a hand on Bobby's shoulder. "I miss her, too."

14   Back to The Lost Station

It was just after 10am when Bobby heard his mother calling to him and he was glad for the interruption. He had been reading one of the books from the thrift store but the old western was not a page-turner. The cover art was of a gunfighter facing off in a dusty street against a man dressed in black pointing a rifle in his direction but the story was boring so far, about a ranch woman who had just lost her husband in a range war.

Bobby tossed the book aside, doubtful if he would ever pick it up again except to throw it in the trash. He walked over to the banister and shouted down, "I'll be there in a minute, mom. Okay?"

Jenny appeared at the bottom of the stairs and made an urgent motion for him to come down now. So, he made a 'why' motion with his arms. Jenny pointed a finger at him, then indicated that he should 'come down right now, young man'. Bobby dragged down the stairs like a captive slave, bound in servitude to a ruthless master.

Bobby reached the stair bottom and stood before his mother, waiting on her demands. Again, without talking, Jenny pointed her finger upward to the ceiling, then slowly moved it around until it was pointing to the front room. Bobby followed the line of direction that she wanted him to take and mindfully went there. He slumped his shoulders as he walked away, just for effect. There was little else he could do. He heard his mother humming and the soft steps that she made as she returned to the kitchen.

When Bobby entered the front living room, he could see no reason to be there. It appeared to be empty. There was no mop pail waiting for him to swab the deck and no vacuum cleaner either. Then, he heard an odd clicking noise like peanuts being cracked open. Bobby knew that his grandfather kept a straw basket of fresh peanuts by his easy chair, so he stepped around expecting to see him but it was Kelly. And, sure enough, she was cracking nuts. She had a big pile of empty peanut shells in her lap, nestled in a crater between her legs to hold them from dropping to the floor. Kelly was either a fast eater or she had been here a while, maybe chatting with his mother. She tossed a handful of peanuts into her mouth and started chewing.

Kelly was dressed up today, wearing a pink cotton skirt and a white puffy-sleeve blouse with yellow flowers on it. Her hair was tied back in a pony-tail with accent strands that had either escaped the rubber band or were meant to be cascading as an accent to her face. She was wearing high top cowboy boots that were worn and scuffed, every bit the country girl impression she was trying to make.

"Is there a trash can around?" she asked him.

Kelly stood up without waiting for an answer, holding the pink skirt out in front of her like a tray to keep the shells from falling onto the floor. Bobby found an oblong bin under a table. It didn't have any trash in it but he held it out for Kelly to use. She dropped the peanut shells in the bin, then brushed the small bits and pieces off from her skirt.

"Do you want to go on an adventure?" Kelly asked when she was finished.

"Maybe," he said, after considering it, then he put the bin back under the table. "Maybe I do."

Kelly motioned for him and her to go outside, to the porch for more privacy he guessed. Kelly went first with Bobby close behind.

Kelly went to the porch swing, sat down and pushed off. Bobby waited for the right swing and sat down beside her.

"I'm going out to the gas station in the desert," Kelly told him. "I just wanted to know if you would like to go along."

"Kelly, there's nothing out there," Bobby told her.

"You were busy looking for your sister," she said. "You weren't looking for evidence".

"You'll be wasting your time," he complained.

Kelly suddenly dragged her boots on the porch floor and the swing abruptly stopped.

"I'll let you know if I find anything," she told him. Then, she got up and walked away, down the steps and out into the yard. On her way, just like that. Bobby ran after her but she was moving fast.

"Wait, Kelly. Will you wait up," Bobby called to her.

Kelly did stop but didn't turn around to face him so that Bobby had to walk around her. He could tell by her face that she was angry, disappointed in his reluctance to go with her.

After a moment, Bobby said, "I'll have to ask my mom."

"Go," said Kelly, as she brushed away more peanut shell crumbs from her skirt.

Bobby did tell his mother that he and Kelly were going to hang out for a while but he didn't mention the gas station in the desert because then she would have certainly said no.

"Will you be back by lunch?" she asked him.

He lied and said "yeah, probably," but he was was almost sure that he wouldn't be.

"If I'm not, I can grab a burger."

Okay," Jenny said, "that's alright."

Bobby had lied to his mother before about silly and stupid things that he had done before but nothing on this scale. Going out into the desert without supervision, that would most certainly result in severe punishment if his mother ever found out. Still, he wanted to go because Kelly wanted him to and he didn't want her to be angry with him. Guilt and worry went with him on that trip back to the Inyo Desert where Alice disappeared but he was excited, too.

The man that was going to take them was named Frank Bodine, a neighbor of Kelly's, she told Bobby as they walked down the street. He had parked some distance away because he didn't want Uncle to know that he was doing this.

"Best to keep it quiet," Frank told Kelly, "I don't want no trouble."

Kelly knew that Frank had been fired from a job recently and that he needed money, so she offered him forty dollars plus money for gas to get them out there and back.

When Bobby saw Frank's truck, he almost turned around and went home. It was the kind of truck you would see in a junkyard. It had no rear fenders and no tailgate. Most of the paint on the truck had been burned away by the sun. It had probably been red at one time but now it was a dirty faint rust color, except for the passenger door. That door had obviously been replaced by a black one from another truck and even that door was damaged with a big dent in it.

Frank called over to him as Bobby appeared at the passenger window.

"You gotta reach inside to open it, that outside handle don't work," Frank said in a loud voice.

As Bobby reached inside the open window, something grabbed his arm and he jerked back, surprised. Then, Andy's head appeared in the window and he was laughing.

"Gotcha," Andy exclaimed.

Andy had been slouched down out of view. Kelly should have told him, he thought. Bobby didn't like being made to look like a fool.

Andy opened the door and could see that Bobby was upset.

"Hey, I'm sorry," Andy apologized. "I thought it would be funny is all."

Kelly slid into the front seat next to Andy who was next to Frank. The back jump seat was full of boxes, tools and all manner of junk that Frank needed to carry with him at all times, so Bobby got in next to Kelly and the front truck seat immediately became crowded.

Frank went around corners as if the police were chasing him. On one sharp left turn, Bobby's hand reached out for support and his hand landed on Kelly's leg. He took it away fast and Kelly didn't seem to notice, just kept staring at the open road leading out into the desert.

There was a hot wind blowing that day and the breeze coming through the open windows of the truck was stifling.

"Do you have air conditioning?" Bobby shouted over the noise of the racing engine.

Frank just shook his head 'no' and kept driving.

One strong wind that jumped into the passenger window swirled in the cab with genuine force. That wind lifted Kelly's skirt like a sheet on an open clothes line and Bobby was able to catch a glimpse of white panties with blue trim before Kelly managed to press the dress back down.

After that, Bobby tried hard to watch the desert landscape out the passenger window. After a time, he did look back at Kelly but only after he had stifled his arousal. Most of the time, Kelly looked straight ahead as if excited by the adventure they were all about to experience. But sometimes she did look at him, straight at him with her sparkling, intense eyes as though thrilled beyond reason and Kelly could see that he was excited, too. And that made Bobby go dumb, because he was excited for an entirely different reason than her.

He felt Kelly shift as she leaned in close to him and felt her warm breath on his neck.

She spoke into his ear as if sharing a secret.

"Almost there," Kelly said to him. "Are you ready for this?"

Bobby could smell her, a fresh airy smell like she had just stepped out of the shower to dry off. He turned to Kelly and his face was so close to hers, like they were getting ready to kiss.

"I'm ready for this, Kelly," he told her.

Kelly didn't pull away too quickly but seemed to enjoy this moment, her body tightly pressed against his in the bouncing truck.

Frank hit a pothole that jolted all of them and they turned to face the road ahead. But Kelly didn't move back across the seat. She remained leaning in toward Bobby as if reluctant to lose that intimate moment with him.

The truck arrived at the derelict gas station too soon for Bobby. Frank and Andy had vanished from his mind and Bobby was glad that they had been quiet for most of the trip. He didn't want the intimacy to end, how he felt with Kelly sitting so near to him in the truck.

"There it is," shouted Andy.

Frank nodded, shifted gears to slow down and the truck coasted in under the outlying roof where cars used to fill up with gas, out of the desert sun. Bobby opened the black replacement door and stepped out first, quickly followed by Kelly dragging a small backpack from the floorboard with her and Andy with his black camera bag that he had been tightly holding on his lap the entire trip.

Frank leaned over to them and said, "I'll just wait here while you kids do it." Then, to Kelly, "you've got one hour, like I said. If you're late, the bus leaves without you."

Kelly pulled Bobby aside and asked, "where did Alice see the balloon?"

"Not sure, really," he admitted. "But it must have been in that direction," pointing to the northeast. "That's where I found her."

"Let's get on the roof," Kelly said, "where's the ladder?"

Kelly didn't wait but turned and dashed around to the back side of the gas station. Bobby ran after her.

Bobby saw that the ladder was still upright against the back wall. Kelly already had one foot on the bottom rung and was staring up at the roof edge.

"Wait, Kelly," shouted Bobby. He grabbed her arm to stop her from climbing.

"That ladder is rickety and rotten, just like I said," he cautioned her. "And look, there are two rungs missing."

"I can do it, Bobby," she pleaded. "I want to go up there."

Bobby held onto Kelly's arm still. He was going to let her go, just wanted to hold onto her a little bit longer while he told the rules.

"You hold on with both arms and only take a step up when your other foot is firmly planted on a rung. If you feel like you're going to fall..."

Kelly put her hand on Bobby's chest and said, "I'm not going to fall. I'm a good climber. You just watch."

Bobby let go of her then and she went up like an expert at ladder climbing. Bobby held the ladder steady for her in case it should slip. He was only mildly worried that it would break apart. After all, it had held his greater weight. But as he thought about it, he had absolutely no recollection of climbing the ladder on the day Alice went missing. Bobby just remembered suddenly being on the roof, searching for her.

He was not watching Kelly ascend as those thoughts bubbled in his brain, and almost missed the opportunity to confirm his suspicions. But then, he looked. Yes, tiny blue flowers all around the edges and he smiled.

Bobby followed Kelly up and found her looking at the desert landscape with binoculars.

He walked across the roof slowly so that he didn't startle her, she was that close to the edge and it was a long fall, high enough to break a leg for sure.

"Kelly," he said. "Can you step back a little? You're making me nervous."

Kelly took a step back for him but kept looking out at the desert, as if an enemy was approaching and she didn't want to lose sight of the bad guy.

Bobby stood right behind Kelly with his arms ready to grab her if she became dizzy or lost her balance.

"What's out there, Kelly?" he asked her. "What are you not telling me?"

Kelly lowered the binoculars but still did not look at Bobby.

"Strange things have happened in this desert," she told him as she turned her head to look at him, "since the crash that Pete Selby saw all those years ago."

Bobby looked at Kelly in a confused way that was telling her to spill it.

"It's all in the 'Restricted' folder that you were about to open on the computer," she explained. "That's why I stopped you when I did. I didn't want to frighten you."

Kelly raised the binoculars and watched the desert again but there was nothing for her to see. She really didn't think there would be; she was only hoping for a miracle moment.

After one more look around in all directions, Bobby and Kelly climbed back down to the ground. Bobby went first so that he could hold the ladder for her.

"I wonder what Andy is up to?" Kelly asked.

They found him inside the gas station. He was taking pictures of the inside walls, the counter top and whatever else that interested him. Bobby slid through the door and Kelly came after.

"Watch where you step," Andy warned them. They both froze in position and waited for him to tell them why.

"There are footprints in the dust... on the floor," he told them.

"Those are my footprints," said Bobby and took a step.

"No," exclaimed Andy, then in a calmer voice, "not yours, others."

Andy pointed to the dirty tiles on the floor in front of them and said, "most are behind and in front of this counter but there are more in other places... a lot more, the garage."

"I don't see any footprints except mine," snorted Bobby.

Andy looked at Bobby as if he were stupid and recklessly intent on ignoring his warning.

"You're not looking close enough," said Andy. He used a flashlight to illuminate the shadows on the floor. Kelly saw the footprints before Bobby and she gasped.

"Look," Kelly said in a low voice and she bumped Bobby's shoulder with hers for effect. "Footprints!"

"Those are animal tracks," Bobby scoffed, "probably a raccoon or, I don't know, a lizard got in here looking for food or water."

"No, not animal tracks, something else," Andy told him. "Go down on your knees, right where you are, and look closer." Before either of them moved, Andy cautioned them, "be careful not to smudge any."

"You've taken pictures, Andy?" Kelly asked him.

"Yes, I have pictures, the ones in here. But outside, you know, the wind, other disturbances." He shook his head, "not gonna find any out there."

Amazingly, the footprints seemed to have patterns, much like the bottom of a bare foot would make if it disturbed the dust but these were much smaller than a human foot could possibly make.

Kelly and Bobby, on hands and knees, moved across the room as if the floor had hidden explosives and one wrong move would send all of them to oblivion.

Kelly pointed to a perfectly shaped circular pattern in a mound of dirt, like someone had pressed a large beach ball into the ground but none of them could even guess on what made that.

Bobby was still skeptical until Andy moved the flashlight to a dark recess at the furthest back corner of the lobby, on the floor.

"Over here, look," said Andy, sounding proud that he had discovered such a wondrous thing.

The single hand print on the dirty floor was almost perfect, deep enough to show exact measurements, as if it had been left on purpose to be found and marveled at. The finger spread was wide and the impression was solid enough to see a pattern of ridges and whorls but this hand print was only the size of one that a nurse might make from a newborn baby on a birth certificate.

"Okay, yeah, that is strange," thought Bobby but he kept his mouth shut. Then he smiled. It was Andy that was the joker, not Kelly like he had assumed with the toilet paper prank. He must have a small imprint stamp of some kind and had made this perfect 'evidence' while Kelly and him were up on the roof.

"If I only had the right tools," Andy said quietly, "plaster of Paris or melted wax even, I could take a mold."

Kelly stood up and looked around the room, searching. She found an empty metal bucket that would safely cover the hand print with room to spare.

"What are you doing?" Andy asked, worried that she was going to disturb the find.

Kelly explained, "we put the can over the print to keep it safe, from the wind or anything else that might disturb it. When we come back, you'll have the right material to get the evidence, won't you?"

Andy gave her a 'thumbs up' as an answer.

When they went into the mechanic's bay there were more of the same tiny footprints all around the car bays and on the squalid unkempt cement floor.

"They're all over the place," Kelly marveled, "like they were wandering or maybe looking for something."

"Yes, recent, too," Andy sounded confident. "Wind hasn't erased them yet."

Andy waited for Kelly and Bobby to look at him before he went on. He wanted all their attention before the big surprise.

But he had to say, "there's more," before they would stop searching and look in his direction.

Andy waved his hand theatrically as if he were preparing to show them the absolute finest and best previously owned car on the lot.

Kelly walked with him to a far corner of the garage, a dark spot that light couldn't quite reach into. Andy turned the flashlight on and the reveal astounded Kelly but not Bobby who still thought this was just a joke being played on him. He stood a small distance away with his arms crossed, waiting for the prank to be over. Kelly looked back at Bobby and waved for him to come closer.

"Bobby, c'mere, look," Kelly insisted. And he went to her, ready to call out and expose the ridiculous charade. He was pissed that Kelly would do this to him but then thought, maybe she was unaware of Andy's betrayal of her sincere quest for answers. When he saw the strange design on the wall, however, he quite suddenly changed his mind. Dan could have possibly conceived this fakery since he was skilled as an artist but Andy? No, Bobby thought, he couldn't have done such an intricate sketch in the short time that he had been alone.

The markings were similar in ways to the petroglyphs Bobby had looked at on the club's computer but this 'writing' appeared to be more distinct and busy. It couldn't be described as an easy smooth style but was more rough and abstract, like an imaginative child might do if handed a crayon and a blank sheet of paper.

There were lines – some jagged, others wavy, two big circles at the top, triangular shapes and odd symbols that were unusual. The drawing was not on the ground like the footprints but up on the wall of the garage about 14 inches high above the floor.

"Nothing giant about this one," Bobby thought. It probably measured only 9 inches by 5.

"It's scorched," said Andy, "or burnt into the wall, by a flame or something hot."

"No, no," Kelly said, "this is a drawing done by hand, maybe using charcoal or graphite, I'm not sure. Look at the lines and overall design. This is intricate, maybe a message or telling a story like aborigines do."

"That could be right," Andy agreed. "There is a problem, though. See the outlines here and here," Andy said pointing to specific features of the design, "it's already smudged, degrading. It isn't meant to last over time like a petroglyph. We need a sealant, something that will protect and cover it without destroying it.

"What about lacquer or a clear coat spray paint, that would do it, wouldn't it?" Bobby asked.

"Yeah, that would be good, I think," Andy replied.

"You've got enough pictures, Andy, just in case?" Kelly asked again, needing to be reassured.

"Yeah, I do," Andy replied, "but, Kelly, we need to cut out this section of wall and recover it. This is too important, an actual artifact found by us, The UFO Bureau. And yeah, it's probably illegal but I know a guy," said Andy. "He'll do it for a price."

"No," said Kelly shaking her head. "We need to do this ourselves. Nobody can know about this."

Kelly looked at each of the boys, her expression one that said 'please, guys', hoping that she wouldn't have to convince them more than that.

"We'll find a way, Kelly, if that's what you want," Bobby said to her.

"Yeah, Kelly, we can do it," Andy chimed in. "How hard could it be? The right tools, a little muscle..."

"Transport might be a problem," said Bobby. "None of us are old enough to drive, huh?"

"We'll do a work-around," Kelly smiled at them.

The honking horn dissolved any thoughts and plans to talk about right now. Anything that they could do would have to happen another time.

On the ride back to town, the UFObians were excited and enthusiastic about the discovery, although they didn't reveal any details because Frank was there with them. Kelly was positively giddy, bouncing around on the truck seat, poking at Andy and Bobby. She even reached up to Bobby's head, mussed up his hair, then hugged him after.

Frank was sullen on the way back, because Kelly was not showing him any attention. If she asked him to give her a ride to the desert again, she was going to have to pay more than money next time. "Fun time out in the desert." he muttered once, wishing he was a teenager again like the boys who just had Kelly out in the Inyo Desert.

None of them thought to look up during this event. If they had, they might have seen the two orbs silently hovering over the abandoned station, one large which was primary and another of a lesser size. The orbs did not move during the entire time that the team was exploring the station. Only when the car began to travel west away from the location did the ancillary orb break from position and follow it for a distance of 4.7 miles, then the orb stopped, as if that was the limit of its directive dictated by whatever force was controlling the thing. The secondary orb then returned to its original position above the gas station with the primary and they both hovered over the Inyo Desert like two metallic moons, sentinels patiently waiting and watching.

15   A Serious Talk

Bobby ran up the front steps and went into the house as if the police were chasing him and he was desperate for sanctuary. He was in such a hurry because of the worry that was swirling in his mind. Although there had been fun, and excitement, on the desert journey, his guilt for deceiving his mother was smothering those other emotions now. He had considered telling her, confessing to his crime but knew he wouldn't. And even more bothersome, Bobby felt sure that his involvement with Kelly was leading him down a dark path and he was probably going to get into more trouble before the mystery was solved.

Jenny heard him come in and looked down the hall from the kitchen.

"Bobby, is that you?" she called to him.

Bobby was halfway up the staircase when he heard her and stopped abruptly.

"Yeah, Mom, I'm back," he shouted.

"Did you eat?" she asked.

Bobby jumped down the stairs and hurried into the kitchen.

"I could eat something," he grinned at her, then plopped down in a chair at the table

Jenny had been washing dishes at the sink. She dried her hands on a dish towel, then reached into the oven for Bobby's plate. The meal was his favorite – a cheeseburger with waffle fries and it was still warm.

"I just put it in there five minutes ago," his mother said as he put the plate in front of him. "Do you want ketchup, mayo, mustard?" she asked Bobby.

"Mm-hmm," Bobby grunted from a mouth full of burger, then bobbed his head up and down to make sure that she understood.

By the time Jenny placed the condiments to the side of his plate, Bobby had consumed most of the burger and a good handful of 'potato shakes' as he called them.

Jenny watched him eat for a few moments, then went back to the kitchen sink to wash the last dishes.

She could hear her son engrossed in his food but disturbed him anyway.

"Did you have fun with Kelly?" she asked him.

"Yeah," was all he said back to her.

"Bobby," said Jenny.

Bobby made a noise to tell her that he was listening but still eating.

"Bobby," she said cautiously, "you do know that you can get a girl pregnant?"

The silence from her son told her that he had stopped eating but he didn't say anything to her question. When she turned around to face him, Jenny noticed that Bobby had stopped mid-chew and was looking at her as if to say 'please don't go there'.

"I know you like Kelly..." Jenny went on in a motherly tone.

"Pregnant? What are you talking about? I'm just a kid," Bobby said.

"Hasn't your father talked to you?" she asked him. "No, he wouldn't," she thought. "But they teach it in school, don't they? Hygiene class?"

Bobby was wondering just how far his mother would go in this talk about sex, and he was curious to find out.

But, then he said, "I know about sex, Mom. I do."

"You can't know everything," she went on, "and I don't know how much to tell you."

Bobby didn't say anything, just took the last waffle cut and put it in his mouth.

"Maybe you should talk to your grandfather," his mother said to him.

"No," Bobby said looking directly at her, "if we're going to have the sex talk thing, I want you to do it, not Grampa."

Jenny sat down at the table but didn't believe that she was actually ready to have this serious talk with Bobby yet. But, she was worried about that Kelly girl. She was just so cute and Jenny was still concerned about what Bobby had been doing in bed yesterday when she burst into his room unexpectedly.

"You're going to have to help me here, Bobby," she sighed. "I don't know where to start."

When Bobby realized that his mother was on the verge of tears, he said, "Mom, I already know a lot. I'm fourteen."

Jenny looked at him waiting for the boom and hoping that it wouldn't happen.

"I do know that I can get a girl pregnant if I go too far," he admitted, being serious now.

"Oh my God, he's having sex already... at fourteen!" Jenny silently screamed.

And, Bobby could see that his mother was stunned by his admission. So, he quickly said, "I haven't had sex yet," and he saw the look of relief on her face.

"I'm not ready yet," he explained. "I wouldn't know how to... what to do, really. Yes, I've got the information but to actually... do it. No, mom, I'm not ready."

"Kelly," his mother said, only that.

"I like Kelly. She's fun," he told her. "but she's like one of the guys, you know? Like a buddy." And, here he was, lying to his mother again, not wanting her to know the truth about him and Kelly. He didn't want to put that problem on her, not now with all that's been happening – the divorce, running away to Grampa's house, all the worry and stress that his mother had. It was enough.

"If you want, we can have this talk when I am ready," he said to her. "Okay, Mom?"

"And, you'll tell me when that is?" she asked him.

"I will tell you," Bobby promised, lying one more time.

"Okay, then," Jenny said reaching across the table to squeeze her son's hand.

"I love you," Jenny smiled at him and he said it back to her because she needed to hear it.

"I love you, too, Mom," Bobby said knowing that was true. "No lies that time," he thought.

Alice came into the kitchen, opened the refrigerator door and looked inside.

Jenny and Bobby's talk was over, for now, and both of them were thankful for Alice's intrusion.

"What are you looking for, baby?" asked Jenny.

"Don't know yet," replied Alice, "something good."

"I can make you something," Jenny said as she stood up from the table. "What would you like?"

"I don't know 'zactly' what I want, though," Alice said.

"Alice honey, you just ate. Are you still hungry?"

"One of my dollies is hungry but he is a picky eater," complained Alice.

"How about a cookie?" Jenny said to her daughter. "Do you want a cookie?"

"Maybe," replied Alice, "what kind?"

Jenny opened a cabinet and moved some packages, then found cookies.

"Let's see, there's peanut butter and chocolate chip," she told the little girl now standing at her feet, waiting.

"No," Alice said sadly. "He likes green stuff."

Bobby reached across the table for the chocolate chip cookies.

"Well, honey, we don't have any green cookies," Jenny told her.

Alice marched back to the refrigerator to look for proper food that her dolly would eat without making faces at her. Jenny didn't see what Alice took from the refrigerator but the little girl had something green in her hands when she left the kitchen.

16 A Factual Account of An Ingling Lost

Kelly was early for supper, showing up even before Jenny had started preparations for the evening meal. Kelly apologized saying that she needed to speak with Uncle for a few minutes if he wasn't busy.

Uncle must have heard the conversation, because he shouted from the den, "I'm in here, Kelly."

As Kelly came into the room, Uncle waved an arm for her to come closer.

"As it happens, I'm not busy at all, Kelly, so take a seat and let's talk," he told her.

Kelly came around to see that Uncle was cracking peanuts just as she done earlier that day. He had a bowl in his lap that was mixed with shelled peanuts and empty shells together. As they talked, he would unconsciously search for a fresh peanut shell hidden among the discards but, he kept his attention on her since Kelly was more important than peanuts.

"I was just watchin' some tv show on fishin'," he said to Kelly, "but I lost interest a good while back."

Uncle lowered the volume on the tv set with the remote but didn't turn it off.

"You go first," Uncle said to Kelly.

She sat down on the foot stool next to Uncle's chair, since he wasn't using it and it was convenient.

"So, I wanted to ask you about the fish tank upstairs, Kelly began. "It's really big, like some giant scooped up part of the ocean and dropped it in your room."

"It's a 90 gallon," Uncle boasted, "but I've seen bigger."

"It's a saltwater tank?" Kelly asked.

"Yes, it is saltwater," Uncle admitted.

"I looked it up on the internet," she explained. "YouTube has some videos."

"YouTube?" Uncle seemed to be clueless.

"It's a video website, Grampa," said Bobby who had just come in to join them. People take videos of just about everything now," he explained as simply as he could, "then upload them to the internet for people to look at on their computers."

"Yeah," Uncle said, "I think I saw a story about that on a tv show, lots of fights and arguing as I recall."

Bobby nodded at Kelly to go on.

"This one girl," Kelly told Uncle, "she has a really big tank. It almost takes up the one whole side of her garage."

Uncle nodded, wondering where this was going.

"My mother took me to Yuma one time and we went in to an aquarium store but there wasn't anything like what you have."

"I'm not surprised, Kelly," said Uncle. "Salt water tanks, well, that's a specialty hobby for people who've got a lot of money to waste."

"I want one as big as yours," Kelly went on. "Oh, not anytime soon but, you know, someday."

"I'll help you any way I can," Uncle said, "but really I'm just a novice. I don't know all, no matter what some folks think. I've got an old Navy buddy in San Diego. He came out and helped me get started."

"Can we go look at it?" Kelly asked. "I only got a glimpse the other day."

"The day of the accident," Uncle thought but just said, "well, sure."

Bobby and Kelly followed Uncle up the stairs and into his bedroom. Alice was already there, staring into the front glass of the tank like she was looking at a toy store window, wondering what she could convince her mother to buy for her.

Alice didn't greet them or seem upset as Bobby, Kelly and Gumpa crowded in close to the aquarium, violating her space. She just said, "that yellow one is funny. She will come right up to the glass and try to bump your finger. Watch."

Alice pressed a finger to the tank and sure enough, the yellow fish came at it bumping into the glass once, then again as if saying "yes, I see you still there, little girl."

"It probably thinks your finger is a worm and wants to eat it," Bobby said to his sister.

"No, not," squealed Alice. She knew her finger didn't look like a worm but Alice still examined it to be sure.

"Where is the octopus?" Kelly asked. "I saw it the other day."

"Cathy is a timid creature, Kelly. I imagine she's hiding out under the rock garden, most likely."

"You name all the fish… and octopus?" Kelly asked him.

"I do." Uncle responded but didn't explain any more about that.

"I don't see the turtle," Kelly said sounding disappointed.

"That's because I don't have a turtle," he told her.

"Maybe it wasn't a turtle; it was mostly hiding behind the rocks and weeds. Was it a salamander, maybe?" Kelly guessed.

"No, huh uh," said Uncle.

"I know I saw it, whatever it was," insisted Kelly.

"What color was it?" Bobby asked her.

"Gray like the octopus but lighter with spots sorta like on a giraffe, orange spots or maybe yellow?" Kelly said uncertain.

Kelly noticed that Alice was looking up at her in a hurt way, as if Kelly had stepped on her toe or something.

"He's not in there right now," she said to Kelly.

"Who, Alice?" Kelly asked the little girl. "Who's not in there right now?"

"Abernathy," Alice said, then she twirled around once as if to magically disappear like fairies do and left the room in a flurry.

Kelly wanted to run after the little girl but Uncle was still pointing out details about the colorful fish and coral to Bobby and her. Kelly forced herself to seem interested in his descriptions but it was hard to keep pretending that she was fascinated.

Kelly did watch carefully once more, when Uncle used a long round wood stick to lightly tap on an outcrop of rocks. The tiny octopus did come out of a dark hole then so that they all could see her. Cathy moved over the rocks almost as if she were dancing, her many delicate tentacles going this way and that as if keeping time with music that only she could hear. And as beautiful as Cathy was, Kelly was disappointed in her appearance. She had been secretly hoping that Abernathy would come out from the rocks, now that she knew he was real and not imagined.

Kelly was polite and talkative during supper but Bobby knew that she would be. It was her 'good girl' role presented for Grampa and his mother. Bobby had come to think that Kelly had a different personality for each day of the week, maybe more. When he had first met her, she was the nasty local girl, wary of intruders, protecting her domain. The following day she was the gang leader attempting to recruit Bobby into combat against rivals. On the journey to the desert, Kelly was flirtatious and bubbly without being outright comical, except when she tousled his hair. Kelly must have studied Pegs for a long while to get that persona just right but was sure to discard the ridiculous mannerisms that made Pegs such an outrageous tart.

After supper, Kelly and Bobby went to his room and Bobby left the door open for his mother's sake, and maybe his own. Kelly's costume today was prim and proper, the good girl personified. She had on a simple white dress with a blue sweater for accent. She had short ankle high kitty cat socks on with simple black pumps that wouldn't offend anyone.

Kelly sat on Bobby's bed just like she had done the other day, legs crossed, the upper one slightly bouncing in a slow rhythm as if a fly had landed on her foot and she was trying to softly shoo it away.

"I can whistle," Bobby told Kelly as he stood tall above her.

"What?" Kelly asked but she knew.

"Lauren Bacall to Humphrey Bogart," Bobby accused her. "To Have and Have Not, 1944."

Kelly smiled at him and said, "you're wrong about me, Mr. Bogart and I will admit to nothing." Kelly was impressed that he had looked that up for her or maybe he was an old movie buff like her. And, she wanted to know.

"You had to look that up. Am I right?" Kelly said.

Bobby didn't answer the question. He was looking at Kelly in a way that made her slightly uncomfortable.

"Are you going to arrest me, sheriff?" Kelly asked and held out her wrists to be handcuffed.

Bobby was being sincere when he said, "I just want to know which one is the real Kelly. I want to know you as you really are."

Kelly stood up and walked across the room so that her back was to him. She gazed out the window for a few moments, then said, "I really don't know," she said softly as if speaking to the dark night outside. "I seem to adapt to a situation and do what seems necessary right at that moment."

She turned to Bobby then and said, "I'm still searching, I guess for who I want to be... at the end, whenever that is going to happen."

"How you act with other people, I don't care," he said to her, "but I want you to be honest with me. Can you do that?"

"Yes, I think now I can," she told him but Bobby detected an uncertainty in her voice.

"Maybe tone it down a bit with my mom and grandfather, yeah?" he asked.

Kelly smiled and nodded.

"I can do that," she said with more conviction. "Alice?" she asked him.

"Alice?" he said, not understanding right away. "Oh, Alice. You need to be the fairy princess that grants her every wish but you're going to have a problem there, because she wants to fly just like Tinker Bell."

Then a clouded look was on Kelly's face as she said, "I need to tell you what really happened the day that I fell."

Bobby sat down on the bed because he had a feeling that what Kelly was about to tell him was serious. Kelly came and sat beside him.

Kelly smoothed her dress down, wiping away imagined peanut shell crumbs, then with a sigh, she said, "After I fell, there was someone... some thing hiding under the bed, watching me. It was Abernathy."

Bobby stared at her in obvious disbelief.

"I know how ridiculous that sounds, Bobby, I do," she said, sounding just as confused as Bobby was. "I wasn't sure at first but now..."

Kelly turned to Bobby and grabbed both of his hands in hers.

"I was scared," Kelly said. "I thought if I told anyone, they would send me away to the hospital for more tests. Bump on the head, brain concussion, hallucinations."

Bobby saw that Kelly was genuinely scared.

"I know what I saw was real, Bobby," she said to him but he thought maybe Kelly was trying to convince herself as much as she was him.

Then it all came out of her in a rush like she had to make a final best effort for him or all was lost.

"It was Abernathy," she swore, "standing near me. And, he wanted to help me after the fall when I was hurt but he didn't know how. He was so small, see, and I was so big."

Bobby was getting frightened now, because Kelly was behaving so unlike he had ever seen her before, scared and tearful as she gripped his hands tighter.

Bobby felt that he needed an adult in this situation, didn't feel confident enough to handle the trauma Kelly seemed to be having. He was about to call for his mother when Kelly said, "we need to talk to Alice. Can we do that?"

"No" was his immediate thought. Bobby didn't want his little sister to see how Kelly was acting. It would frighten her.

Seeing his face, Kelly knew that he was long past believing anything she said now but she tried anyway.

"In the desert, when she was lost, Alice told me that she found something. It was Abernathy and he fell from the sky," Kelly implored, wanting to shake him, slap him, something to make him wake up and believe her. "Yes, I thought it was just make-believe at first but now? I saw Abernathy under the bed after I fell, Bobby."

Kelly could see in his eyes as he looked at her with a grim expression of sorrow that it was useless. Kelly let go of Bobby's hands and slumped over as if all her energy had suddenly vanished.

"I knew you wouldn't believe me," she accused him. "I knew."

Bobby put his arm around her shoulder to comfort Kelly.

"Kelly please, listen," he said calmly to sooth her.

"Alice was lost in the desert, just for a short time that day," Bobby said in a soft voice. "Do you really believe that she captured some creature while she was out there, because...?"

Kelly wouldn't allow him to say anything more, terrified of what that might be.

"She came out of the desert with something," Kelly said, seeming to gain more composure.

To appease Kelly, he tried to think back to that awful day. He recalled a fuzzy image of Alice strolling out of the desert. She was holding that big shoulder bag that she was always carrying but cradling it like an infant in a blanket.

"There could have been something," Bobby said, then he paused.

"What?" Kelly asked. "What was it?"

"Her carry-all, that big bag that she takes wherever she goes. There could have been something in it."

Alice mostly carried her dolls and stuffed animals in that bag for traveling to the playground or on other day trips but it was also useful for hiding things, Bobby knew. Once she had cats – not kittens, regular size housecats – and no one even noticed until they started yowling and howling, trying to escape from the little girl's custody.

Kelly saw that he remembered something else by his confused expression.

As Kelly watched for a reaction, Bobby slowly sat up, his hands tightly gripping the edge of the bed.

"She was telling a story in the back of the car, talking to one of her dolls. It was hurt or broken. I don't know."

"What?" Kelly asked excitedly.

"It got injured, I think, when a bird dropped the doll and she was going to make it well. She... she was gonna..."

"What? Tell me, Bobby," Kelly implored.

"It likes to eat green things," Bobby said softly.

"What?" Kelly asked. "What did you say?"

Bobby turned to Kelly with an odd expression on his face as if experiencing a sudden revelation, or maybe wonderment at what he now believed could be happening.

"It wanted a green cookie," Bobby said, feeling as if he were in a dream. "Abernathy likes to eat green things. Alice is feeding it."

Bobby and Kelly looked at each other amazed but finally accepting that fantasy had just become reality for both of them.

"They're gonna lock us both up in the asylum, Kelly," said Bobby offhandedly.

Kelly nodded vigorously, then said, "we need to talk to Alice."

"Yeah," he replied, "I know."

As they were on their way to find Alice, Kelly grabbed Bobby's arm to stop him.

"What?" he asked her.

"It might be... " Kelly bit a lip to stop her talking but then continued because he needed to know. "It might be better if I talked to Alice alone."

"What? Why?" Bobby blurted out.

"She doesn't like you very much," Kelly said. "Alice told me, that first day, that you're mean to her. She wanted me to beat you up and seemed real excited when I told her that I'd do it."

"I'm not mean to Alice," Bobby argued. "It's just, well, she's a little girl, she irritates me sometimes."

"You're her big brother," Kelly said to him. "You're the one that's supposed to be her champion, not me."

"Okay, yeah, she might respond to you better than me, I'll give you that," he finally admitted, "but there's no way that I'm not coming with you. No way, no how."

"You'll be nice to her tonight?" Kelly asked him.

Bobby nodded.

Kelly just had to add "you can go back to being mean Bobby tomorrow."

Then, Bobby and Kelly went off together in search of a little girl who had all the answers, they hoped.

Alice was already dressed in her nightgown, ready for sleep, just waiting for Mommy to come with her 'good night pleasant dreams' kiss. Seeing Alice scowling at him, Bobby sat as far away as he could on Alice's toy chest. Kelly sat on the bed next to Alice, who wondered if Kelly was going to 'goodnight' kiss her.

"Alice," she said softly, "can I talk to Abernathy before you go to bed?" Kelly asked her sweetly.

"He's not here right now," Alice said with assurance but she didn't really know where he was. He could be under the bed or snuggled in with the other dolls. She reminded herself to look after Kelly and Bobby were gone.

"Is he hiding?" Kelly asked.

"That's what he does," Alice said, in a sort of sing-songy way. "He will not stay put."

"Do you talk to him often?" Kelly said.

"Sometimes," Alice answered, "but he doesn't really talk except to make funny noises and go like this."

Alice moved her hands and arms in slow, easy movements like a circus clown that was trying to regain balance on a tightrope and not doing very good, at all. Then, Alice looked at Kelly, opened her mouth wide and used one hand near her own face, then moved that hand in and out, in and out.

"That," Alice stated with certainty, "means that Abernathy wants some food."

Kelly turned her head to look at Bobby with big eyes and a wide open mouth like Alice had just demonstrated to her.

"You found him in the desert," Kelly said, hoping the child would elaborate.

Alice nodded, then said, "he was injured by the bird but he only limped for a little while. All better now."

"Does he go swimming a lot?" Kelly asked her.

Kelly knew that the little girl must be tired and ready for sleep but she couldn't stop now.

"I don't know," Alice said yawning. "I can't keep my eyes on him all day long."

"What was that about a bird, Alice?" Bobby asked from across the room.

"A big bird was carrying him off for her baby chicks to eat but he fought the bird and they both fell out of the sky. I told you about that, Bobby, in the car," she said, unhappy that he had just forgotten.

Just one last question and she would leave Alice alone, Kelly promised herself but she needed to know this one for sure.

"What color is Abernathy, Alice," she asked.

"Mostly he is gray," she explained, "but he can go black when he is sick or unhappy. You can't see the spots when he's that way."

"Spots?" said Kelly.

"He has spots like a giraffe," Alice said, "orange, and green sometimes."

Then Alice seemed to become excited as she spoke.

"He vomited once," Alice said, "when he ate corn and peas. Abernathy won't eat corn anymore or just plain grass from the yard but I like to see the funny face he makes when I give it to him."

Alice giggled a little as if remembering Abernathy doing just that. Kelly reached out and hugged the little girl because she deserved a big reward but a hug was all that Kelly could offer right now.

Bobby and Kelly went back to his room while Alice was being tucked in by her mother. They both sat down on the bed as they had done before, silent at first, each one thinking their own thoughts about this revelation.

Bobby spoke first in a hushed tone and said, "there is a creature in the house, right now... in my Grampa's house."

Kelly was quiet still, until she slowly turned to look at Bobby with a sad expression on her face.

"Oh, Bobby," she said.

When he saw tears start to form in her eyes, he reached out and took her hand; it was trembling.

"What, Kelly, tell me," he urged her.

"He's lost, Bobby," she said as she began to cry. "Abernathy is lost."

She leaned in to Bobby as if falling but a slow fall into his arms and Bobby held her close for a short while letting her weep on his shoulder.

It wasn't a long cry, just enough to get rid of a mild sadness.

When she did rise up, out of his arms, Kelly looked at Bobby, not sad but hopeful that that she could convince Bobby of her belief that a rescue was needed to save Abernathy.

"The footprints in the gas station, so many of them," she said. "and... and the message on the wall. They left it for him."

"Who?" Bobby asked, not understanding.

"His people," she said, "they're still out there and they've been searching for Abernathy. That's why so many footprints were there but they can't find him. Abernathy is lost somewhere in this house and he doesn't know how to get back home."

17 Night Crawlers

Kelly didn't think she was going to be able to sleep later that night but she was wrong, so wrong. As soon as her head hit the pillow, she was out like a light bulb suddenly gone dark, as if her brain were exhausted by the mish-mash thoughts, plans and feelings that Kelly had forced upon it.

"Enough" said her brain, "I need sleep and I need it right now," and it just shut down and Kelly was taken with it into a deep but satisfying slumber much needed by both of them. She dreamed during the night, her closed eyes active as if a movie was playing on the inside of her eyelids, watching whatever images were there.

In one dream Kelly was a cloud, drifting high over a landscape filled with pink trees and wild animal herds watching her from far below. She was a happy cloud and didn't want to scare the beasts with her thunder and lightening but only wanted to offer them shade from the hot sun but she couldn't linger too long in one place, the wind told her. Kelly was alone; there were no other clouds with her and she needed to find some and so, she drifted away. Kelly wouldn't remember that dream when she woke up, like so many dreams that are lost by all of us.

It was Albino Man that woke her. Kelly sat up as if she had been yanked by a rope that had been tied around her chest while she was asleep but she could not see who was pulling at her. In her stupor, Kelly even tried to untie the rope binding her chest but when she felt for it, there was nothing there. There was a void of blackness around her, so that if anyone had been in the room pulling on the rope, Kelly wouldn't have been able to see them anyway.

She reached for the pencil and notepad on the dresser table next to her bed but her hand found nothing but emptiness. And then, Kelly remembered that she was not at home in her own bed like she should be. Kelly was at the spa, sleeping on the cot in her secret place. Kelly hadn't gone home after supper at Uncle's house. She had told her mother earlier that day that she was going to a sleep-over with one of her friends. Her mother didn't even ask who it was or when she would come home, as if she didn't need to know, or just didn't care.

Kelly quickly lay back down, closed her eyes and tried to grab the dream before it got away. She lay very still for what seemed like a very long time but it was actually not even a minute.

Kelly got up, slid her legs over the edge of the cot and planted her bare feet on the cold cement floor. The dream had escaped, after all. Kelly stomped her feet like a petulant child will do when having a tantrum. She could only remember Albino Man but didn't know more than that. He had come back to her in the dream, Kelly knew but what he was doing or what he was telling her – no, that was gone.

Wide awake now, Kelly tiptoed across the floor and opened the secret room door. It was not as dark in the next room because there was a window that let in what light the night could provide.

She didn't bother to put on any more clothes than she already had on. Kelly leaned against the door frame for just a few moments to gather her thoughts, then straightened up and walked out.

All the computers were still asleep in the tactical room, not disturbed by dreams like the one Kelly just had. She didn't turn on any lights, not wanting to be dazzled just yet. But, when she opened the refrigerator door, the light that came on was blinding. After her eyes had adjusted to the bright, Kelly reached in and took an orange soda out. The door closed and she was grateful for the darkness.

Kelly drank the soda as she wandered around the room. She stepped on an object hiding on the floor. It wasn't sharp, like a tack or a nail but she jumped anyway as if stung. Then, she reached down and found a pencil.

"Too late," she thought, "I needed you before but not now." If she had a pocket, Kelly would have put the pencil in it for later use. She tucked it in the elastic waistband of her underwear, not really thinking about it, just doing it.

Kelly held the drink can upside down to get the few remaining drops of soda. She would have stomped on the empty can to crush it, if she had been wearing any shoes which she wasn't.

Kelly set the empty can on a table as she passed close to one, still wandering. She didn't want to go back to sleep just yet, though she was tired. Her brain tried to resist but Kelly was thinking again, about Abernathy.

"I wonder what he's doing right now, this late at night?" she asked herself.

Kelly had a sudden urge to grab her bike and race over to Uncle's house, sneak in while everyone was sleeping. Maybe she would find Abernathy swimming with the octopus, like lovers off on a midnight skinny-dip in the pool.

That image of the two creatures, cavorting together naked, caused her to laugh. It wasn't a hearty guffaw but just a light laughter like she might do in a school classroom so that the teacher wouldn't hear.

Kelly yawned a great big yawn, knowing that she had to go back to bed soon. She was not going on a daring midnight adventure to find Abernathy, though she wanted very much to do just that.

She would go back to her secret room, lay down and hope Albino Man would meet with her again in another dream. Kelly wanted to ask him a lot of questions and maybe this time, she would remember what he told her, if he had a voice.

Kelly would have been surprised to know that Bobby was awake, too. He was standing in the hallway just outside his grandfather's door, listening. He heard the sounds of the humming aquarium with its filters and wave motion motor but no unusual noises of splashing that warranted him to venture inside. The door was slightly ajar but not open enough for Bobby to stick his head inside to look and he wasn't about to push the door wider open. That would be wrong for so many reasons. His grandfather could be awake just like he was or the door could make noise and that could wake Grampa. No, the door would stay as it was and Bobby moved on quietly down the hall.

Bobby didn't know what had awakened him. He couldn't remember a sudden sound like Kelly tap-tap-tapping at his bedroom window, wanting him to open it and let her in. Anyway, the window was already open when he looked, for the night breezes to waft through. Kelly would have just climbed on in, she was so brazen, Bobby knew. He did look out at the yard, just to make sure that Kelly wasn't out there tossing pebbles at the house. He was actually disappointed not to find her there, smiling up at him and waving.

Bobby went to Alice's room next and he did open that door. He could always argue that he was just making sure that Alice was safe, he reasoned.

"A nightmare woke me," he would say to his mother. "I just wanted to make sure that everyone was okay."

And, he thought, "now I"m making plans to lie to her. How bad is that?"

Alice was sound asleep. She had two dolls next to her, one asleep but the other one was sitting up against the pillow, wide awake and staring right at him.

"Go away, you bad boy," Jim-Jim said to him. "You are not supposed to be here."

The doll didn't actually talk to him; it was just an awake dream but Bobby did feel like a bad boy. "Was he really mean to Alice all the time like Kelly had accused him?" he thought. Sometimes, yes, he was. Like out in the desert, Bobby had been so angry with Alice for getting lost and upsetting Mom. He had never seen his mother in such a hysterical state and that had scared the wits out of him.

Bobby slipped inside and quietly stepped over until he could look down at his sister.

"Alice, I"m sorry," Bobby whispered to her. "I promise I'll be a better big brother from now on."

Alice didn't wake up but she made a noise in her sleep, sounding like "m'kay" or maybe it was just another awake dream for Bobby but he hoped not.

Bobby made a silent and short inspection of Alice's room, just on the off chance that Abernathy was there somewhere. He even bent down to look under the bed but he wasn't about to scrunch under like Kelly had done the other day.

Bobby went back to his own room without checking on his mother. Her door was closed, too, just like Alice's but he didn't open it. He felt that everyone was safe in the house and it was okay to go back to bed.

Bobby didn't know that Spylgyn was in Alice's room while he was searching. Spylgyn watched Bobby's feet go this way and that, ready to run if the youngling found him. Spylgyn remained still and quiet, even when Bobby looked under the bed where he was hiding in the darkest recess against the wall.

Only after Bobby left, did Spylgyn move to find a more secure nestling place. The fluid that he had taken earlier from the water pool would sustain him for a time but he needed to eat. The small amount of food that the spryling had left for him smelled rancid and was sour to the taste. Spylgyn had eaten some of it anyway but it caused sickness and he vomited it out.

Spylgyn decided that he must search for some nutrients that he could eat soon or he would become weak and expire. Spylgyn was not ready to go beyond but he felt that time was coming if he didn't do something soon. There were plants above ground outside that were edible and seemed to give him moderate strength. The cuts and abrasions from the feathered one's talons had already mended but his leg was still bruised from the fall and caused pain when moving. The healings that he tried seemed to have poor effect on that injury, possibly because of the poor nutrients that he had been intaking.

Spylgyn dropped to all four appendages and darted out from under the bed taking care to limit the use of his left leg. He jumped on the wall, then sprang to the crevice opening of the cube. On the ledge, he looked back quickly to see if the spryling had been disturbed but she still slept quietly. Then, Spylgyn spun around and jumped out from the cube into the wilderness arena.

Once on ground he lay flat in the cool grass, waiting. After a minute he stood upright and searched in all directions for possible threat. He knew that he was too far from cavern for an orb to locate him and without a stone to show him the way, he was trapped in this strange forbidden land.

He was not fearful of the spryling anymore as she seemed to be of a complacent manner and did not interfere with too much of his movements. He made it clear to her in the beginning that he did not want grasps and holdings after he fought against that. Spylgyn only hissed and struggled in a way that would not cause her body harm although he could have stung her. But, in such an early life, a sting could possibly kill a spryling of her youth. It was frustrating that she still was not receptive to the thought clouds he was giving her. She did mimic some of his body intuits but the only ones that she seemed to actually have understanding of were "eat" and "no".

The younglings and larger Oolongs still caused fear and concern for his safety. He had smelled the feastings that this tribe were burning and didn't want to be taken for such a horrible ending. So, he continued to hide from them until he could make plans for escape and attempt return to cavern, or beyond if that was to be the final journey.

Spylgyn did find some edibles in the yard and gorged on various plants, roots and danglers. Although the food had peculiar odors and tastes, he was delighted that this nourishment did not cause him to expel remnants.

Spylgyn did not linger any longer than to gain adequate sustenance to survive in the open arena near the cubes. There was much danger here; he could smell beasts within range though he was unable to identify the kind or species. One that startled him made noises like a belching frog but so much louder it stung his earholes.

He returned to the spryling's cube. Under the bed no longer seemed a safe hide. Another opening in the cube revealed an enclosed space with fluffs and nesting material. He gather some of these into a corner of the cubit and dug a tunnel to hide. The smell was disturbing to Spylgyn but he felt safer in this close, dark environment and he slept.

18 The Push Button Option

When Bobby entered the kitchen the next morning, he could sense a somber mood was clouding the room. It was the quiet that struck him first, as though someone had died and a funeral was going to take place later that day.

His grandfather was sitting at the table in his usual chair but he was holding his head down as if he was going over the eulogy in his mind and wondering what he would say when asked to step up to the podium.

His mother was seated at her spot, one hand placed under her chin, elbow on the table, seeming to hold up her weary head to keep it from collapsing. Although his mother was smiling as she watched Alice eat her morning cereal, there was a sadness in her expression.

Apparently, Alice didn't know the person that had died, because she was her usual happy self, no cares but those of a playful child anxious to quit breakfast so that she could rush away to coloring books and dolls as quickly as she could.

"Who died?" Bobby asked, while standing at the kitchen door.

The grown-ups looked at him in a way that shook him for a few seconds, thinking "oh crap, somebody did die," and wondering who it was.

Uncle said, "mornin', son," then went back to his sad place, working out the oration for the recently departed.

His mother just smiled at him, a crooked smile that could only mean bad news was on the way.

Bobby slid his chair out and sat down, anxious for answers.

"I've got scrambled eggs and sausage," said his mother and she got up from the table and went to the stove.

"Yeah," Bobby said, "I'll have some of that."

Alice had a dripping spoon of milk cereal ready to eat but first said "Daddy's coming today," before she shoved the spoon into her mouth.

"Dad is coming here?" Bobby asked his mother.

"Yes, your father's coming by today," Jenny told him as she placed a plate of food in front of him.

"I'm going out," Uncle said, then got up from the table and walked out the back door, seeming not quite irate but close to it.

Jenny watched him leave, not upset that he left but obviously wanting him to stay.

"He wants to see you guys," Jenny said, not looking at Bobby.

She went to the stove to do busy work, moving pans from one place to another, keeping her hands going for distraction but what she really wanted to do was go back to bed and drift into a deep sleep where there were no more exhausting problems to confront her.

"I've got a lot of things to do today, Mom," Bobby told her.

"You can spare some time for your father, can't you?" Jenny asked with her back to him.

"When is he coming?" he asked.

"This afternoon, I imagine," she replied. "I'm not sure. He's just coming."

Bobby ate his breakfast in silence with no more questions.

Alice said, "finished", got out of her chair and bobbled off to her daily duties that were important to only her, she thought.

Bobby knew that he would be interrupting those activities, whatever they were, because he wanted to have a sit-down chat with his little sister later that morning. He had questions for Alice, questions that he had formulated during the night when he couldn't sleep.

Bobby had a spoonful of scrambled eggs scooped ready for eating, held it poised just like Alice had done with her cereal. He was looking across the table to the screen door that his grandfather has rushed out of and saw Kelly standing there, waving at him.

"Good morning," she said cheerfully.

Kelly was dressed in her mobility outfit – high-up cut-off jeans that adults would consider shameful, a loose fitting t-shirt with a mynah bird design, knotted at the bottom revealing her slim waist, bottomed out with white socks and low-riders to complete the look of a daring young girl destined for excitement and adventure.

"Goodness, you're early today," Jenny said as she invited Bobby's 'girlfriend' in. Bobby couldn't help but notice that his mother was a little shocked when she saw Kelly's gear.

"Have you had breakfast?" Jenny asked her.

"Yes ma'am, I had a burrito at the diner," Kelly told her.

It was the way his mother looked at Kelly as she walked over to sit at the kitchen table next to him that concerned Bobby.

"Why, you little slut, his mother was thinking," he thought.

Bobby got the distinct impression that his mother didn't think Kelly was so cute anymore, now that she knew for a fact that the local girl was lusting for her innocent child.

"What are you guys going to do today?" Jenny asked them, knowing that they probably wouldn't tell her the truth."

"No plans yet," Kelly answered cheerfully and took a piece of sausage from Bobby's plate, tossing it quickly into her mouth before he could stop her.

Bobby saw his mother bristle.

"She took food from my child's plate," his mother was thinking, "right off the plate and in front of me!"

Jenny was leaning back on the stove front, her eyes glazed, arms braced like she was getting ready for a sudden rush at Kelly.

Bobby knew he had to stop his mother from attacking, so he said "we're going to the clubhouse, Mom. All the other guys are going to be there, you know, just hanging out, nothing going on, really."

Bobby didn't really think he had calmed his mother's protective stance but, at least, she stopped gawking at Kelly with such disdain. Jenny turned away from them, back to the stove, as if she was unable to watch their lustful mating posture any longer.

"Are you gonna eat that?" Kelly pointed to the last piece of sausage.

Bobby glanced at Kelly, then to his mother, who was still turned away from them.

"Would he run or defend Kelly if his mother attacked?" Bobby asked himself but he wasn't sure. Then, he pushed back from the table, grabbing Kelly's arm as he stood up and decided that it was best for them to run. Bobby dragged Kelly out of the kitchen before that disaster could happen.

"I asked you to tone it down, Kelly, didn't I?" said Bobby as he continued to drag Kelly up the staircase.

"What are you talking about?" Kelly asked him with feigned innocence.

He stopped on the steps and looked down at her in amazement.

Words were not forthcoming, so Bobby pumped his arms up and down at her in a comical way, kinda like a magician would present his lovely assistant on stage before sawing her in half for the audience. And that gave him the idea of how to tell her.

"Now presenting, ladies and gentleman, Kelly, the wonder of the world."

Kelly just looked at him without expression as if she really didn't understand.

"Look folks, the legs go all the way up to paradise. Turn around for the audience, Kelly. Make sure they all get a good look, hold nothing back."

Bobby knew that he was pissing Kelly off now but he was unable to stop.

"The lovely Kelly has an on and off button, too," he exclaimed.

Bobby used a finger to lightly push at Kelly's navel like it was a button.

"On, sexy. Off cute. On hot. Off cold," Bobby demonstrated for her. He wanted to push more buttons but Kelly grabbed his arm to stop him from poking at her belly.

Bobby knew there was a slap coming and knew that he deserved a hard one, too.

He braced himself for the impact but Kelly just held onto his arm and looked at him pleasantly.

"You think I'm sexy?" Hot?" Kelly asked him.

"Well, my mother thinks you're sexy and hot. Yesterday, she only thought you were cute," he told her.

"All mothers think like that when their little boy is being chased by a vixen," Kelly said calmly.

"Vixen, did you have to look that up?" Bobby asked.

"No, Bobby," I know all the words. "Bitch, tramp, harlot... trouble-maker."

Kelly turned around and ran down the staircase and out the front door, not looking back at him even once.

Bobby just stood on the stairs, uncertain if he should chase after Kelly. He decided not to, knowing that Kelly would no longer be the cute, lovable girl that he liked so much. If he was able to catch up to her, Kelly would be the fighter then and that would only cause more hurt and anger between them. Better to let her calm down for a while, he thought. Then, he realized that he needed time to calm down as well. He couldn't talk to Alice when he was this way, so angry and agitated. He went on up the staircase, walked down the quiet hallway and went into his room, closing the door behind him.

19   Dancing with Tigers

Kelly was zooming on her bike but it was not a happy zoom like it had been the other day This time it was an angry zoom, the everybody get out of her way zoom. She raced down Crystal Lane, ripped around the corner and almost crashed into Mr. Peterson as he was crossing Main Street on his way to mail a letter at the post office.

"Watch out, you damn fool," he shouted after her, not realizing that it was the Alban girl until it was too late. Peterson galloped across the street to safe haven, hoping Kelly didn't look back to see who it was that yelled at her. He got to the post office and pushed through the door, afraid that Ms. Gurdy would lock him out if she saw what had just happened in the street.

Kelly raced on, pedaling furiously as if lives were in danger and she had to get there to rescue them before they perished. She didn't even slow down to jump the curb into the city park, almost losing control then, and again as she dodged a German Shepard that was intent on biting her leg as she passed by but Kelly was moving too fast for the startled dog.

Officer Reynolds was sitting in his patrol car on the far side of the park when Kelly flew past him. He almost spilled the hot coffee in his lap as he tried to put it back in the cup holder. Reynolds hit the switch for the siren, slapped the car into gear and took off after the reckless speeder. He lost sight of her when she went through the alley behind The Chicken Coop, since he was unable to follow through that narrow space. Good police work and a little luck allowed the policeman to run her down before she managed to escape in the woods just north of town.

It was only when she heard the 'whoop, whoop, whoop' of the siren right behind her that Kelly knew that she was caught and couldn't get away.

"Give it up, Kelly. I got you," came Reynolds' voice from the loud speaker. "Take it to the curb and show me your hands."

Kelly turned in to the sidewalk and lay the bike down to rest against the curb. She could see the flashing lights of the police car were still turning but at least the policeman had cut off the offending siren.

"So close," Kelly said wistfully, looking at the woods just a few hundred feet away. She went to her knees and placed a sorrowful hand on the bike frame. "We almost made it." Kelly looked up at her captor and slowly raised her arms to surrender. Kelly was smiling at the big man when he came to stand over her but Officer Reynolds wasn't smiling back at her. He looked angry and pissed off.

It was almost like before an earthquake when dogs run in circles and jungle monkeys scamper away to find the strongest branch of the tree before there is even the slightest tremor.

It was Dan the Man that looked up first wondering what was happening, then Martin and Andy raised their heads from their work and looked around as if sensing a violent storm approaching. Pegs only looked away from her computer game when the entry door was slammed shut, that being the first quake that startled everyone.

When Kelly swung the inner door wide and stepped inside the tactical room, all the UFObians were attentive. Later each one would have their own version of what happened that morning.

It was Andy who told Bobby, "Kelly looked like a wild animal, all angry and shit, you know?"

"Oh, yeah, man!" Dan would say. "Kelly looked at us like she wanted to fight but didn't know which one of us she was gonna swing at first."

"Always wear good running shoes, Bobby, 'cause you never know when she's gonna come at you."

Bobby couldn't remember who said that to him but it was really good advice as he later found out.

Kelly didn't attack anyone. She just reached back for the door and quietly closed it shut. All of them watched cautiously as Kelly trod past them ready to dive under a table if her claws came out. She held her fists out in front of her as she walked the room, like a prize fighter about to enter the boxing ring for a championship match. Then, it looked as if she was in a heated argument with an invisible someone, pointing accusingly, slapping at the air and throwing her arms up in frustration. Then, she just silently walked away.

It stayed silent in the tactical room for several minutes after Kelly was gone. Everyone stayed where they were except Pegs. She got up quickly and ran for the door, escaping before Kelly could come back.

Kelly was in her secret room that was only open to her. Still agitated by the argument with Bobby and the policeman's lecture, Kelly was smoldering with anger. She stomped back and forth, sat down on the bed, stood up, kicked the wastebasket across the floor, then decided that her safe haven was too confining for her fury. Kelly took a baseball bat with her when she went out into the forbidden zone.

The pool area was a large open arena with high ceilings and plenty of empty space, although the swimming pool took up most of the expanse. There were tile mosaics on the walls with colorful and artistic designs from a past era Uncle would have told her if she had asked. Kelly was saving all the tiles that had fallen away over the years and was keeping them in boxes, safe from further damage. When Kelly owned the spa, she intended to put the tiles back up in the vacant squares.

Kelly tossed the baseball bat into the empty pool and climbed down the ladder at the shallow end. Now, she had fighting room. Kelly grabbed the bat and swung away at invisible baseballs that were floating in the air around her. Every hit was a home run in her mind but she didn't want applause from the stands and no hearty pats on the back from her teammates. It didn't take long for her to become exhausted. The bike ride and the baseball game had sapped all her energy.

Kelly dropped the bat when she hit a foul ball that flew into the stands and hit Officer Reynolds right in the head. The ambulance took him away and Kelly jumped up and down with excitement. That foul ball was way better than any of the home runs that she had slammed over the fence.

Kelly sat down on the tiles but then scooted over a bit so that she wasn't sitting on the 'Blue Darling' mermaid's head. She felt like crying but couldn't make any tears come out but the sadness and despair were there, nevertheless. Kelly raised her knees up for elbow support, then plopped her head in hands that were no longer fisted. She stared down at the deep end where the swamp water had pooled.

"It's getting deeper," she thought, "but what could she do?"

Kelly was not supposed to have access to this area; no one was. That's why she called it the forbidden zone. Uncle would be angry if he knew that Kelly had found another way in, maybe even evict all of them. That's why she didn't tell anyone about the secret places that she found.

Kelly got up and, being mindful of the slippery slope, carefully walked down to the edge of the swamp. Sure enough, she saw that her marker was underwater, only by a few inches but that was still troublesome. Kelly couldn't remember exactly when she last checked the depth of the swamp, so it must have been some time ago. The leak was obviously coming from the pipe under the diving platform. Looking up at it, she could see that the tile wall below the opening was moist and stained from drainage. Kelly kept meaning to plug it up with something but it was too high to reach without a ladder and she wasn't about to hang over the pool edge without someone holding onto her legs.

"Another day," she thought.

"But when, Kelly?" her brain demanded an answer.

"Later," Kelly told it.

Kelly noticed that the cattail plants were much bigger now. Growing in one corner of the swamp, the stalks were almost as tall as a person now. The leaves were a healthy green color and the brown fuzzys at the top looked soft to the touch, though she had never done that. There were other plants beneath the surface of the water, weeds that swayed as if in the gentle current of a creek or large pond. Kelly had found a frog once, happily sitting on one of the lily pads floating on the surface. She tried to rescue it but it jumped away and hid from her in the muddy bottom of the swamp. Kelly never saw it again but she hadn't looked very hard.

That lost frog brought her thoughts back to Abernathy, another amphibian that needed rescue. That's how Kelly thought of him now, as a water creature that somehow was found wandering in a dry, hot desert. Abernathy must need the water in Uncle's fish tank to stay wet, maybe even to breathe. So, swimming wasn't a fun activity for the amphibian, it was necessary for its survival.

Kelly had to get back into Uncle's house somehow.

She climbed out of the swimming pool and wandered around the walls while thinking about what to do. Sometimes Kelly would place a hand on a mosaic when she passed by a favorite image, the cool tiles seeming to give her solace. She stopped at the seashore scene and looked up at the slim blonde lady in the yellow swimsuit. leaning over, reaching out her hand to pet a jumping puppy. Kelly turned around, placed her back against that wall then, slowly slid to the floor. She stared across the pool to the ocean mosaic – an underwater design of fish, turtles and whales cavorting in the sea. Kelly imagined that it was somewhere far away, maybe in the Mediterranean because the water was so clear and serene.

"Abernathy would like it there," she thought.

If anyone had been looking across from the far side of the pool, it would appear that the blonde beauty at the seashore was reaching down to comfort Kelly.

20   The Tale of Big Black Joe

Bobby's parents were arguing downstairs. He could hear their voices occasionally but it had been quiet for the last few minutes, as if they were between rounds. It was his father who raised his voice in anger most of the time but his mother wasn't being the quiet and obedient wife today. Bobby couldn't follow just how the argument was going, their voices were only noises without words, none that he could make out anyway. They had been going at it for 12 minutes now, after he and Alice had been dismissed to their rooms so that his parents 'could talk' as his father had explained to them.

Bobby wanted to go down and tell them to stop but he knew that would only make his father even more angry. His grandfather had taken Alice to his room and closed the door behind them, probably to protect the child from angry voices that might upset her. Bobby had gone to his own room but he didn't want to be alone anymore. It was the quiet that got to him, not the yelling. He had become used to the arguments in the past couple of years but they still upset him.

Bobby lightly knocked on his grandfather's door and heard Grampa's voice say, "come on in, Bobby."

His grandfather was seated in the highback patchwork chair. Alice was sitting on his lap and there was an open scrapbook laying on the bed that they were looking at. Bobby sat on a footstool near them and gave his grandfather a 'what are we supposed to do?' gesture and the old man gave him a 'I don't know, just wait and see' shrug.

"Turn the page, Gumpa," Alice demanded.

Uncle turned the page and Alice gave all her attention to the revealed photos.

"Grampa...," Bobby said but his grandfather shook his head to stop the boy, then indicated Alice with a nod. Bobby understood, nodding. They shouldn't talk about anything that might upset his little sister. There would be time for that later.

"What's that?" Alice asked with enthusiasm.

Alice was pointing at something in the photo and when Gumpa didn't answer fast enough, she squirmed and raised her head to look at his bearded face.

"Why, that's a big black snake that your great-grandfather found out in the desert."

"A snake!" Alice exclaimed and bent over to get a closer look at the snake in the photo.

His grandfather winked at Bobby to let him know that was only a tale for Alice, a fantasy to keep the little girl interested.

"Yes ma'am. Big Black Joe they named it," he said. "Biggest snake ever caught in the world."

"Is it dead? Did they kill it?" she asked sounding concerned.

"Why, no," Gumpa told her. "You don't kill a big snake like that, because it's a wonder, see?"

Alice waited patiently for the story to go on.

"Well, they sent Big Joe off to a zoo, all the way over to Germany."

Bobby could see that his grandfather was making it all up, enjoying the story almost as much as Alice.

Uncle went on, saying, "they had a big black lady snake there named Sally and she needed a proper fella so that she could lay eggs and hatch some babies."

"Snakes don't lay eggs, Gumpa, that's chickens," Alice corrected him.

"Snakes lay eggs just like chickens, Alice. Turtles too," he explained.

"Nuh-uh," Alice said.

Bobby wanted to look at the photo of the big black snake, so he slid the stool over, nearer to his grandfather and Alice.

The old black and white photo showed a young man who was sitting astride what did looked like a big snake. Bobby's great-grandfather had his boot heels dug into the snake's belly and was raising his hat in an upward motion like cowboys do when they're riding bulls at the rodeo. Bobby knew that it really wasn't a giant snake but couldn't quite figure out what it was.

As Bobby was about to ask his grandfather, a loud voice from downstairs shattered their fantasy about Big Black Joe.

Uncle picked Alice up and set her down. Then, he motioned for Bobby to come over and take possession of his little sister. Bobby sat in the patchwork chair, his grandmother's chair. He could still remember how she looked, always doing some busy work with her hands when she sat in it. His grandfather had taken it out of the front room and moved it to his bedroom after she passed away.

Bobby didn't take Alice into his lap but kept her between his legs as he moved the patchwork chair closer, so that he could see the photos over her shoulder.

His grandfather left the room, probably going down to break up the argument. At least, that's what Bobby hoped.

"Is it really a black snake, Bobby?" Alice asked her brother.

"Yes, it is," he told her. "You just don't know because you're still in first grade. They don't teach about Big Black Joe snakes until the 3rd grade."

"Oh," said Alice, as if that reason seemed good enough for her.

Alice turned all the pages after that but they never found any other photos that were as fascinating as the one of the giant reptile that had been captured in the desert so long ago. There were a few others that caught Bobby's attention, though. In one, his great-grandfather was sitting on the bank of a pond with rocks and boulders in the background. His pants were rolled up to the knees with his bare legs submerged in what looked like cool and refreshing water. There was a young woman standing in the water with her back to the camera. She was naked. "Jaybird naked," Alice had pointed out for Bobby.

Bobby and Kelly would study this photo book together with Uncle later on, searching for the solution to a riddle that confused them all.

Still waiting for a resolution from below, Bobby and Alice found other things to do. His sister seemed to be accepting her brother's new friendly attitude toward her, even allowing him to comb and shape twin ponytails into her hair, instructing him, "just like the forest fairies wear their hair."

While he was doing that, Bobby felt that she might be open to answering just a few questions but promised himself to stop if she became pouty.

"I wonder what Abernathy is doing right now?" he said.

"His name is not Abernathy anymore," Alice said, all the while looking into the dresser mirror at their reflections.

"It's not?" is all that Bobby said, hoping to hear more about it.

"No," sighed Alice, "he didn't like that name."

"So, what is his name now?" Bobby asked her.

"Spylgyn," Alice replied.

"Spill-gen?" Bobby asked.

"Spyl-gyn," Alice said again when Bobby didn't pronounce it right.

"Oh, Spylgyn," Bobby said and made it sound right this time.

"Yes, just like that. Spylgyn," Alice said the name again because she liked the way it sounded.

"That's an unusual name," Bobby told her.

"Yes, I know but he likes it," Alice sighed.

"How did you come up with that name?" Bobby asked Alice.

"I didn't," Alice confessed, "he did. He said Spylgyn, Spylgyn, Spylgyn, like that" making it sound like music on a record that was skipping."

"What does it mean?" Bobby asked, more to himself than to Alice.

"I don't know," Alice said, "but when I said it back to him, he smiled at me and did a happy dance."

Actually, Spylgyn was laughing uproariously at Alice because of the peculiar noise that the spryling made when she tried to sound his name. He hopped, spun and bounced on all fours, much to her amusement. And, yes, it could be called a happy dance because it was pleasurable for both of them.

"Now when I call out Spylgyn Spylgyn Spylgyn, he will come out of his hiding place... sometimes," Alice said.

Bobby had finished the ponytails a while back but had kept his hands moving on her head to keep Alice distracted, wanting her to give him more details.

"Aren't you done yet?" she asked him. Alice was pouting at him in the mirror.

Bobby held both of his hands up to show his sister that he hadn't pulled out a single hair from her head.

"All done," said Bobby.

A few minutes later, Jenny came up to tell Bobby and Alice that their father was taking her out for lunch so that they could have some private time together and that Bobby would be responsible to look after Alice while they were gone.

"Mom, I need to go to the clubhouse," he said to her.

"No," said his mother, "you are to watch Alice while I'm gone. I can't put this on your grandfather."

Bobby nodded in agreement but he was not real happy about it.

21   Chasing Butterflies

Kelly rode by Uncle's house fast the first time, hoping that Bobby wouldn't come out and chase after her. When he didn't, she circled around a few blocks just to give it time, then passed by the house again but much slower. She was hoping that Bobby would come out and chase after her this time. Kelly was ready for Bobby to apologize to her and this was her way of giving the boy an opportunity.

He would run out of Uncle's house, down the steps and into the street, yelling at her departing figure.

"Wait, Kelly! Oh wait, please," Bobby would plead to her and she would stop for him but wouldn't get off the bike. She wouldn't ride off until he had properly made amends for assaulting her, poking at her like a child poking a stuffed animal to see if it would make a funny noise. Kelly wanted him to be very sorry for doing that to her, even though she thought it was kinda funny, in a way.

Kelly casually pressed a finger into her belly button and said with a whisper, "on, off, on, off."

Kelly had coasted into the vacant lot just up the street from Uncle's house when Bobby didn't run after her. She was at a loss for what to do next. Uncle's truck was there and Jenny's car too; they weren't all gone into town for ice cream and lollipops.

"Why wasn't Alice on the front porch swing?" Kelly wondered.

She could have rode into the yard then, just to make silly talk with the little girl and their conversation would prompt Bobby to come out of hiding. Were they all inside because they had found Abernathy and were already making plans to present him to the world on Dr. Phil?

"Well, that's not gonna happen," Kelly said as if talking to the sapling across from her. "Abernathy is mine as much as anybody's."

Kelly lay down on the grass, staring up at the branches of a big shade tree. The wind was cool on her belly and legs; the ground was not as soft as a mattress but it was not uncomfortable. She winched in pain when the back of her head touched ground because of the still sensitive bump that refused to 'get lost'. Running her hand over the bulging area she thought, "why is it not getting smaller and healing?"

Kelly turned her head so that the injury was no longer against the ground. It didn't hurt as much if she didn't put any pressure on it.

It had taken Kelly a long time to get her anger and frustration under control. Her isolation time in the forbidden zone had helped. There was no one there to say mean things to her and point out her faults, though she knew there were a few that rankled some people.

"I am who I am," Kelly said to the sky. "You're either with it or you ain't."

She could feel the anger pulsing deep inside her but she easily stifled it and shoved it back down into a deep hole. It was tightly wrapped as Kelly saw it in her mind, like a firecracker waiting to explode. The fuse was still winking at her, so eager to be lit but Kelly refused.

Clouds drifted by as she looked up at them but there were no interesting shapes to guess at. They were wispy clouds without any puff.

Kelly rolled over on her belly then reached beneath her to remove an offending rock. She tossed it aside without even looking at it, not caring if it was a pretty one that deserved to be in her collection. Face in hands, elbows resting in the soft grass, Kelly began to hum a tune, keeping time with her upraised legs.

"I need some advice, Uncle," Kelly would say to him.

"Yes, that was a good reason to knock on the door and gain entrance," she thought.

"Bobby is angry at me because I'm hot and sexy." she would tell him. "He's worried that his mother thinks that we're gonna do it!"

Kelly had to chuckle aloud as she imagined Uncle's reaction to that news.

"Well, it's okay with me, Kelly," Uncle would say to her or maybe "you're a shameless little hussy, girl," but she couldn't decide if he would be smiling or frowning when he said that.

Kelly tossed that scheme aside just as she had done to the rock and played out other scenes with Uncle. It was like a fast moving locomotive was racing through her mind. One boxcar with an idea would appear, then another and another as they sped by on the tracks until the red caboose went past, leaving her at the station.

The only idea that seemed solid to Kelly would need to be something about the spa but she didn't want to tell Uncle about the swamp in the pool. She didn't want her secret places to be discovered, especially not by the man who very well might lock her out of the spa for breaking the rules.

"His name is Spylgyn," Bobby said to her.

Startled from her thoughts, Kelly rolled over quickly and saw Bobby staring down at her.

"What?" Kelly said with shock, wondering how he had snuck up on her.

"We surprised you!" Alice exclaimed.

Bobby was holding his little sister's hand like he had been taking her out for a stroll when they just happened to find her lolling about in the woods counting ants.

"Say that again," Kelly said to him.

"Spylgyn, Spylgyn, Spylgyn," Alice sang.

Alice pulled away from Bobby's hand to chase after a butterfly because that's what little girls do.

"Don't go far, Alice," Bobby shouted after her.

"I'm sorry," Bobby said to Kelly and she could see that he meant it but she needed to punish him more.

Bobby sat close next to her in the grass, wanting to put his arm around her but didn't. There would come a time for that when they declared affection for each other as boyfriend+girlfriend. Bobby wanted that to happen soon because he really wanted to touch her. Surprisingly, that opportunity happened for him, like he was granted a fairy wish from one of Alice's friends. An ant was crawling on Kelly's arm and he reached over to brush it off.

"Ant," he said to her.

"I probably have some in my pants," Kelly said, although she was only wearing the cut-offs.

"I saw you ride by," Bobby said.

Kelly didn't answer, just hugged her knees to her chest and waited for Bobby to go on.

"Don't be mad at me, Kelly, please," Bobby said. "I shouldn't have acted out like that."

"You poked my belly button," she accused him.

"Well, it was right there, Kelly," he explained. "It wanted to be poked and you know it."

He held up a finger, ready to be of service but the belly button was hiding behind her knees. So, Kelly stretched out her legs as far as they would go.

"Do it again and see what happens," Kelly challenged.

Bobby moved the finger toward her on-off switch, then pulled it back, laughing. Kelly had planned to jump at him when he hit the button then, decided to do it anyway.

Bobby fell back with Kelly on top of him. She straddled him like a pony, grabbing at his tucked-in shirt.

"Where's yours?" she asked him as he lay back in surprise. "What happens when I push your button?"

Kelly yanked the shirt tail out, exposing his belly.

"You don't want to do that, Kelly," Bobby warned her as she wiggled a finger at him.

Kelly didn't make idle threats. She pushed deep as if she was turning on an airplane propeller, ready to fly away on an adventure.

Bobby suffered for just a moment while his engine started then he grabbed Kelly by the waist and flipped her over until he was sitting atop her, roles reversed.

She lay there looking up at him, wondering what he was going to do now.

"Kiss me, Bobby," she wanted to say to him. "Kiss me now," but didn't.

"Are you guys 'wrastling'?" Alice asked them.

Alice was looking at them as if she really expected an answer.

"Were there no more butterflies in the woods?" thought Kelly but the moment was lost.

Bobby got off Kelly and they both stood up, looking at each other and wondering what would have happened if they had been left alone just a little longer.

Bobby put both of his hands on Kelly's shoulders and turned her around to brush dirt and grass off of her back and she allowed him to do it, even when he was touching her butt.

Alice saw their parents driving down the street first and shouted, "Bobby, it's Mommy and Daddy" but they passed by without stopping. Knowing Alice would run after them, Bobby quickly scooped her up and held her tight.

"I want to go, Bobby. Let me go," she squealed, struggling against his grasp.

"Alice, quit it," he scolded her when she began to kick him.

Alice went limp, defeated.

"Kelly, I gotta go," Bobby said to the confused girl. "I'll explain later."

"Wait, Bobby," and Kelly grabbed his arm. "Come to the spa, soon as you can."

"If I can, Kelly," he told her. "I don't know; there's some drama going on."

As he walked away with Alice tugging at him, he looked back over his shoulder and said, "I'll try."

"Bobby," she called to him but he kept going away from her, without looking back.

"I have so much to tell you," Kelly said as if he was standing right next her.

22   Green Apples and Vanilla Ice Cream

Uncle was sitting at the kitchen table eating peanut butter and crackers when Bobby came in through the back door.

"What's doin', Bobby?" his grandfather asked him before he even looked to see who it was.

Bobby still stood just inside the screen door.

"How'd you know it was me?" Bobby asked.

"Why, I smelt you," the old man said. "Everybody goin' around has a certain smell attached to 'em."

Bobby walked around and sat at the table close to his grandfather in the chair usually reserved for his mother because it was close to her station, the kitchen sink.

"I gotta say, I was confused at first," Uncle said. "I thought it was Kelly. Wanna cracker?"

Uncle didn't wait for Bobby to answer, just slid the plate across to him.

Bobby took a cracker sandwich and began eating; that would give him time to decide if his grandfather was really able to smell him or was it a 'black snake'.

When Uncle didn't say anything more, as if there were no more to tell, Bobby asked, "what does Kelly smell like?"

"Kelly smells like vanilla ice cream on a hot summer day," he said with certainty.

"And me?" Bobby asked while eating another cracker.

"Well, I don't mean to offend you, son but you smell like an old baseball that's been hit over the fence too many times."

"I don't even know what a baseball smells like," Bobby said.

"You never took a whiff when you were tossin' one around?" Uncle asked.

Bobby shook his head 'no'.

"It's got an earthy smell to it," Uncle said and went on with more since the boy seemed to have an interest. Uncle waved his hand at his face as if he were pulling Bobby's scent toward him, then took a deep sniff of the passing wind.

"It's not a bad smell, Bobby," he told him. "There's a tangy odor of green apples, not quite ripe but almost there... and wind, yeah, strong wind that smells... smells like vanilla ice cream." Uncle took a cracker from the plate and began eating it, as if the discussion was over on the subject of what people smell like.

"Tell me about Big Black Joe," Bobby said.

"Oh, that was just a tale for your little sister, Bobby," Uncle confessed.

"I know, Grampa. I think it's a pipe or maybe a hose, a big hose," Bobby told him.

"It was," his grandfather told him, "but my grandfather did name that hose Big Black Joe like it was a thing alive. He used it to pump water out of the grotto"

"There's water out in the desert?" Bobby asked.

"There was, long time ago," Uncle said.

"Not now?" Bobby asked him.

"No," Uncle kinda chuckled, "just come up dry one day. So long ago, I can't even remember when."

"I saw the picture of the pond, and the naked lady," Bobby said.

"Oh," Uncle said, as if he had forgotten that photo was still in the album.

"That was my mother, Lula Mae," Uncle told the boy.

A sort of sadness could be seen on Uncle's face as he talked about his mother but he was smiling from the good memories that were being recalled.

"I wish you kids could'a known her. She was a special lady," Uncle told Bobby, "but she died young when I was just a boy."

They were quiet after that. Bobby could see that his grandfather was thinking back to the years that he had with his mother and he didn't want to take that away from him.

Bobby took that time to choose the words that he needed to say to his grandfather about what he wanted to do.

"I want to stay here, Grampa, with you," Bobby said.

"Humph, what?," Uncle asked. "What was that, son?"

The words just ran out of his mouth, like they were escaping, "If Mom decides to go back, you know, with Dad, I want to stay here. With you, just for the summer."

"You do?" his grandfather asked him.

"She's gonna go back, Grampa," Bobby paused, then went on, "and I don't want to go."

Bobby didn't know what his grandfather was thinking, so he pressed his case.

"There's Kelly. I like her, better than any other girl I've ever known," Bobby told him. "And the club, it's fun, you know, like an adventure."

"It would have to be up to your mom, Bobby," he said but wanted to say "yes, you can do that."

The disappointment on Bobby's face hurt Uncle, so he tried to make amends.

"I can talk to her, Bobby," Uncle told him. "She might go along. It would just be for the summer."

Bobby nodded solemnly but he knew there wasn't much hope of that happening. "Yeah, just for the summer."

"Hey, hon," Uncle said.

Bobby looked up to see his mother standing at the kitchen door and he wondered if she had heard him and Grampa talking. She was looking at Bobby and Uncle as if not really seeing them, her thoughts being elsewhere.

Then, in a soft voice, Jenny said, "can I talk to you, Dad?"

His mother looked at Bobby and he could see that she didn't want to say anything while he was there.

"Can I use your bicycle, Grampa?" Bobby asked as he got up from the table.

"Yeah," Uncle said while still looking at his daughter, a worried look. "It's in the shed behind the work shack." He looked at Bobby then and said, "uh, you might need help to get it down. It's up on the wall."

"No, that's okay. I can get it," Bobby said as he went out the back door.

"Don't go far, Bobby," his mother shouted after him but he didn't answer.

Bobby opened the shed door and went inside. It was a dark and gloomy room but it had a pleasant smell that was somehow inviting. Bobby couldn't find the light switch. He seemed to remember that there was a pull cord that turned it on. He waved his arm in the air but felt no string hanging down from the rafters. He could see the bicycle and tried to take it down in the dark but was unable to figure out how to release it.

"What are you doing?" asked Kelly.

Bobby hadn't heard Kelly follow him inside and she was standing right next to him, so close it scared the crap out of him and he jumped back right into her. Kelly grabbed at him to keep from falling and Bobby reached for her at the same time. They were close together in a dark room, chest to chest, their faces almost touching.

Kelly whispered, "what are you doing, Bobby?"

"I'm getting the bicycle," he stammered, "my grandfather's bicycle."

Kelly wasn't going to tell him to turn on the light, secretly hoping that he wouldn't.

"I can't find the light," he said but didn't let go of her right away.

She wasn't going to lose a magic moment again, so Kelly kissed Bobby. It wasn't a passionate kiss but it was a special kiss. That first kiss is always remembered by a boy, the gentle softness of her lips, a taste of ripe peaches or vanilla ice cream and the soft, shuddering sensation that sweeps through his body as he moves closer in to the girl.

It was Kelly that drew back first but not too far, just enough to whisper to Bobby, "you're going to remember that kiss for the rest of your life."

They still held each other close as if each one was waiting to see what the other one would do. Bobby leaned in and kissed her again. As any young boy would do, he moved his hands over Kelly's slender back, feeling her softness, the ridges of her shoulder blades and the valley of her spine and, eventually, found the bra strap that was hidden beneath her shirt.

They touched each other in a tenuous way, as if fearful of how far to go with their first experience. Kelly was the adventurous one and she would go as far as Bobby wanted to take her. Any thoughts of another life outside the bike shed were forgotten by both of them but, the worry and guilt that Bobby was feeling made him step away from Kelly.

"Help me get the bike down," he whispered to her as if that were a sin and not what he had been about to do to Kelly, if she let him.

They worked close together to lift the bicycle off the hooks that were high up on the wall but that was grunt work, not intimate at all.

Kelly walked out backwards from Uncle's shed, holding onto the handle bars to guide the bicycle out the door. Bobby lifted the bike wheels over the chock at the bottom of the door and pushed the bike out. He quickly looked at the house to see if anyone might have been watching them but didn't see Uncle or his mother at any of the windows.

They ran the bike over to the vacant lot before anyone could tell them to stop. Kelly jumped on her bike and they rode off together going away from Uncle's house.

23 What's This? What's That?

When Bobby and Kelly came into the tactical room, everyone seemed to be busy on personal tasks.

Martin was looking in at the website chat room to see if anything interesting was going on but his primary focus was writing a descriptive about what happened at the 'Lost Station', as they were now calling it. Of course, he hadn't been there for the discovery but he was able to get enough facts from Andy and Kelly to do a rough draft about the recon team's experience out there. More details would be added or deleted during a group discussion of the event at some later time.

Dan the Man had the 'alien' drawing enlarged on his computer screen, going over the finer details of the strange symbols, looking closely for any hidden codes that might not be visible on the photographs that Martin had printed out for all of them. He was currently looking at the two shapes inside the shed structure. To his eye, there were obvious differences that could be significant. The right triangle was slightly larger than the left and the lines were drawn thicker as well. The small triangle was partially hidden, placed behind the larger one for some unknown reason. Dan was measuring the height and width of the symbols with specific attention to relative size and depth of the not-quite-the-same twins.

Pegs was listening to a lively tune that was playing in her earbuds, lip syncing to the song, swaying with the music like a Taylor Swift back-up dancer. In a way, Kelly was envious of her mate since she seemed to have already chosen a definite path of evolution – fabulous, flirtatious ingenue with developing but already awesome, talent. Pegs waved to Kelly from her station at the conference table where she was sorting pages into stacks, that morning's event either forgiven or forgotten.

At another table, Andy was studying several photos and documents that seemed haphazardly thrown all over the place. He was writing in a thick notepad; he always seemed to have one with him or close by, so that he could write notes or jot down any ideas that might suddenly come to him. Andy was very secretive about his journals and became upset at Pegs when he had found her reading one that he had left unguarded.

When Martin looked up and saw Kelly, he waved frantically for her to come over as though he needed to talk with her right away before anyone else could signal and take her away on their less important task.

Kelly sauntered on over but didn't rush. Martin sometimes could get overly excited about the littlest things and Kelly didn't want to encourage any impulsive or delusional behavior from him this afternoon.

She looked back at Bobby who was still standing at the entry door as if feeling like an interloper. Kelly motioned a 'come with me' gesture with her hand and Bobby went with her obediently.

"Kelly," Martin said as he turned the computer monitor for her to see, "Kelly, you gotta see this. We've been getting all kinds of hits on the website about the pictograph."

"What's that, pictograph?" asked Kelly.

Martin explained, "that's the closest term that we could find to describe the art. It's not a petroglyph, that has to be ancient. This is a new find, recent, not old. I'm calling it the 'Inyo Cipher', unless somebody can come up with a better way to identify it."

"So, anyway," he went on, without pausing, "there's this guy in Japan. His name is Fujikawa Sumiso and he..."

"Say that again, Martin but spit the gum out of your mouth this time," Bobby said, smiling at his own joke.

Martin just waved a hand at Bobby in a 'shut up, just listen' way and went on with his very important explanation.

This guy, Fuji..." Martin said looking directly at Bobby like he was an idiot, then looked back to Kelly as he went on, "he's got a theory, what I think very well could be a valid translation.

"Yeah, go on," Kelly said with a little interest.

Martin rolled out an oversized paper drawing of the pictograph that Andy had made earlier and began to point at the different symbols on the page.

"These here with the tentacles," Martin said pointing to the two circles at the top of the drawing, "could be the sun and moon. And all of this below, that's the Inyo desert."

Martin waved a hand over the lower part of the drawing to demonstrate for Kelly the vastness of the terrain, as he saw it.

"It could be..." Bobby hesitated, then said, "balloons."

"Don't encourage him, Bobby," Kelly said trying to be humorous but Martin was offended.

"Hey, you got better things to do, go," Martin said, snatching the paper away and turning his back to them.

"I was just making a joke, Martin," Kelly apologized. "Don't be so serious all the time."

"But, this is serious, Kelly, don't you get that?" Martin said with cautious enthusiasm.

Kelly put on her serious face for Martin and said. "I do, Martin, really I do. Go on. Tell me."

"Here," Martin began, "these could represent heat or possibly solar bursts," indicating the wavy lines near the center of the art. He used a finger to point at the interspersed dots drawn in the pattern but not counting out loud. He just said, "there are seven drops. Seven, that's a prime number!"

Bobby almost lost interest and walked away from the table. He didn't like math, didn't like math at all. He almost failed algebra last year in school, just sliding by with a poor D- grade and he was pretty sure that was only because the teacher liked him.

"You said they're drops?" Bobby asked him.

"Rain, don't you see? Drops of rain beneath the solar," Martin said, believing that it was so, then added, "bad weather, storm," in an eerie and ominous way.

"That's a reach, Martin," Kelly said to him.

"It could be bubbles, or some kind of alien ray fired from that spaceship," Bobby said, just making things up.

"You know, Bobby, maybe you should go help Pegs out," Martin said in a dismissive way. "She's all alone over there."

Bobby turned around to look at Pegs who was standing idle in the room. She was looking around as if wanting to do something but didn't know whatever that could be. When she saw Bobby looking at her, Pegs took that as an invitation to join him at Martin's table. She rushed over and stood next to Bobby, putting an arm around his waist but let him go when she saw the look that Kelly gave her.

"Should I even go on?" Martin muttered.

Martin offered a few wild speculations to satisfy Bobby.

"That's the spaceship and those are gravity rays that keeps the UFO aloft. This is a fence and that's a road."

Bobby interrupted saying, "no, that's the gas station," indicating the shed-like structure, "and that," pointing to the thick wavy line, "that's Big Black Joe."

Martin leaned back in his chair and angrily folded his arms across his chest indicating that class was over.

Kelly gave Bobby a look that asked him 'did you really have to say something so ridiculous?'

'What?' Bobby gestured back to her, then said, "I'm being serious. My grandfather told me all about that snake."

Kelly, Pegs and Martin stared at him, waiting for him to explain.

"Snake," said Martin.

"It was the largest snake ever caught, that's what I was told," Bobby told them.

"Uncle told you that?" asked Kelly.

"Sure did," Bobby said. "He even showed me a picture of Big Black Joe from when he was captured somewhere out in the Inyo desert."

"It does look like a snake," Pegs said pointing to the image on the pictograph. "A big black snake."

"Tell the rest of it," Kelly ordered him.

"It's an industrial hose, military surplus from after World War 2," Bobby confessed. "My great-grandfather, he built the spa. That giant hose was used to pump water from a grotto somewhere out in the desert, mineral water maybe or, I don't know, special water, anyway... for the spa."

"Special water?" Kelly said to Bobby.

"Yeah" Bobby said offhandedly, "or it could be a road. We're all just guessing here, right?"

24   Into the Forbidden Zone

Bobby couldn't say what the tiny room had been used for when the Inyo Desert Spa and Health Resort was still operating but it struck him that it looked exactly like a prison cell. There was a black steel cot in one corner that took up most of the floor space, leaving only a minimal area to walk around. There were pillows and blankets on the bed as if the prisoner was either out to lunch or walking the yard during his exercise period.

Kelly revealed a dark hole when she removed the air vent grill that was low on a bare wall of the inmate's cell.

"And that's how Curly escaped, Warden, through the air-conditioning vent," Bobby said to Kelly in a way that a prison guard would've used in a Stooges short.

"It's tight," she said, "but I think you can squeeze through."

Then, before he could say 'lickety-split', Kelly dropped down on hands and knees and quickly scooted into the vent opening and was gone. Bobby didn't think about it more than a few seconds and he got down low and went in after her.

After a few feet the tunnel became completely dark, no light at all. He could hear Kelly in front of him but it sounded like she was far away so he moved faster to catch up, too fast. Not realizing that she had stopped for him, Bobby stumbled abruptly into her backside.

"Sorry, sorry," Bobby said. "I thought you were getting away from me."

When she didn't answer, Bobby reached a hand out and firmly grabbed onto her leg.

"Kelly?" Bobby said quietly as if people might be listening for them scampering through the tunnel. "Why are you stopping?" he whispered. "What's wrong?"

Then, suddenly, there was a blinding light that startled him. Kelly moved fast then, out of the tunnel and into the light. Bobby scrambled after her.

After the dark, it took a few moments for Bobby's eyes to adjust to the bright sunlight coming in through the massive skylights way up high in the ceiling. Kelly had led him out from the tunnel into an enclosed alcove at the base of the diving platform. The platform was high enough for him to get up but he still had to stay in a stooped position to come out into what looked to him like an arena.

"Watch your step or you'll go in the pool," Kelly warned him.

Bobby was standing just a few steps away from falling into the empty pool. If he had kept walking straight while still blinded, he might have ended up in the swamp 12 feet below the edge of the swimming pool.

Bobby looked around the arena searching for Kelly. He couldn't find her at first but then saw her leaning against the wall with the Happy Beach scenes. Kelly had been so still that she blended in with the art. She had one leg crooked under her, braced against the wall as if she was just waiting for a bus to arrive.

Bobby looked around the arena, staring at Kelly's wall first with its bathing beauties, musclemen, children playing volleyball and colorful beach umbrellas. Although it was only a mural, the scene seemed to be alive with activity. All the people seemed to be having so much fun and the frothing ocean waves seemed to be moving inward like it would occur at a real beach.

"This is my special place," said Kelly. "I've never brought anyone here before."

"There are mermaids in the pool," Bobby said to Kelly. "They're... very attractive."

"Do you think so, Bobby?" sincerely was how Kelly asked him. "I mean, really?"

"Yes," Bobby said as he began walking toward her. "This place...it's awesome, Kelly. I've never seen anything like it."

Kelly ran to Bobby, practically jumping into his arms.

"I knew you would like it," she said as she looked up at him. "I knew it."

Kelly took his arm and guided him around the walkway. Either Bobby would stop at a mural to ask her a question or marvel at an image or she would show him a delicate form that might be overlooked against the large scale.

Kelly took him to all the off-rooms where there were soaking tubs for mud baths and a proper sweat room with wooden benches for people to sit on. There was even a communal shower with even more murals on the wall that were just as stunning as the pool arena paintings.

All this beauty had been locked away as if these abandoned rooms were buried, not to be seen, like a pharaoh's tomb. Kelly was an interloper, having discovered the ancient treasures but wanting to keep the secrets of the tomb hidden from thieves and barbarians. Only now, she was sharing her secrets with another, a boy that she trusted, a boy that she was falling in love with.

Eventually, Kelly took Bobby back to the arena where they paused at the deep end of the pool. Kelly reached down, slipped off her shoes and socks, tossed them a few feet away. Then, she sat down at the edge of the pool and dangled her bare feet into the cool water that wasn't there. Bobby didn't take off his shoes; he just sat down next to her.

"What are we doing, Kelly?" he asked her.

"Why, falling in love, Bobby," she wanted to say to him but didn't.

"We don't have much time," Bobby told her.

"Time," Kelly said. "Time for what, Bobby?"

"I might have to go back to Texas. My father, he wants us to come back home."

"No, Bobby, you can't," Kelly told him. "not now!"

Bobby moved closer to Kelly until their shoulders were touching and said, "Mom and Alice, they can go back if they want to. I want to stay. My grandfather is going to ask my mother if I can stay here, with him, for the rest of the summer at least."

Kelly's thoughts held back an immediate response to this disastrous news. Then, when she spoke, there was a certain authority to the way she said, "No, you're not leaving. No."

Then, Kelly seemed to just collapse against Bobby, as if all of her strength had just casually wandered away. Bobby put his arms around Kelly and drew her in to him.

"I won't let them take you," she said wistfully.

A quiet softness seemed to surround the young lovers as they were holding each other there at the edge of the pool. It was a silent sound, like snow falling in a forest but if someone were listening closely, they could almost hear the mermaids weeping at the bottom of the pool.

"We need to do it, Bobby," Kelly said while her head was cradled in his chest. "We need to do it before they can take you away."

"What... " Bobby said. "Do what, Kelly?"

144

Bobby could feel the sudden tension in her body. Then Kelly suddenly sprang to her feet and said, "come with me."

She took Bobby's hand and pulled at him.

"Come on, Bobby," Kelly pleaded.

Bobby quickly got up as Kelly yanked at him. He was dragged along as Kelly hurried into the mud room. She let him go to open a storage door at the back of the room. At first uncertain if he was ready for this, Bobby hesitated at the entrance, then took that fateful step, going in to be with the girl.

Kelly shoved him aside as she burst out of the room carrying a plastic bucket. She ran back toward the pool arena, swinging the pail like a small child would do when hurrying to build a sand castle at the beach.

Bobby just stood at the storage door watching Kelly run away from him. There was a blank stare on his face that could have been expressing confusion, shock... or disappointment.

"Bobby, c'mere, hurry," Kelly implored.

Bobby went back to the pool arena because Kelly seemed insistent, enthusiastic as a kid at the circus. He stood near the diving platform but couldn't see Kelly anywhere in the arena.

"Kelly, where are you?" he hollered in a loud voice.

"Down here," Kelly answered, "I'm down here in the pool."

Bobby looked over the edge and there she was standing at in the deep end of the swimming pool. Kelly looked up at him, as if wondering why he was being so reluctant to be with her.

"Hurry up, Bobby," she called to him and pointed at the shallow end of the pool. "There are steps."

"I don't want to, Kelly," he said to her.

Now, Kelly was the one that was confused. She walked over to a spot right below him and looked up.

"Oh, Bobby, you have to. Please come down."

"That water looks nasty," Bobby said.

Kelly gave him a moment to change his mind, then said, "fine, be a jerk then."

Bobby watched her go back to where the bucket was laying. She snatched it up and slung it like she was going to throw it at him in frustration. Kelly stared up at him, waiting but Bobby boldly crossed his arms, a way of saying, "nuh uh, Kelly, not gonna."

Kelly waded into the swamp, first scooping up some of the murky water, then began pulling up weeds, mossy growths and just because she could, one of the floating lily pads. She moved her feet through the water as if not wanting to step on anything that was alive, thinking of the frog. She grabbed one of the cattail stalks and ripped it out. Then, Kelly waded across the swamp to where Bobby was looking down at her.

"Can you help me?" Kelly asked him.

Bobby shook his head 'no'.

"Please, Bobby," she pleaded. "I need the rope."

There was a rope laying on the pool walkway that he hadn't noticed before. Bobby got it for her and was going to toss it down, still coiled, to Kelly.

"You need to hold one end of it!"

Bobby held a knotted end of the sisal rope and dropped the rest of the coil down to Kelly. She hurriedly looped her end around the pail handle and tied it up. Kelly stepped back and looked up at him again.

"Pull it up, silly," Kelly instructed him.

Bobby worked hand over hand as he pulled the heavy pail up to where he was. Kelly watched until the treasure was safe, then quickly ran to the steps at the shallow end.

Bobby moved away from the bucket of crap that Kelly had gathered from the swamp, as if it was something of disgust and he didn't want to be anywhere near it.

Kelly ran to the bucket, sat down and pulled the swamp pot between her legs where it would be safe from spillage.

Bobby stood clear away from the mud bucket, thinking 'strange Kelly' might be getting ready to throw some of that gunk at him.

"What's wrong with you?" Kelly asked him sincerely. "C'mere, look."

Again, Bobby just shook his head 'no'.

Kelly reached one hand into the murky water and took out a round puffy thing that looked like a moldy biscuit, one that had been left out far too long and wasn't really food anymore.

"It's green," Kelly told him thinking he would get it, then again, "green, Bobby."

There was a great big smile on her face as Kelly looked at him.

"Abernathy likes to eat green things."

"Spylgyn. His name is Spylgyn," said Bobby, finally understanding.

After that, he wasn't so afraid of Kelly's bucket anymore.

25   Details and Stuff

When Kelly went over her plan to capture Spylgyn, Bobby pretty much agreed with most of her ideas but was quick to point out some flaws in the details. Kelly wanted to rush right over to Uncle's house and just go at it. Bobby thought it was better to take action the next morning, when they would probably be more calm in the situation.

"You think I'm not calm?" Kelly asked him.

Kelly was agitated but Bobby wasn't about to tell her that he thought that.

"I'm talking about the situation with my mother and father," he replied.

"We're not going to tell them. They can't know. And Uncle, he certainly can't know," Kelly pointed out. "We sneak in, go to Alice's room and get her to coax Spylgyn out from hiding," Kelly said as if it was going to be as simple at that.

"She's not just going to give him up, Kelly," argued Bobby. "Spylgyn is... well, he's hers, her... I don't know what? Pet?"

Kelly insisted saying, "Alice is a bright kid, Bobby. I've talked to her, she has good common sense. If I tell her the right way, she'll do it."

"Then, when Spylgyn comes out, you just toss the little guy into the bucket and make a run for it?" Bobby asked. "You're gonna hold your hand over the bucket, so Spylgyn doesn't jump out, right? How are we going to transport the bucket from the house to the spa, our bikes?"

Bobby could see the disappointment in her face but he also saw anger and frustration.

"Look, Kelly, the plan is good, we just need to refine a few details, you know," Bobby spoke in a soothing voice hoping that would calm Kelly down. "We just need to think things over so that we can do this right."

Kelly didn't calm down, though. She began to pace, going in one direction, then another. as a myriad of thoughts raced through her mind.

Bobby knew that now was a good time for him to shut up. Kelly stopped pacing, and came at him. Bobby almost raised his arms in a defensive stance, thinking Kelly might hit him, so he showed her his palms to stop her advance, a way to say 'I don't have any weapons, Kelly, please don't hurt me'.

Kelly stepped right up to him and said, "don't go timid on me, Bobby."

"I'm not, Kelly," Bobby replied but he could see that she was still angry.

Although she didn't shove him out of her way, it seemed that way to Bobby as she walked past him. Kelly was on her way to the mud room, fast walking like an Olympian at a track meet. He considered going after her, then tossed aside that idea as foolish. Better to let Kelly vent without him as an easy target.

Bobby heard loud noises coming from the mud room, like things being thrown and torn apart. There was a fury happening in that room and Bobby didn't want to be vulnerable when Kelly came out from there. He moved quickly away to the far side of the swimming pool, thinking she might come out with a baseball bat, eager to crush any enemy that stood in her path.

There was a quiet then, so maybe the conflict was over. That silence was just as foreboding as the noises had been. Bobby remained where he was in what he thought was a safe zone.

Kelly came out of the mud room carrying an ice chest like the ones people take to the beach to keep sodas and sandwiches cold. She looked at Bobby standing where he was, seeming confused by his departure.

"What are you doing over there?" Kelly asked him.

"I thought you might be going for a weapon," Bobby said sheepishly.

"C'mere," Kelly said in a sweet voice. "Bobby, come here."

Bobby wasn't going to fall for that tune. He stayed where he was. That ice chest looked heavy and could cause damage if Kelly swung it at him.

Kelly set the ice chest down next to the bucket and waited for Bobby to come back. When he didn't, Kelly reached down and opened the lid of the ice chest, showing him how it worked.

"Look, it opens. It closes. Open. Closed," Kelly demonstrated as if instructing a child. "It's got a lid with a snap-lock. Spylgyn can't jump out."

Since Kelly appeared normal again, not raging, Bobby came back to her.

"We'll need more water and something soft to cushion the ride, a towel or clothing maybe. There are bungee cords in Uncle's tool shed. I can get them."

"Bungee cords?" Bobby said, not understanding.

"Yes, to fasten the icebox to your bike, your grandfather's bike, on the back plate. It'll work, Bobby," she said, smiling.

"You really want to do this tonight," Bobby said, knowing now that it was going to happen just like Kelly wanted, no matter what he said.

Kelly was standing with her hands on her hips as if she was waiting for Bobby's next argument about her plan and ready to refute any remark that might leak out of his mouth. But, the way she was looking at him, all sweet and lovable like she was, Bobby would have jumped into a lake full of alligators to save all the ducks, if she only asked him to.

Bobby had to lift more water out of the swamp to dump into the ice chest until it was a third full. Kelly found a large patch of grayish moss and some deep green fibrous things to add as a soft buffer for the amphibian during the bike ride. And then, there were the cattails, weeds and puffy green biscuits that they both hoped would be a food source for the amphibian.

All the while they were working, they would talk about what they were going to do, what could go wrong and what might possibly happen when they got Spylgyn to the spa. Bobby had heard her use the word amphibian instead of creature, so he asked Kelly about that.

Kelly said, "I'm thinking that he might be an unknown species or evolution."

Neither one of them could decide if the amphibian was an air breather or a water breather. Kelly suggested that it's possible that Spylgyn could do both. After some thought, Bobby was convinced that he was an air breather, like whales or Galapagos lizards that can stay underwater for a long time.

Kelly told Bobby about her theory that the water they were using was actual source water from his great-grandfathers sinkhole and it could be that the grotto out in the desert was Spylgyn's home.

When Bobby scoffed at that, telling her that the water had dried up years and years ago, she replied, "but, what if it didn't? The sinkhole may be dry, yes but only on the surface. Nobody knows how deep that water source is or how big. It could be an ocean, or an underground lake!"

Her enthusiasm was infectious. And, she was right, Bobby thought. How deep, how wet was the cavern below the desert? He didn't know.

"I've seen videos of divers with scuba gear going deep into underground caverns, big caves that can stretch for miles and miles," Kelly told him.

Actually, Bobby had seen something like that on The Discovery Channel, so maybe Kelly's theory was possible.

When the ice chest was ready to go, Bobby grabbed it up and headed for the door that led out from the pool arena.

"Stop," Kelly said loudly as he turned the lock to open the door. "We can't go out that way."

"What," Bobby said, "why not? Kelly, we can't crawl through the tunnel with this," indicating the heavy ice chest.

"I can't," Kelly said, "I promised Uncle. I can't use that door."

Kelly's logic amazed Bobby.

"Kelly, my grandfather wanted you to stay out of this place, obviously," he explained to her. "You're already here, in the forbidden zone. Promise broken."

Bobby unlocked the door and swung it open. Kelly actually gasped in shock. She remained some distance from the door as if the opening was a monster's gaping maw and would swallow her whole if she attempted to step out from the pool arena.

"I didn't make any promises to my grandfather," he said, smiling at her.

Bobby stepped out into the hallway but held the door open for Kelly.

"You can go out the tunnel if you want to. I'll wait for you here," Bobby said.

As Bobby let go of the door, Kelly ran for it and managed to step out just in time before it closed. There was a whoosh of air that followed after Kelly like the breath of a beast coming after her. Kelly squealed out a tiny scream and grabbed onto Bobby for protection.

26 The Burgle

The bungee cords were right where Kelly said they were, hanging on the work shop wall, ready to use. They were both sneaking as though it was criminal, what they were doing.

"We're not stealing," Kelly told Bobby, "just borrowing. Uncle lets me use things all the time."

"Then, why are we whispering and sneaking?" Bobby asked her.

"It's more fun this way," she told him.

Bobby led the way with Kelly close behind him when they went in through the back door of Uncle's house. No one was in the kitchen to confront them. The house was still and quiet, almost like no one was there. Kelly urged Bobby to move faster by putting a hand on his back and pushing.

"Go," she whispered.

They were just a short few steps into the hallway below the staircase when Bobby heard muffled voices coming from the front room. He stopped and turned to Kelly who was crouched down in her creeper stance. Using only gestures, Bobby told Kelly that she should sneak upstairs with the ice chest, while he tried to distract the occupants with misdirection. Kelly nodded, indicating that what they were about to do would be a good burgle.

Bobby and Kelly positioned themselves just beyond the sight line for anyone in the front room but Kelly went too soon. Bobby had to quickly jump into the entry doorway, exposing himself to anyone that was looking in that direction. His grandfather was in the big chair with his back to Bobby, so he couldn't have seen Kelly go around the banister and scamper upstairs. His mother, however, could have if she had been looking. Her head was lowered though, like she was staring at something that she had dropped on the floor. Bobby must have made noise when he jumped because his mother looked up to see him standing at the entry opening.

"Bobby, where have you been?" his mother asked him, though she didn't seem to be genuinely alarmed like he thought she'd be.

"Your father wanted to say good-bye before he left," she said.

"He's gone?" Bobby asked.

"Yes, he had to go back," she told him.

Jenny didn't say 'back to his new girlfriend' but that's what she was thinking.

"We're not going?" Bobby asked but didn't make it sound too hopeful.

"No," was all his mother said.

Uncle got up from his chair and turned so he could look at Jenny and Bobby at the same time.

"I'm gonna get the grill started, my turn to cook tonight," he said to them. "Hot dogs, burgers and all the fixin's, done proper," then added, "burnt and crispy."

His mother was looking for the dropped item on the floor again, not saying anything. Uncle walked over to Bobby and put a hand on his shoulder.

"I always have good dreams after I eat hot dogs and porkers," Uncle said to him, "and just a little bit of flatulence. You can look that word up later."

"I know what flatulence is, Grampa," replied Bobby.

After his grandfather left, Bobby stood at the doorway, uncertain what he should do next. Bobby wanted to hurry after Kelly but his mother seemed so distracted and forlorn. And, he knew that he should stay and try to comfort her. He went to sit on the footstool and sat down facing his mother.

"What's happening, Mom?" he asked her. "Are you okay?"

"Your father..." Jenny began but was uncertain how much to say to him right now.

"Mom. I know already," he said to her.

"What do you know?" Jenny asked.

"I've seen him with her. I know what they're doing," he told her.

"What did you see?" Jenny asked Bobby.

"I saw them in the car together. They were kissing," Bobby replied.

"Where?" Jenny said to him.

"At the school, Alice's school," Bobby said.

"Alice was with them?" she said, shocked.

"No, Mom, I was waiting for Alice," Bobby explained. "She hadn't come out yet. I didn't know Dad was gonna be there to pick her up. I was gonna take her home with me."

Jenny wanted to know more, all that Bobby saw or heard but didn't ask him for details. There were enough rotten images in her head anyway about what her husband was doing with that woman.

"Why on earth would I want anymore?" Jenny thought.

"What are we gonna do?" Bobby asked her.

"Stay here for a while, with Grampa," she said easily.

"Yeah," Bobby said, "that's what I want to do, too."

"We'll be okay, Bobby," she told him and reached a hand to him.

Bobby took her hand but it wasn't enough. He stood up and leaned over his mother to give her a hug.

"Yeah, Mom, we're gonna be okay," he told her.

Jenny hugged her son, giving him that long hug that mothers sometimes give to their children, a hug that lasts a good while. When she did release him, Jenny placed her hand on Bobby's cheek, looking into his eyes that were so like hers.

"I love you, Bobby," she told him.

"I love you, too, Mom," Bobby said back to her.

"Now, go," Jenny said, sort of pushing him away. "Go be with your girlfriend. She went upstairs."

"Kelly's not my girlfriend, Mom", Bobby said.

"That's right, just a buddy," Jenny said smiling.

Bobby did leave but not quickly. He looked back once at his mother sitting quietly in the chair. She was still watching him, so he gave her a little wave goodbye.

"You may not know it yet but she is your girlfriend," Jenny said but Bobby was already gone and didn't hear her.

27 What's in the Closet, Alice?

Bobby went to his room first to see if Kelly was waiting for him there. She wasn't. He went back to Alice's room and listened in at the closed door but it was quiet. He couldn't hear if Kelly was in there or not. If she was already engaged in convincing Alice to let them take Spylgyn, he didn't want to disturb the negotiations.

Next Bobby went to his grandfather's room. The door was open, so he went inside to look at the fish tank. It's possible that Spylgyn could be in there for one of his water treatments. Bobby looked all over, searching every cranny and behind ever rock but no amphibian. The octopus watched the intruder ominously from its perch on a rock pile, then silently slid off and backed into her cave, out of sight.

Bobby returned to Alice's room and the closed door. He knocked softly, then opened the door before anyone could refuse him entry.

Kelly and Alice were sitting on the bed doing the girl talk thing. His sister had a doll in her lap and was gently brushing her hair. Kelly was sort of half stretched laying down like she might be considering a nap.

"All okay in here?" Bobby asked.

Kelly got up from the bed, took a moment to brush at her clothes, then turned to Bobby with a 'what are you doing?' expression on her face. Kelly rounded the bed and went to meet Bobby at the door. Kelly took his arm and pulled him outside into the hallway, closing Alice's door behind them.

"Kelly, I just want to know what's going on," Bobby said to her.

Kelly laid a hand on his chest and said, "I know, Bobby, you want to help."

Then, she sighed, and told him the truth. "But, you've got to remember that you're the big, bad brother who wants to take away one of her toys."

"Well, that's what you're trying to do, isn't it?" Bobby said to her.

"No," Kelly answered. "I'm not going to take Spylgyn away from her. I want her to give him to me."

"And just how are you going to do that?" Bobby asked.

Kelly didn't want to get into a long discussion about it but she knew that Bobby needed to be soothed at the moment.

"Little girls have different emotions and thoughts than little boys," she explained.

Bobby wanted to say that he wasn't a little boy but he didn't.

Kelly felt something in Bobby's shirt pocket, so she reached in to see what it was.

"If someone tries to take a toy away from a child, a boy will usually fight or argue with them," Kelly said as she removed her black rock from his pocket.

"You need to keep this in a safer place. Don't want to lose it," Kelly told him.

She took the small rock and put it in the watch pocket of Bobby's jeans as she went on with her explanation.

"A little girl, well, she might cry, maybe have a temper tantrum if it's a special toy like Spylgyn. But, little girls are generous, too. I was a little girl once, so I know what I'm talking about."

"You were never a little girl, Kelly," he said to her.

"Was too, and I've got pictures to prove it," she said petulantly.

Bobby reached up and moved an errant strand of hair off from Kelly's face.

"One day a toy is special, much more special than any of her other toys," Kelly said looking into Bobby's eyes. "but, a day later, or maybe a few days, that toy just becomes regular, not really special anymore."

Bobby wasn't really listening to Kelly anymore. He was watching her lips while she spoke, the words no longer important to him. He was back in the bike shed with her, the kiss that he would remember for the rest of his life, vanilla ice cream. Her voice was like the sound that clouds might make as they drifted across a clear blue sky, he thought, soft and soothing.

Bobby leaned down and kissed Kelly while she was still talking.

After a moment, Kelly pushed him away, gently.

"She'll give him to me, Bobby, if I ask her," Kelly said softly.

"I know," said Bobby.

Bobby didn't want to leave her but he did. Kelly gave him a little push to send him along. Neither one of them said 'I love you' when they parted. That wouldn't happen until Thursday.

Uncle was in the backyard at the barrel grill when Bobby came out the back door.

"Grab the dogs and meat before you come out, Bobby," his grandfather said. "I'm about ready for 'em here."

Bobby turned on the spot and went back into the kitchen. He returned with a package of hot dogs and ready-made burgers in plastic. Bobby put them on the folding table right next to the grill so that they were an easy reach for the cook.

"I seem to recall that you like your burgers well done," his grandfather said to Bobby.

"I just want hot dogs tonight," Bobby replied. "you're gonna grill some onions, right?"

"It's not done any other way, unless you're an amateur," Uncle chuckled. "Maybe you can do the chopping chores, help your mom out some."

"Yeah I can do that," Bobby said.

Jenny was at the picnic table setting out place mats and utensils on the table top. There was a chopping board with 3 already peeled onions and a sharp knife waiting for Bobby. He didn't work fast, having decided to take it slow and easy. His grandfather was just now putting the hot dogs and burgers on the grill. He tried to calculate the time factor and guessed that it would be about 20 minutes until feeding time. Bobby hoped that would be enough time for Kelly to convince Alice to give up one of her dollies.

Spylgyn lay in the cubit listening to the spryling sing to him. He knew she was calling to him, wanting him to come out from hiding but he wouldn't. There was another with Ayeece in the outer cube and Spylgyn was afraid of what would happen if that other one saw him. The spryling would not harm him, of that Spylgyn was certain but he didn't know what this other creature would do to him.

Spylgyn had accepted that he was lost to the others of his kind. G'Thorpe and Neela must have returned to cavern when they couldn't locate him. The orbs had gone with them as they should have. Spylgyn knew that he had been taken far past safe haven, deep into the world of the Oolongs, those who eat creatures like him.

By sniffing the air of her passage when the other one came near, Spylgyn determined that it was probably the female youngling that Ayeece called Keeyee. When he heard the other one speak to Ayeece, her tonal noise was fresh and not of a harsh nature.

Another odor had wafted through to the amphibian, a deep rich aroma that reminded him of cavern. Intrigued but still wary, Spylgyn came out from under the nest he had made and crept closer to the cubit opening.

"Call to him again, Alice," Kelly told the little girl.
"Spylgyn, Spylgyn, Spylgyn," Alice sang quietly.
Kelly was laying flat out on her belly because Alice had told her to 'go smaller'.
"He will think you are too big," Alice said, "You need to be small, like me. Big people scare him. He runs away when he hears big people coming."
Alice was sitting cross-legged right in front of the closet door opening. Kelly was stretched out, hiding behind the little girl so that she would not frighten Spylgyn by being too big. Most of Kelly's body would be hidden from view if the creature happened to look out. At least, that's what Kelly hoped.

158

"Spylgyn, Spylgyn, Spylgyn," Kelly called softly to the amphibian. She waved the cattail at the dark opening like it was a wand that a fairy would wave when summoning magic. To her nose the plant's smell was not pleasant but she thought that Spylgyn might like the odorous aroma.

As she continued to pass the plant back and forth, Kelly thought she might have seen some movement but couldn't be sure.

"There he is," said Alice.

"What, where?" Kelly almost shouted.

"Right there," Alice said. "Spylgyn, come out."

Kelly's eyes were straining to see into the dark recesses of the closet but she saw nothing but a pile of clothing on the floor. Then, the clothing moved ever so slightly.

"Ask him to come out again, Alice," Kelly whispered.

"I don't know how," she whined.

Alice began to move her hands and arms like she had seen Spylgyn do when he was trying to communicate with her.

"Come out, Spylgyn, come out," Alice said louder.

"Alice, ssssssh." Kelly said to her. "He's scared. We don't want to frighten him."

"I know," said Alice and scooted over to the ice chest before Kelly could stop her.

Alice searched the container to find just the right thing that would appeal to Spylgyn. Her hand came out with what looked like a tiny pea pod. She moved back to her spot in front of Kelly but closer to the opening, then held her hand out, reaching into the dark space where Spylgyn was hiding. When Alice removed her hand, Kelly could see that the pea pod was gone.

"He took it, just like that," Alice said. "He likes green things, I told you."

"Alice," Kelly said softly, "would you get me one of those bean pods."

Alice got another plant from the ice chest and handed it to Kelly.

"Can I do it, Alice?" she asked. "Can I give it to him?"

Alice nodded so Kelly scrooched in closer to the closet and held her hand out with the pea pod in her palm. She didn't put it all the way in as Alice had done but kept her hand a few inches away from the opening. Then, they waited.

Spylgyn shelled the pod that Ayeece had given him and ate the peas one after the other. It was good food, like nothing she had ever given him before. Then, he ate the pod casing even though that was something that he usually didn't do. "This is from cavern," he thought as he chewed vigorously. When he finished eating, he looked out to the cube dwellers. Now, it was the other one, Keeyee, that held her hand out to him with a fragrant seed pod in her hand. Spylgyn crawled out from the nest and went to get it.

The amphibian came out from hiding and Kelly got her first good look at Spylgyn. The first thing that sprang to her mind was, "oh my God, he's so cute."
Spylgyn stood at that line between darkness and light but did not go out to the youngling's hand right away. To Kelly, it seemed as if Spylgyn was deciding if he would trust her or go back to hiding in the dark closet. The amphibian cocked his head slightly and made a hand gesture to the one called Keeyee. When Keeyee didn't respond, Spylgyn looked at Alice then, made the same hand gesture to her.
Alice wiggled her fingers to Spylgyn and said, "Kelly won't hurt you, Spylgyn, I promise. You won't hurt him, will you, Kelly?"
"No, Alice," Kelly promised. Then looking at Spylgyn, she said "I won't hurt you, Spylgyn."
Kelly cautiously moved her hand closer to the amphibian but not too close. As fortune would have it, she held her hand with the palm up which was a clear sign of peace to the Ingling. Then, as if the creature sensed that it was safe, Spylgyn hopped out of the closet and went right to Kelly's face. He reached up one hand

and placed it on her face, moving its fingers in a soft, pleasant way.

"He's just saying hello, Kelly," Alice said, "that's what he does when he likes you."

Kelly remained very still and accepted Spylgyn's caress. In her mind, Kelly was saying to herself, "this is happening, this is really happening to me, right now."

Spylgyn hopped over to the pea pod in Kelly's hand. He looked at Kelly before reaching for the food, as if asking if it was okay. Kelly wiggled her fingers to say "yes, tiny creature, take the food, it's for you."

Spylgyn took the pea pod and sliced open the shell. He tossed the peas one at a time into his mouth and ate them quickly. Then, he sat down and waited to see what else Keeyee was going to do.

Alice," Kelly whispered, "would you give me some more food from the ice chest?"

Alice chose different things this time. She gave Kelly a green biscuit, a lily pad and a lichen covered rock. Kelly took them in her right hand and passed them over to her left hand. She laid that hand down right in front of Spylgyn so that he could choose from the plate.

Spylgyn reached into her palm and scraped some green powder off the biscuit and licked the stuff from his fingers like it was sugar on a powdered doughnut. The powder must be good because he came back for more. The lily pad must not have been food because he let it lay. Spylgyn picked up the rock but seemed confused why this non-edible was presented to him. It wasn't a finder stone, just ordinary.

Spylgyn looked at Kelly and made a hand gesture, his palm turning up, then down and back up again.

Alice, what does that mean?" Kelly asked the little girl.

"I don't know," Alice replied. "He does a lot of things like that but I don't understand."

Then, Spylgyn stood straight up and ran across Alice's lap to get to the ice chest. The little girl squealed in surprise but the amphibian paid no attention to that.

He was used to her peculiar noises and had heard that one many times during his stay with her.

The amphibian sprang onto the lip of the container and looked inside at the contents. There were things there that could only have come from cavern and that confused Spylgyn. If the Oolongs had been to cavern, that would be a disaster for all. Cavern was sanctuary for his tribe and all the other Inglings that dwelt there. He wanted to question Keeyee about this matter but Spylgyn knew that the youngling would not understand. Their language was coarse and distorted as he heard it. He had struggled with the spryling for a long time trying to get her to understand simple hand signals but eventually had given up on Ayeece.

Kelly got up from the floor and sat cross-legged to see what Spylgyn was doing at the ice chest. The amphibian was perched at the top of the opening and was looking inside at her miniature swamp.

Balanced on the ice chest rim, Spylgyn looked back at Keeyee. He raised one arm to the youngling, showing her the question hand signal to ask how she had found cavern. Keeyee just looked at him stupidly and Spylgyn became frustrated.

"Keeyee," he whistled, "Keeyee!"

Spylgyn jumped off the ice chest and went back across Alice's lap to confront the youngling. He jumped up onto her leg and looked up at her face. Using hand signals and his own very odd language, the amphibian tried to convey his request for her to take him to cavern but it was quickly apparent that she was ignorant also, and this frustrated Spylgyn so much that he became angry. He jumped from one of Kelly's legs to the other, then back again. Spylgyn slapped one hand repeatedly on her leg, as one would do when trying to wake up a lazy dog.

"Oh, my God, Alice, what is he doing?" asked Kelly.

"He's not happy," Alice said.

"I can see that," Kelly said. "What am I supposed to do?"

Alice just shrugged as if this unusual occurrence happened to her all the time with Spylgyn.

The amphibian lay down almost like he was exhausted. He stretched out on Kelly's leg and rested. Her skin was warm to him, soft like Neela's, and that gave Spylgyn a sense of comfort. The Ingling wanted to nestle there, sleep on the youngling if he could.

Kelly let him lay on her leg for a long time. She wanted so badly to take one hand and pet him like a kitten but didn't. She was worried about his erratic behavior when Spylgyn was jumping on her and making those strange noises. Kelly knew that must be how he spoke but it just sounded like whistles, bubbles and clicks to her and how could she know what that meant?

Spylgyn got up on all fours and moved closer to stand on Kelly's denim shorts. He made a hand signal to the youngling but knew it was pointless because she just couldn't understand. He tried sending thought clouds as he had done before when the youngling toppled but, again, she wasn't able to grasp any.

"I want to help you, Spylgyn," Kelly whispered softly to him. "Will you let me help you?"

Spylgyn reshaped his vocal cavity and made one last attempt to mimic the Oolong sound that was her name.

"Keeyee," he whistled," Keeyee."

Kelly heard him that time. It was her name. Spylgyn was saying her name! She looked down at the tiny creature and tried to whistle like he had just done, "Keeyee...Spylgyn...Keeyee."

Kelly put her right hand on her chest as if showing him where her heart was and said, "Keeyee."

Spylgyn cocked his head at the youngling when he heard how she said the names.

This youngling can understand, he reasoned but not enough for them to actually talk to each other. The amphibian decided to show her by action instead of words. Spylgyn began hopping and spinning and to Kelly it looked like he was dancing like an enthusiastic puppy would do.

"Happy dance, that's the happy dance," said Alice.

Spylgyn jumped off Kelly's leg and onto Alice's lap. He didn't stay with her very long, just long enough to lick one of her fingers like he did with the green sugar. Then, Spylgyn sprang onto the ice chest and jumped inside.

Both Alice and Kelly looked in to see what the amphibian was doing.

"He's making a nest," Alice said.

Spylgyn had burrowed into the mossy growth and was making a nest, just as Alice told Kelly. He wiggled and squirmed until his lower body was immersed in the cool water, then pulled a lily pad over his chest as a comfort. The amphibian looked up at Ayeece and Keeyee and chirped a few noises at the Oolongs which, of course, they couldn't understand. Then, he lay back and closed his eyes like he was going to sleep.

Kelly watched Spylgyn for a few moments but the amphibian remained still and quiet. Then, she gently closed the lid of the ice chest.

28   More Lies for Jenny

Alice came running down the back steps like a dog running after a thrown ball. She went right up to Uncle and placed her order.

"I want a hot dog and curly fries," Alice told her grandfather.

I don't have any curly fries, only spuds," he told her.

"Are there onions in with them?" Alice asked.

"Yes, I thought you liked my spuds," Uncle said.

"I may want to kiss a boy later and I don't want nasty breath," Alice said.

Uncle handed her a hot dog and bun and Alice went to the picnic table hoping there would be at least some potato chips to go with her meal.

"What boy?" Jenny asked her daughter.

Alice forgot to be polite and responded with a mouthful of hot dog.

"When I find one," Alice admitted to her mother and that seemed to be an acceptable explanation because Jenny didn't ask Alice any more questions about that.

Bobby had questions for Alice, though. He leaned across the table and used his mouth to express, "Where is Kelly?"

Alice gave him a look like he was a crazy person but she mouthed words back to him in response but there were only the nonsense words of a little girl who didn't understand what he was asking.

"Alice, where is Kelly?" he whispered to her.

"Oh, she's gone," Alice said.

"Gone," Bobby said in a regular voice.

"She said you are to come to her later after barbecue," Alice told him.

"Are you going out with Kelly tonight, Bobby?" Jenny asked her son.

"Uh, yeah, Mom," he replied, "if that's okay."

His mother looked disturbed at this news, so Bobby said, "all us guys are going to a movie."

"I think you'd better alter those plans, son," Uncle said. "That theater is closed on account of the fire."

"Fire?" Jenny said, sounding concerned.

"Yeah, popcorn machine caught on fire or something. It's been closed about two weeks now, I guess."

Bobby went on with the lie, saying "I meant we're gonna watch a dvd movie, over at Dan's house."

"Dan?" his mother asked because this was the first time she had heard the name.

"It's okay now. Dan's a good kid, I know him," Uncle said to Jenny.

"Who else is going to be there?" Jenny asked Bobby.

"Just the guys, you know, "Andy, Martin and Dan."

"And Kelly," his mother said.

"Yeah, Kelly, too," Bobby told her. Bobby saw that his mother was not thrilled about her son going out at night, unsupervised, although she had let him do that all the time back in Texas. He thought she might be thinking of what Kelly and him might do if given a convenient opportunity, so he elaborated to make the tale more innocent.

"Dan's got this dvd about scuba divers that explore underground caves."

"Scuba divers in a cave?" she said as if not believing him.

"Now, I've heard of that," Uncle said. "Big caves with underground pools and lakes and divers going exploring down there."

"Maybe your friends could come over here and watch it," his mother said to Bobby.

"Oh, hon, let the boy go," Uncle said to Jenny. "You worry about too many inconsequential things. Don't mess up the boy's life."

"Mess up his life," Jenny said with muffled fury, while giving her father an angry look. "Is that what I'm doing, messing up his life just like I messed up mine?"

Uncle leaned back and tried to apologize. "Jenny, I just meant…"

"Inconsequential." Jenny sat up straight and repeated the word as if it suddenly had a new meaning for her. "Inconsequential," she said slowly, "that's my life, meaningless.

Uncle leaned in to the table and moved the food around on his plate. He knew that any further discussion between him and his daughter right now would only make matters worse.

Jenny got up from the table and walked away, leaving behind a stunned audience.

After his mother was gone and a proper time for silence was over, Bobby said, "I guess that means I can't go."

"No, you ahead on," his grandfather said. "I'll talk to her when she's calmed down."

Bobby didn't rush off to go be with Kelly right at that moment but he wanted to. Instead he waited for what he thought was a proper and acceptable time to leave.

His grandfather left first without saying anything, just went into the house like a man would walk into church, with quiet dignity but, maybe, a little sad.

Bobby went to sit next to his little sister and said, "What happened, Alice? Why did Kelly leave?"

"She went to take Spylgyn home," Alice said without emotion.

"She took him?" Bobby asked.

Alice gave him the short version, the way a little girl will leave out too many details of a fairy story that she has only heard once. Bobby wanted to know more but Alice was getting pouty on him and he would just have to get the whole story from Kelly when he saw her.

Bobby found Kelly's bike just where she had left it in the vacant lot. She must have taken his grandfather's bike because she would have to strap the ice chest onto the back plate for the ride back to the spa. The wheels on her tightly trimmed bike were bare as was the rest of the speeder; no unnecessary fenders or appliances that could catch the wind and slow her down. Bobby grabbed the bike, ran it down the pavement then jumped on like a cowboy would do with a galloping horse. He lost the pedals once in his impatience to ride away and almost fell off the unwieldy beast. Bobby didn't know that he was supposed to shout 'Zoom!' when he finally got the bike going really fast.

29 Policeman Delany

It was just coming on dusk when Kelly rode through the center of town on her way to the spa. She was careful to avoid rough spots and potholes in the roads and took all the curves wide in such a way that the trip would be as comfortable as possible for her passenger. Traffic was light on the main streets but Kelly took what back roads she could to avoid people when possible. She didn't want any upsets on this bike ride.

The Inyo Spa and Health Resort was built in the late 1960's when the town was still thriving because of its close proximity to the military base just 18 miles north. When that base was closed in 1975, the town of Inyo suffered a serious loss of revenue from the soldiers coming in for entertainment and supplies. Many businesses closed as a result, leaving behind empty buildings and barren parking lots. But the Inyo Spa was not affected that much when the army left. People still came from all over the world to experience the healing powers of the source water. When the sinkhole suddenly dried up, so did that section of town where the spa was.

Kelly thought of Farren Street as her territory and didn't like interlopers wandering around on the street where the spa was located. So, when she saw the police car parked in front of the spa, she slowed down and rode in to the curb, stopping under the street lamp with the burnt out bulb.

Kelly could see that the police car was just parked at the yellow loading zone but there were no flashing lights and no police officers in sight. The street was quiet and still as it was supposed to be, except for the invader.

Kelly leaned over the handle bars of the bike and waited, watching for any movement or disturbance that might cause her to ride away and come back later. It wouldn't be her arch-enemy Officer Reynolds that was lurking in her domain; Kelly knew his shift ended at 4pm. It was either Malloy or the new guy, Delany, that was here to cause trouble.

"No way around it," Kelly thought, "I've got to go in and find out what's happening."

The front doors to the spa were unlocked. Kelly went into the lobby foyer with Uncle's bike and stood it against a wall. She removed the ice chest from the rack and carried it with her when she went in to the tactical room.

Officer Delany was sitting at one of the computer terminals, just staring at the screen like he was watching a tv program. There was a soda on the table and a single snowball cupcake still in the torn wrapper close to him. Delany looked over at Kelly when she came inside but didn't say anything to her.

"How are you this evening, Officer Delany?" Kelly asked him.

"I don't suppose you want to give me the password here, huh?" Officer Delany said casually.

Kelly casually tilted her head but gave him no answer.

"Yeah, neither did Martin Goren before he scampered away," scoffed Delany. "Late for supper, he said."

She walked behind the policeman to the refrigerator and placed the ice chest on the floor next to it.

"Do you have a search warrant?" Kelly asked while she was doing that.

"Don't need one in this circumstance," Delany said

"What circumstance is that?" Kelly asked.

"Missing person, possible kidnap or foul play," Delany said to her.

"Who's missing?" Kelly asked but she knew.

"You are," the policeman said as he rotated in the computer chair to confront her.

"I'm right here, case solved," Kelly remarked.

"I see that." Delany pointed a finger at her. "You're right there."

Kelly smiled at him but soon realized that was a big mistake. She was leaning against the fridge door in an innocent way but Kelly could see trouble in the way the policeman was looking at her.

Delany looked right at her face at first, meeting her blank stare with his own. Then his eyes moved down, looking at her shirt and cut-offs in a way that said, "I like the way you dress, Kelly." When his gaze traveled down to her bare legs, Kelly moved and went to sit at Dan's drawing desk. That gave her enough space so that the guy couldn't grab at her and hid most of her body from his view.

"What are you doing, Officer Delany?" Kelly asked.

"Just making sure you're okay," he told her. "Your mother has been calling the police station because she was worried about you, said she hadn't seen you for 24 hours and wanted to file a missing person's report on you."

"I'll call her, let her know I'm okay," Kelly said. "Is that all?"

"Yeah," Delany said but he didn't get up to leave.

"What are you doing here so late, Kelly?" he asked her.

Kelly wanted to look surprised and say, "is it past curfew, Officer Delany? I'm so sorry," but she didn't.

"Things to do, always things to do," Kelly said off-handedly. "Don't you have things to do, Officer Delany? I mean, other than baby-sit me."

Delany didn't react to that barb, just stood up and looked at her for a few more moments, then said, "go on home, Kelly."

Delany took the cupcake with him but left the empty soda can on the table.

Kelly stayed where she was at Dan's drawing desk long enough for Delany to get in his police car and drive away. Then, she went to the door and locked it.

30 That's So Cool

Kelly carried the ice chest with her when she descended the steps into the swimming pool then walked across to center stage and set the container down next to Milly, the mermaid with the red hair. Kelly didn't open the lid right away but sat down next to it as if she was reluctant to open the lid to let Spylgyn out.

Kelly drew her knees up to her chest and wrapped her arms around her legs, holding them tight. It was the memory of Officer Delany that caused her to do that. Kelly had a notion that she had just been violated by that man and the way he had looked at her.

"I'm not candy, Officer Delany" Kelly said softly. "So, you just need to back off, man."

Kelly closed her eyes and began to sway back and forth like she was sitting in a rocking chair.

"Am I candy?" she asked herself and admitted that sometimes that was how she behaved, how she dressed. Kelly wouldn't have gone so far as to dress up in a Halloween costume and go around town like a French maid in a too short skirt with fish-net stockings and a dust fluffer but, she did have a need to be noticed, just not by people like Officer Delany and the bald clerk at Sodas and Creme.

Kelly reached down with one hand and felt for the frayed strings on her cut-off jeans. She could feel that her panties were not 'out there' for the crowd to see but she knew that some people looked at her as though they were, men and women alike.

She did want to be eye candy in the right situation, Kelly thought but didn't think that was so wrong. It was in all the movies and magazines wasn't it? Sex sells and there was no way around that in her mind. Kelly knew that she was intelligent, could be funny when she needed to be or moderately sweet if that was called for.

But for this boy, she wanted to be a delicious treat, a thing to be kissed and touched. Kelly wanted Bobby to be in awe of her. That's why she was behaving like a racy pop star, for him, wearing 'so tight' cut-offs and a t-shirt tied up to show off her waist and midriff.

But, he had also shown a good amount of interest when she was playing the Sandra Dee innocent on the field trip into the desert.

Kelly dropped her legs down, then stretched out on the cool tiles of the swimming pool deck and lay there. Officer Delany was gone from her mind now, like a mosquito that had tried to take a bite out of her but had been slapped away just in time.

Kelly felt a sense of freedom and abandonment when she was alone like this, especially in the pool. She wanted to take all of her clothes off to feel the sensation of cool tiles pressing against her body, like an icy massage. Kelly had only done that once, not long after she had first violated the forbidden zone. Even now, as she lay there, that sensual feeling from long ago gave her goosebumps. Kelly could feel them forming on her forearms and went looking for them with her hands, hoping that would make this special memory more pleasurable to her.

Kelly didn't hear Bobby come into the pool arena. He was just suddenly there, sitting on the edge of the pool above her, watching.

"How long have you been there?" Kelly asked.

"Not long," Bobby told her but she had a sneaky suspicion that he was lying to her.

"Okay, if I come down?" he asked.

Kelly sat up and waved a hand to him.

"I've been waiting for you," Kelly said.

"You could have left the door unlocked," Bobby said as he climbed down the ladder. .

"Oh, I forgot. You don't have a key," she apologized. "How did you get in?"

"I crawled through a window around back like a burglar," he confessed.

Bobby sat down beside her saying, "is he really in there?"

Kelly nodded, smiling.

"What... how did you...?" Bobby stammered.

"Spylgyn got in all by himself, just climbed in like he knew he was going on a trip," she said to him.

Bobby didn't know what to say.

"And listen... Spylgyn knows my name. He said my name to me," she exclaimed.

"He talked to you?" Bobby asked.

"Well, no," Kelly said, "not really. He makes sounds, chirping and whistling like a bird, and there's music like, I don't know, he's singing. And he makes movements with his arms and hands just like Alice told us."

"Sign language, like a deaf person?" Bobby asked.

"Yeah," Kelly said, "like that but more expressive, especially when he's upset."

"He got upset?" Bobby asked.

"He said my name," Bobby, she exclaimed. "He knows who I am."

Kelly reached over and hugged Bobby but that didn't last long. She was too excited to remain still. She scooted back and tried to make the musical sounds of how Spylgyn said her name.

"Keeyee, Keeyee," Kelly sang to Bobby.

"Keeyee, Keeyee," came a muted voice from the ice chest.

Spylgyn was answering her call.

31 The Swamp

Kelly and Bobby sat facing the ice chest so that they both could look inside when the lid was opened.

"Are you ready?" she asked him.

Bobby nodded and said, "Do it."

Spylgyn hadn't made any other sounds from inside the container since he had called out to Kelly a minute ago. She undid the locking clasp and slowly lifted the lid.

Spylgyn lept out, a terrific jump that landed him a good 7 feet away from his captors.

Kelly screamed like a little girl would if she saw a spider on the toilet seat when she went into a bathroom. Bobby jerked like he had been shocked by electricity.

Spylgyn spun around to face the Oolongs, as if the amphibian expected an attack and was ready to fight or run.

"He's fast," Bobby exclaimed.

This was Bobby's first look at Spylgyn and his first impression was that the creature looked like a hairless squirrel but with skin that appeared to be smooth and moist like an eel or salamander..

Spylgyn had his arms stretched outward in a defensive posture, hands flared forward revealing webbed fingers that were most certainly amphibian. A formidable raised dorsal fin from shoulders to lower back appeared to have sharp spikes that quivered and jerked as if alive. The Ingling was on bent knee, crouched low, confronting the unfamiliar male Oolong, wary of his intent. Spylgyn's long tail was whipping about rapidly, an agitated motion that was not unlike a cat getting ready to pounce on a mouse.

"What's he doing?" Bobby whispered to Kelly.

"He doesn't know you, Bobby," she said in a low voice. "He's just scared maybe. Here, hold your hands out like this."

Bobby didn't look at her because he saw rightly that the amphibian was in a fighting stance and he didn't want to look away, worried that Spylgyn might jump at him suddenly.

"Look, Bobby, like this," she said to him.

Bobby glanced over at her, then quickly back at the amphibian. Kelly was holding her hands out in front of her with the palms up. Bobby slowly raised his arms and did his hands just like Kelly but he thought it was a stupid thing to do.

After a few seconds of this stand-off, Spylgyn seemed to accept that Bobby was not a threat. The dorsal fin receded into the amphibian's back, vanishing as if it never even existed. Spylgyn moved his head to the left then across to the right, eyes darting rapidly to look at one location, then another, as if wary of the unfamiliar surroundings of this strange place. He suddenly spun around to look behind him at the swamp. Spylgyn looked in that direction a long time, leaving his back vulnerable.

"Wonder what he's up to?" Bobby whispered.

"Sssshhhh," Kelly shushed him.

Bobby lowered his arms and put his hands in his lap.

"Enough of that," he thought.

Spylgyn heard the movement and spun back around to face them. He looked at each one, then stood straight up like a mercat cautiously searching its domain for threats. Spylgyn held out both of his arms and turned his hands palms up to show them that he also did not have any weapons, none that were visible to them.

Spylgyn jumped up suddenly, twisted his body around while in the air and landed a few feet closer to the swamp. Then, he scampered across the floor and dove into the water.

Bobby breathed a sigh of relief.

"Well, I'm glad that's over," he said to Kelly. "I thought the little guy was gonna attack me. Didn't it look like that to you?"

"He was just making sure it was safe, I think," Kelly told him. "Remember, he doesn't know you yet. You could be an enemy."

"I'm not gonna hurt him, Kelly," Bobby said, sounding annoyed.

"But, he can't know that, Bobby." Kelly spoke in a soothing way. "Alice said that he runs away when he hears big people coming."

"I'm not much bigger than you are, Kelly," Bobby said. "So, why am I a threat and you're not?"

Kelly thought about it, then said, "mmmm, let's see... you stomp when you walk and your voice is deeper than mine, kinda growly sometimes. You're a man; I'm a woman. I am a soft sweet nester and you, you are the agressive hunter that gathers food for the tribe. Spylgyn might think that you want to eat him for dinner with some peas and carrots."

Bobby wanted to laugh at her comical description of him but didn't. He just smiled at Kelly in a lopsided way.

"We really must look like giants to Spylgyn," Bobby said.

"We've got to find a way to communicate with him, Bobby," Kelly said. "you know, find out what he's thinking about us and tell him what we're thinking."

"What are we thinking, Kelly?" asked Bobby. "I don't know. When it comes right down to it, this is your game. You're the experienced alien hunter and finder of unusual phenomenon, not me. I'm just an interested observer."

"You're more than that, Bobby, and you know it," she said to him.

Bobby shrugged his shoulders in a way that said, 'prove it, go ahead, convince me'.

Kelly scooted over to him and sat in the space between his outstretched legs. She lifted her legs over his so that hers were around his waist, creating an intimate closeness. It was an awkward position for Kelly so she held onto Bobby so as not to fall backwards. Bobby wrapped his arms around her and held her close.

"I don't know what's going to happen, Bobby," she said softly. "Between you and me, with Spylgyn. I don't know."

Bobby didn't say anything in reply.

"Do you have any ideas?" she asked him.

Bobby started by just saying her name, "Kelly..."

"Hhumm", Kelly said softly.

"Spylgyn is on your shoulder," he told her.

"Is he?" Kelly said, not understanding.

"Yeah," Bobby told her, "he's on your right shoulder, looking at me."

Kelly had thought that the soft touches on her back was Bobby trying to find her bra strap again. She didn't move but remained still with her head buried in Bobby's shoulder. She didn't want to frighten the amphibian with any sudden movements.

"What's he doing?" Kelly asked softly.

"Nothing, just looking at me," Bobby said to her.

Kelly felt Spylgyn move then. He was pulling at her hair with his fingers as if he was searching for fleas like a monkey might do for a friend. Kelly felt Spylgyn's still wet fingers near her ear. She held her breath while the amphibian studied her head.

Spylgyn's inspection went on too long and Kelly had to breathe or she would pass out. She sucked in air like a person coming up from underwater, a big breath that rushed in so fast that her chest heaved. After that, Kelly decided to breathe normally and hope for the best.

She felt the amphibian on her neck now, then higher as he climbed onto the very top of her head.

Spylgyn began smelling, then feeling at the irregular bump on the back of Kelly's head. Then he turned, squatted and urinated on her injury.

"Well, thank you," Kelly blurted out. "Thank you for that."

"What's he doing?" Bobby whispered to her.

"I'm pretty sure he just peed on my head," Kelly grumbled.

"Yeah, that's uh, that's unusual," replied Bobby.

"All done, there he goes," Bobby announced, too loud.

Kelly turned around just in time to see Spylgyn leap onto the wall of the swimming pool at the deep end. He sprang from low to high until the amphibian was able to jump over the edge and out of sight.

"I didn't know he could do that," Bobby said, sounding a little stunned by what he just saw.

"Me, neither," Kelly said in a similar way.

"Did you close the arena off?" Bobby asked her. "There's no way he can get out, is there?"

Kelly had a shocked looked on her face. "I forgot to do that."

They searched the place for over an hour, looking first as a team, then splitting up thinking that might give them fresh eyes. There was no sign of Spylgyn, no tiny wet tracks that would lead them to his hiding place.

"I've got to go home," Kelly finally said to Bobby. "It's late."

"Yeah, me too," he said. "Tomorrow, early, we'll both come early. We'll find him, Kelly."

"Unless he got out," Kelly thought but didn't say it.

They both kissed and hugged before they went their separate ways, Kelly and her bike going northwest.

Bobby watched her ride away until she turned a corner and was out of sight but she didn't look back and wave at him. He had hoped she would.

As Kelly approached the trailer park, she had, what she could later only describe as an episode of euphoria. The bothersome headache that had been coming and going for the past few days seemed to be gone like a wizard had waved a magic wand at her and shouted. "Begone!"

After she hid her bike underneath the trailer, she sat on the back porch just because she didn't want to go inside yet. Unconsciously, she ran her fingers through her hair then remembered that Spylgyn had pissed on her head. She smelled her fingers but there was no unpleasant odor. And, what about that? The bump on the back of her skull was completely gone and it didn't hurt anymore when she pushed at it. Actually, come to think of it, she felt pretty great all over.

32 A Not Peaceful Night

If anyone had been recording Kelly in a sleep study that night, they would have logged a total of seven dream occurrences where REM was visibly apparent. Any rapid eye movement by the subject of less than 30 seconds would not be considered as relevant. All of the recorded dreams would be less than 1 minute except one. The analyst would have determined that the 83 second episode was most likely a nightmare with the patient making gestures and fists with her hands and several tension jerks of the body during that episode. Of the seven dreams, Kelly would only recall three of them and that was because she wrote notes to herself while still asleep. She didn't remember the nightmare at all.

Albino Man crept into Kelly's dreams while she slept but it was like he was a bit player in the movies, just hired to stand around in the background, careful not to draw attention away from the primary characters.

In the first dream, Kelly was in a small rowboat that was floating in the original source water for the spa. The grotto out in the desert was now full of deep water with a curious indescribable smell that was soft and soothing. She sat on the center board of the boat and looked off in the distance. There were black clouds in the far sky, thunder and lightening monsters like those that could frighten small children and dogs left out in the open with no shelter.

The dark clouds were moving, almost as if they were a muscled beast that was churning and ripping at the usually quiet desert – a maelstrom. Kelly looked for the oars but saw that there were none. She wanted to get to shore before the storm was upon her so began to use her hands as paddles, sweeping at the water from one side of the boat then to the other but soon realized that was a useless endeavor. The storm was coming fast now and Kelly knew that she wouldn't make landfall in time.

It was not light or dark where Kelly was, more like the twilight that happens just before sunset when fireflies suddenly appear, blinking their secret messages to each other. It was then that she saw Albino Man standing on the shore. The ghostly man was holding the boat oars, one at each side, as if using them as crutches to hold up his frail body.

The next occurrence was an ugly and disturbing dream. There were a lot of dusty cowboys, back from a cattle drive, sitting in a smoke-filled saloon drinking whiskey and behaving raucously. An out-of-tune piano was being played by a grizzled old-timer but his fingers weren't touching the keys. "It must be a wind-up piano," Kelly thought, the kind that didn't need a person at all. She knew there was a name for that instrument but couldn't remember what it was. Kelly was on an elevated platform at one end of the saloon with foot lamps around stage front, lighting her up. All of the cowboys in the front row were staring up at Kelly, making whooping noises and clapping their hands with enthusiasm.

When Kelly saw how she was dressed, it was a shock to her. She might as well have been naked on that stage. As she stared out at the audience, Kelly knew that she was supposed to dance for them.

Albino Man was standing at the entrance to the saloon, peering over the swinging gate, watching to see what Kelly was going to do. She felt that if she began to dance and perform for the drunken men, Albino Man would walk away in disgust and Kelly would never see him again, so she ran for the stage wings and fell into a darkness.

Kelly tossed and turned all through the night, a troubled sleep that gave her no peaceful slumber.

In the last dream she could recall the next morning, Kelly was in a jail cell. Her hands held onto the cold bars that confined her and her face was pressed against a narrow opening. She was hoping that someone would come and unlock her cage.

"Her crimes could not be any that warranted prison," she thought.

Kelly heard a shuffling noise in the cell next to her and looked over to see Albino Man sitting on the metal cot in her secret room. He was holding out one hand as if offering her something. Kelly went over to the bars that separated them, reaching her arm as far through as she could to take the key in his open palm. But, Albino Man would not get up from the bed to give her the key.

The scribbled words on the night pad helped Kelly recall all three dreams. She did not get dressed first like she normally would when she first woke up but went directly to her laptop to write out the circumstances of each dream. She didn't want to forget any part of the dreams like she sometimes did if she waited too long.

After Kelly had written out the three occurrences while she was still somewhat befuddled by sleep, Kelly sat at the table just looking at the words on the screen.

"Who is the Albino Man, what does he want?" said Kelly as if someone might answer her.

Kelly could not recall a single instance where any other characters in her dreams appeared more than once. She had read somewhere that all the people in dreams were actually an extension of the person that was dreaming but in her mind that couldn't be a fact. How could she be all the cowboys that were watching her other self performing in the saloon? Kelly reasoned that all those characters were the men in town like Officer Delany, Frank Bodine and Earl the soda shop guy, the ones that looked at her in a disturbing way that was just plain nasty. Hyenas, that's how she thought of them, sly and conniving, ready to pounce quickly if given an opportunity. She tried to avoid them whenever possible.

So, who was Albino Man that was always invading her subconscious? When the connection sparked in her mind, Kelly actually gasped like Minnie Mouse would do if she found Mickey hiding in her closet. 'Eek' she thought to herself but didn't make the sound.

Kelly looked at her reflection in the dresser mirror. That other Kelly was comical, with her eyes wide open and her mouth forming the 'Oh' of surprise. The way mirror Kelly looked almost made Kelly laugh, it was that funny.

33 Olly Olly Oxen Free

The alarm clock went off at 6:13 am, two minutes before it was supposed to happen. Bobby reached over from his bed and stopped the ringing bells. Usually it took some time for him to grasp full awake mode but this morning he was wide awake and ready for the day. He took a quick shower, got dressed and went downstairs to the kitchen.

His grandfather was having morning coffee already but no breakfast.

"You're up early, Bobby," he said to him.

"I was gonna leave a note," Bobby said. "I didn't think anybody would be up yet."

"Oh, I get up early these days. I like the quiet mornings when everybody else is still snoozin'." Uncle explained. "Leave a note?" he asked.

"Kelly and me, we're meeting for breakfast down at the diner."

"That right? Breakfast," Uncle said. "You should get biscuits and gravy. They're the best you'll ever have."

"You'll tell Mom?" Bobby asked.

"Yeah, go ahead on," his grandfather said.

Bobby wanted to sit with his grandfather for just a few minutes and quiz him about the sinkhole and Big Black Joe but the old man seemed like he might be a little grumpy this morning so Bobby just left.

He rode Uncle's bike into town at a good clip but not fast. Kelly wouldn't be there until 7:30 am, so he would be early. Maybe a quick stop at the diner for biscuits and gravy was called for since he still didn't have a key to the spa.

Bobby got two orders of biscuits and gravy, coffee and orange juice. The waitress gave him a cardboard box to carry the food in when she saw that he was on a bike.

Farren Street was usually deserted for most of the day since there were no attractions to draw shoppers to that area of Inyo. There might be one or two cars parked for whatever reason, so Bobby paid no attention to the dirt-covered land rover as he whizzed past on his way to the spa.

Craig Cavanah watched the biker go by but didn't chase after him. He did reach onto the dashboard, though, and pressed a button on the video camera to start recording.

Bobby parked the bike in front of the spa entrance doors to block them off, hoping Kelly would realize that he was not inside. He went around to the sun patio where there were concrete tables and benches that were left standing after the spa closed down. The canvas umbrellas were missing, either taken down or stolen in past years. But, the sky was still opening up and the harsh sun had not really generated any heat yet, so it was cool on the patio.

He put the food on a table, sat down and waited for Kelly. She brought food, too – a sausage and biscuit, a bacon and biscuit, coffee, no orange juice. They sat and ate like it was an every day thing for them.

They had searched for Spylgyn the night before but gave up after it became sure that they would not be able to find the scamp.

Dan was delivered by his father while Kelly was telling Bobby about the rowboat dream and the strange man at the sinkhole. She didn't tell him that the Albino Man was naked, not wanting to complicate the story. In fact, Kelly just kept it simple and told him only what was felt by her, including some imagery about the terrible storm and the eerie desert atmosphere.

"What are you guys doing out here?" Dan asked them.

"We'll be in in a minute, okay?" Kelly said in a dismissive way.

Dan lingered for just a few moments longer hoping someone would offer him a sausage biscuit from one of the open food containers but when that didn't happen, he left.

Kelly wanted to hear Bobby's thoughts about the dream but now that Dan was here, she felt rushed and wanted to get inside the spa. She took a big bite out of her bacon biscuit and stood up.

"We need to go, Bobby," Kelly said to him. "Now!"

Kelly left all the food on the table for someone else to clear away and ran after Dan.

Bobby didn't leave immediately. The biscuits and gravy were delicious just like his grandfather had told him and he wanted to finish eating.

Kelly poked her head back around the corner of the building, waving a 'come on' signal to him. Bobby waved back at her but didn't get up. Exasperated, Kelly stomped back to confront him.

"Are you coming or not?" Kelly asked him.

Bobby forked the last bit of gravy biscuit, dropped it into his mouth, making 'mmmm, mmmm good' sounds while he chewed. And, Kelly waited.

Bobby had noticed that Kelly was dressed conservatively today with full-length blue jeans, though they were a little tight, a poplin lumberjack shirt, tail out, with the sleeves rolled up to her elbows and hiking boots.

"She just needs the double-bladed ax to do it proper," he thought.

Kelly impatiently crossed arms over her chest and scowled at Bobby.

"What if Spylgyn got out, Bobby?" Kelly scolded him.

"Out?" Bobby said looking around the courtyard as if searching for him.

"I'm serious now," Kelly said. "What if he got out of the arena and is running amuck all over town?"

Grunting a 'yeah, okay', Bobby got up and casually walked to the front of the spa but he was going too slow, so Kelly got behind him and started pushing like a farmer would shove a stubborn jackass to get it to going. Bobby played along, leaning back against the pressure but he didn't kick at Kelly like a mule would.

"We're all going out to the 'Lost Station', Kelly," Dan said to her when she came in. "My cousin can give us a ride out later this morning. You want to go? Bobby?"

"Why?" said Bobby.

"Why?" Dan said, a bit shocked at his indifference. "Intel. See if anything has happened, anything altered, gather evidence. Maybe there's another message on the wall or more tracks than before

Andy stepped up and said, "I need to make a wax mold of the handprint before it's gone."

It's a good idea," Dan said as if he was asking permission.

"I can't go," said Kelly. "I've got other things to do."

"Yeah," Bobby agreed, "Me, too... what she said."

Kelly found some busy work, shuffling papers and putting pencils and pens back in their proper places. Bobby went over to the Arizona map tacked to the wall and looked at the desert.

"Okay," Dan said, and began making preparations for the departure.

Kelly managed to slip out first. Bobby went after her a few minutes later.

Dan watched both of them leave, curious about what could be more important to them than the field trip. It took Dan less than a minute to get the idea in his head but once he thought of it, it became a truth to him.

"They're doing it," he said to nobody else in the tactical room.

Kelly didn't crawl in through the tunnel like she always had. She went in to the pool arena through the front entrance, promise broken. She was cautious, pushing in so that only a small crack was open, worried that Spylgyn might lunge through to escape. Kelly poked her head inside to look around first before she finally went in. There was still no sighting of their elusive guest.

When Bobby came in, Kelly was laid out on her stomach at the deep end of the pool, looking down at the swamp.

"Anything?" Bobby asked as he came over to her.

Kelly shook her head sadly.

"He could be underwater. You wouldn't be able to see him," Bobby said. "He can probably stay under a long time without needing air. Like a Galapagos reptile."

"How long can they stay under?" Kelly asked him.

"Long time. Long, long time." Bobby said wistfully.

"You don't even know," Kelly challenged him.

"I can find out," he said to her.

Kelly scooted back from the edge and rolled over to look at him.

"Would you do that for me, Bobby? Would you?" Kelly asked like a giddy little school girl.

Bobby just looked at Kelly without expression, not amused at her childish performance.

"Help me up," Kelly instructed him.

Bobby lifted Kelly to her feet.

She brushed any stray bugs that may have wandered onto her clothes and said, "We need to look around again."

"We're not going to find him, unless he wants us to," he told her.

"I know," Kelly replied, frustrated that what he said was probably true. "Got to look anyway."

They made a quick survey of the pool arena, the mud room and the cluttered storage closet and back rooms. They looked for tracks and checked all vents to make sure that they were still tightly fixed to the wall. Back in the pool arena, Bobby looked up at the massive skylights in the ceiling.

"You don't think he could have got out that way?" Kelly asked him.

"He climbed that pool wall pretty good yesterday," he said to her.

After milling around a short while, they decided to go out to the tactical room again to see if anyone else had come in. Kelly wanted to know who was going on the field trip and she had some instructions to give all of them about the site but not yet ready to offer anything about her and Bobby's recent remarkable discovery – Spylgyn.

Dan was talking to Pegs and Martin as if relaying a confidence to them when Kelly and Bobby came back in. All of them broke apart like they had been caught in a secret conclave. Dan and Martin went to their work stations, leaving Pegs standing alone. She was looking at Bobby and Kelly with her 'what did you do' look. She pursed her lips in a pout, like she was wondering why she hadn't been invited to a party.

Kelly gave her a 'what Pegs?' gesture but the girl didn't respond.

"So, who's going?" she asked all of them. Pegs raised her hand first like a schoolgirl who knew the answer. Martin raised his hand with his back to all of them. Whatever was onscreen at his computer must have been too important for him to turn around. Andy was putting cameras, equipment and supplies into two large duffel bags and raised his hand without looking at Kelly. Dan offered a 'yeah, I'm going' gesture' as if it should've been a foregone conclusion.

It was a loud scream and it scared the hell out of everyone, even Pegs, the girl who screamed. Bobby grabbed onto Kelly by instinct wanting to get her away from the danger. Martin lost interest in the computer and turned around. Dan scrunched his shoulders as if expecting the roof to cave in. Andy only turned his head to see who could have caused such a loud outburst and for what reason.

Pegs was the first one to really commit, though. She screamed once more as she ran across the room and jumped up on the sturdiest table she could get to. She scrambled onto her hands and knees on the desktop, sending papers and objects flying off from her safe spot.

"Pegs, what is it?" Kelly shouted at her.

"There's a rat over there," Pegs screamed, "a big fucking rat!"

"Well," Bobby said to Kelly, "Spylgyn isn't hiding anymore."

Bobby and Kelly went to where Pegs had been just moments ago.

"Don't go over there, it's a rat!" Pegs yelled to them.

Kelly spun around and said, "It's not a rat, Pegs. Calm down and be quiet."

Spylgyn was hiding behind a stack of books but his tail was sticking out from cover. It was snapping and roiling like a snake in a tornado.

"Okay, Spylgyn's upset," Bobby said when he saw the tail doing that.

Without question, Peg's scream had startled Spylgyn as much as the others.

Kelly went right up to the table, leaned over and lay her arm on the table with her palm facing up. Spylgyn darted his head out from hiding to look but pulled it back swiftly.

"Not ready to come out, I guess," Bobby said.

"Spylgyn, Spylgyn, Spylgyn," Kelly sang to the amphibian.

Not right away but Spylgyn did look out again, less cautious this time. He looked at Kelly's hand, then to her face. The amphibian decided not to come out yet and went back behind the stack of books. Bobby noticed that his tail was moving much slower now, more like swaying than twitching.

Bobby took Kelly by the waist and moved her back away from the table but Kelly resisted.

"Bobby, no, what?" Kelly whispered.

"Come with me, okay, just come with me," he said to her.

Kelly went reluctantly. Bobby positioned her a few feet away, then he turned to Dan who was closest to him.

"Come here, Dan," Bobby commanded him.

"Martin, Andy, get over here," he said to the other boys.

All of them, except Pegs, of course, went over to stand with Kelly. Bobby set their positions like a sergeant directing untrained troops in a platoon.

"Pegs, you're up," Bobby said to her. She was still on the desktop on hands and knees.

"No," she yelled at him. "It's a rat!"

"Never mind her," Kelly said to Bobby, then held out both of her hands in front with the palms up.

"Everybody go like this," Kelly told them.

Bobby got in line with the others, then, although confused, they all held out their arms in front of them like Kelly was doing, palms up.

Spylgyn was watching them do all this with what could only be taken as curiosity. The amphibian came out on all fours which was unfortunate for Pegs who tried to climb the high wall behind the table to get further away. Spylgyn didn't slink like a rat would, though; it was more of a hopping and dancing movement like a shy puppy might do.

"A rat," everyone heard Pegs say.

Kelly didn't even shush her. What Kelly really wanted to do was run over, grab Pegs and shake her silly but she didn't.

When Spylgyn reached the table edge closest to the UFObians, he stood up as tall as he could and raised his arms out to them, palms up like they were doing for him.

34   His Name Is Spylgyn

Not quite shouting, Kelly spoke. "Shut up! Enough!"

Everybody got quiet then. She just could not listen to the barrage of questions aimed at her anymore. Even Spylgyn retreated to his stack of books, as if concerned that the younglings with Keeyee might be a threat after all.

Kelly pointed to the far corner of the room where Pegs was still perched at her safe zone.

"Everybody over there. Now." she said in a quieter voice but the tone was presented in a way that said, 'do not disobey me'.

Bobby went first, with Dan, Martin and Andy trailing behind in quick-step. Bobby sat down next to Pegs who was appreciative of his protective cover from the 'rat' across the room.

Kelly turned to Spylgyn who remained in the open but was poised to hide behind the books again or run. She held out her hand in a 'wait' gesture but didn't know if he would understood that signal.

Kelly walked over to the others and stood before them like a school teacher in front of a classroom full of unruly students.

"I know you're all curious and I will explain," she said in a normal voice. "We will explain."

Kelly grabbed Bobby's arm and dragged him away from the others to stand next to her in a position of authority. Kelly nudged Bobby, so he started.

"My little sister found him in the desert. She thought it was a doll."

Astonished, Peg said, "a doll?" then clasped a hand over her mouth.

"Spylgyn," not saying 'that's his name', "is not a doll and he's not a rat."

Their question would be 'what is it then?' and Kelly didn't know what to say.

Bobby said it. "Alien. Spylgyn is an alien from outer space. His spaceship is parked somewhere in the desert just beyond 'The Lost Gas Station of Inyo'."

Kelly didn't nudge him, she shoved Bobby and he had to skip a step to keep from falling over. Kelly took over the story after that, although Bobby stayed by her, occasionally nodding in agreement or shaking his head in disbelief at her wild assumptions. She got all the way to Spylgyn being lost in the pool arena last night, when she was interrupted by Spylgyn.

"Keeyee! Keeyee!" Spylgyn chirped from across the room. "Keeyee!"

Spylgyn had moved to another desk, the one where Andy had a stack of papers and photos that he had taken at the gas station. The amphibian seemed agitated to Kelly, so she went to see what he wanted. The others came after her, not Pegs. The UFObians remained a short distance away from Kelly and the creature so as not to interfere.

Spylgyn had left most of the photos in an irregular pile, choosing only three for her to explain. The photo that held the most interest to the amphibian was a close-up of the message on the wall at the gas station. He was crouched over the photo like a proofreader looking for mistakes on a map. Using one of his hands, he made a circular motion over the entire message.

"Where is it?" she asked him. "Is that what you want to know?"

Spylgyn chirped "Keeyee" again but in a sad way.

Spylgyn started singing then, an explosion of whistles, chirps and an odd bubbling sound. The amphibian swayed side to side like a dancer might do when hearing a favorite tune on the radio.

Pegs, who had finally come closer, gasped when she heard the sound of Spylgyn's musical voice. Bobby leaned in to her and whispered, "still think he's a rat?"

"I don't know what you want, Spylgyn," Kelly told him.

Spylgyn lay down near the photo and put one hand on the triangle that was far away from the other symbols. He patted it several times then said, "Spylgyn, Spylgyn."

"He's the far away triangle," said Dan as if he knew that was right.

"Spylgyn," Kelly said and put a fingertip on the triangle in front of the amphibian. "Spylgyn," she said again.

Spylgyn grabbed onto her finger almost like he was hugging it. Dragging her with him, Spylgyn hopped over to the other two triangles and put her finger in the circle that surrounded those symbols.

Spylgyn croaked like a bullfrog would sound trying to say the name 'G'Thorpe' but it was an unfamiliar sounding for Spylgyn, one that the Oolongs could not possibly translate or understand.

Kelly didn't turn away but said to Andy, "Andy, are there any photos of the gas station, from the road, I mean?"

"Yeah, plenty. Do you need hard prints?" he answered.

"Yes, where are they?" Kelly asked him without excitement but that's how she was feeling – excited.

"The primary drawer at my desk, top drawer on the right, in there," Andy said but didn't move to go get them. He was too fascinated by the 'alien' creature on the tabletop, as were the other UFObians. Martin was the only one who had his arms tightly pressed against his front in a protective way, worried that the creature might be a chest-burster.

Bobby went to Andy's desk and quickly found a large file marked 'Lost Station'. Bobby selected a photo of Kelly with the abandoned gas station in the background that was in direct contrast to Kelly's clean image, appearing derelict and dirty. Bobby went back and placed the photo on the table for Spylgyn.

Spylgyn stared at the image, looked over at Bobby, then back to the photo. Then, he went back to lay down on the photo of the pictograph like he was going to take a nap.

"He's sad," Pegs said even though everybody could see that. Spylgyn didn't move his body but, his left hand was softly touching the small triangle, much like stroking a housecat for comfort. "Neeya," Spylgyn whispered softly, so quiet that none of the UFObians heard.

"I got it," Dan said suddenly, breaking the silence. "I got it, folks."

Dan took steps over to a nearby table to get an art pad. He quickly drew a small triangle with a thick sharpie, then cut the pattern out with scissors so that it was about the same size of the triangles on the photo. Then, he went back to Spylgyn's table to demonstrate.

Dan said, "scuse me, can I get in here?"

Spylgyn moved away as Dan reached in to place his newly drawn triangle on the far away triangle. Dan's drawing was a little larger and completely covered Spylgyn's symbol in the photo. Then, just using a finger, Dan slid the newly drawn triangle across the photo until it was inside the shed with the other two triangles.

Spylgyn stood straight up and wiggled all his fingers at Dan. It looked like he might have nodded too but nobody said anything about that. The wiggling webbed fingers were way too fascinating for all of them. Dan was the only one that wiggled fingers back to Spylgyn.

"He wants to go to 'The Lost Station' with us," Dan said confidently.

What time is your cousin coming?" Kelly asked Dan.

"Anytime now," Dan answered.

"Bobby, can you get the ice chest, maybe put some fresh water and food in it?" Kelly asked him.

Bobby took Kelly's arm and pulled her away from the others.

"Are we really going to do this, Kelly?" he asked. "He'll run away if we take him out there."

"What do you want to do, Bobby?" she asked him.

"I don't know, Kelly," he said. "It just seems like we're rushing into things before we actually think about any consequences."

Kelly thought about that a little, then said, "It seems right to me, Bobby. If Spylgyn wants to go back, shouldn't we take him? I don't want to keep him locked up like a captive."

Kelly leaned in to Bobby wanting him to hug her. And he did.

"I'll save the ducks," Bobby whispered to Kelly.

"What ducks?" Kelly wanted to ask but didn't.

35 The Invader

When Bobby went in to the pool arena, he had a disquieting, uncanny feeling that he was not supposed to be there without Kelly. This was her domain and he felt like he was an interloper and he felt alone. As he walked across to the steps at the shallow end, Bobby felt sure that the beach people were all looking at him with suspicion.

"Why are you here?" they hissed.

"What are you going to do?" the blonde bathing beauty said in a quavering voice.

"Aren't you afraid?" That from the little girl in the blue swimsuit.

"You must go away," they all whispered to him.

"Go away," echoed the mermaids.

Bobby paid no attention to the taunts from the crowd but he kept his eyes on the resentful mural people as he went down into the pool.

The ice chest was near the swamp at the deep end. He knew that the beach people were looking at him as he went to get it. He heard a wet noise behind him and turned quickly to see who it was. His heart was racing and he felt vulnerable. Bobby looked up at the giant images on the wall but none of them had moved. They hadn't stepped out of the wall to come after him.

Bobby made a small slow circle to look at all the murals above the pit.

"Why were they so ominous now?" he asked himself.

"Kelly said I could be here," he wanted to say to them but felt too foolish to do that.

Bobby sat down on the wet tiles near the swamp, resting his back against the pool wall. He pulled the ice chest close, opened it and looked at the contents. No spiders or snakes jumped out at him.

Bobby lifted the ice chest and poured the baby swamp on the pool tiles. The water ran back into the mother swamp but the weeds, moss and pea pods lay on the deck. One by one, he picked up the plant life and tossed them into the source water.

That task completed, Bobby sat back again as if contemplating his next annoying duty – filling the ice chest up again with swamp water, comfortable bedding and green things.

Bobby closed his eyes and thought of Kelly. His image of her was as one of the beach beauties on the pool mural. Kelly was in a polka dot bikini, a white swimsuit with big and little red circles on it. She was waving to him from the shore line, saying, "come on, Bobby, come with me."

A splash from the swamp ripped that fantasy away and Bobby jerked upright. There were ripples in the water like something had been thrown in from above but he didn't see anyone up there. Bobby had a sudden impulse to run to the center of the basin to see which one of the beach-goers had thrown a rock at him but didn't.

Bobby stood up, grabbed the ice chest and went to the water's edge. He scooped up a good amount of source water, then set the ice chest aside. Now, he had to go grocery shopping. Bobby reached into the swamp and began to make selections. Plenty of spongy moss for Spylgyn to lay on went into the container, then a handful of green things. His hands searched the bottom for nuts, pea pods and acorns, whatever. Lots of good stuff he hoped, snacks that the amphibian might like to eat on the journey.

Another splash alerted Bobby and he looked over at the far end of the swamp. Spylgyn was there, standing up in the water with a curious expression on his face.

"You scared me, Spylgyn," Bobby said to him.

Spylgyn chirped back at him, sounding sort of like a dolphin. Then, he disappeared into the murky swamp water, came back up a few seconds later and began swimming, moving his submerged body through the reeds and plants of the swamp as if he wanted to impress the youngling Oolong. The way Spylgyn moved through the water was fascinating, Bobby thought, with a swift but fluid motion like the movements of some of the marvelous creatures that inhabit the lowest depths of an ocean. Spylgyn dove under once more and was out of view for several seconds then suddenly popped up very near to where Bobby was sitting.

Once out of the water, Spylgyn didn't hop on all fours but walked upright. To Bobby, it almost looked like the amphibian was strolling down the avenue. Spylgyn hopped once for attention and chirped again.

Frustrated, Bobby replied, "I don't understand, Spylgyn."

Bobby made some arm movements like Alice had demonstrated but had no idea what he was trying to convey.

But, maybe the gestures meant something because Spylgyn walked closer to Bobby. The Ingling held out his hand showing Bobby a stone. Admittedly, it was a curious rock mostly white with small dark spots as if someone had painted them on the surface.

Spylgyn indicated that he wanted Bobby to have it.

Bobby looked at the rock in his hand, then back at Spylgyn.

"Why is everyone giving me rocks?" Bobby asked.

Lowering his head into his shoulders, Spylgyn made a grunting noise in his throat as if in answer. It sounded like "moow-bee."

Then, as if anxious to go, Spylgyn hopped over to the ice chest and jumped in.

36 Back to Lost

When Dan's cousin arrived to pick them up, Kelly almost canceled the trip. She pulled Dan aside so that the others couldn't hear them.

"Mo-Mike is your cousin?" Kelly asked Dan.

"Mo-Mike?" Dan said to her.

"Mike, Mike, that guy right there," Kelly pointed to the guy in the brand new king-cab truck that was calmly sitting in the driver's seat while every one else was loading up.

"Yeah, he's my cousin. Mike," said Dan, sounding confused.

Kelly stomped her foot on the sidewalk like she was killing a bug that was crawling too close to her. Then, she became lost in thought with a vague look on her face. Her tongue was idly licking at her lower lip as if to feel if it was numb or okay.

"Kelly. What is it?" he asked her.

"Nothing, nothing, let's just go," she said to him.

Martin, Pegs and Bobby and Andy all squeezed into the back seat without complaint. Dan took the front center seat next to Mo-Mike, leaving shotgun for Kelly. When Kelly saw that arrangement, she didn't like it. Kelly stood at the back passenger window staring at Pegs sitting comfortably tight with the boys.

"Pegs, you take the front seat," Kelly said to Pegs.

"I want to sit back here with Andy and Bobby. And Martin," Pegs said to Kelly.

"Fine," Kelly said and gave Bobby a look. He shrugged at Kelly in a 'let's just go' kind of way.

"You can put that chest in the back if you want," said Mo-Mike.

"No, it stays with me," Kelly replied. She placed the ice chest on the front floorboard, straddled it and sat down. She didn't slam the door shut but she wanted to.

Mo-Mike took Kelly's entrance as a signal to go. He gunned the powerful engine a couple of times to show the kids that it was powerful, then jumped the clutch and the truck leaped forward, leaving tire marks on the pavement.

Mo-Mike went north out of town, then circled south on Frontage Road avoiding the town of Inyo as if it were plague-ridden and he didn't want to catch a zombie virus. It was only when they were a few miles out on route 49 that Kelly looked back at Pegs with fire in her eyes. Pegs had been waiting for that look, so she was ready for it.

'We're not doing anything back here, Kelly,' her expression said.

Pegs felt safe in the back with the three boys and the front seat back was a good barrier between them. Kelly didn't actually lean over to find out where Pegs' hands were but she wanted to.

Kelly didn't say one word all the way to the gas station. There was a little conversation in the back seat but it was quiet talk like people do when they're sharing secrets. Maybe that was to keep Mo-Mike in the dark about their mission or maybe it was done that way to keep Kelly from hearing what was being said.

Bobby did reach a hand to touch Kelly's shoulder once during the ride but she ignored him by making no response as if she couldn't feel it or didn't want to.

When they reached the 'Lost Station', the unload was fast. Everyone scrambled out and went to the shade under the jutting roof. It was a stifling, burning hot day. Mo-Mike had just taken the roadside dirt carpet to offload everyone. Once the last person was clear, he spun tires again and sped away.

"Dan," Kelly called to him, "where's he going?"

"Mike's got to go to Buckeye. He's coming back for us in a couple of hours."

"Well, Dan!" Kelly said sounding outraged. "I wish you had told me that before we came out here!"

"It's no big," Dan called to her. "That gives us plenty of time."

Kelly marched right over to him. Dan took a couple of steps back when he saw how angry she was.

"Plenty of time for what?" Kelly demanded an answer but didn't wait for one.

Kelly was on a tirade. "Plenty of time to starve? Plenty of time to bake in the oven? What were you thinking, Dan? What if he doesn't come back, Dan?" Kelly shouted. "Did you even think of that? What if he gets arrested?"

Confused now, Dan asked, "what do you mean arrested? Why would he get arrested?"

Kelly slumped over like a puppet with weak strings.

"I brought food, Kelly," Pegs said in a quiet voice. "We're not going to starve."

"Did you bring snowballs?" Kelly asked her while fuming.

"Yes," said Pegs.

"Give me one, so I can smush it right in Dan's face," she yelled. Then, Kelly stomped off, out into the desert. No one went after her, not even Bobby.

"Well, that was fun," said Martin.

"What is she so pissed about?" asked Dan.

Bobby said. "I'll go talk to her. Get Spylgyn inside, it's probably cooler in there."

Andy instructed the group, "watch your step inside. Follow my footsteps so you don't disturb any track prints."

Bobby stayed under the shade roof as the others all filed in through the leaning door of the gas station after Andy.

Kelly was walking around the desert like a person possessed, circling cactus plants, even stopping to talk to one as if it were a person. She was so far away that he couldn't hear all that she was saying but he was pretty sure that Kelly called the cactus an asshole and a few other derogatory names. Bobby watched her with some concern but he thought that she was behaving badly and that could be funny to watch for a while.

When Kelly took her top shirt off and flung it away, Bobby decided that it was time to step in to the drama. He could only hope that Kelly didn't suddenly turn on him like that poor frightened cactus.

Bobby approached her with some caution, leaving plenty of room to escape if she suddenly came at him. He saw that she was wearing a white cotton undershirt, the kind that old men wear when they go to the barbershop. He didn't think she was going to take off any more clothing but decided to wait just a little longer to see what would happen.

Kelly was slowing down but Bobby could see that she still had a lot of energy left.

When she slumped over like the tired puppet again, Bobby said to her, "you're gonna get sunburn, Kelly. Come back to the shade. All the others went away."

Bobby went to get the top shirt that Kelly had thrown away. She seemed to be calmer now, so he went to her. Bobby put the poplin shirt on her shoulders like a cape. Kelly took it and tossed it aside.

"You're gonna get burnt, Kelly," Bobby said to her but he wasn't going to get the shirt for her again.

With her back to him, Bobby reached an arm around her waist and put his hand on her stomach.

"I'm gonna turn you off for a little while so you can rest, okay?" he said softly.

Bobby found the cleft on her belly with his finger and pressed the button.

"Off," he said to her. He left the hand where it was after she was turned off.

Kelly took some moments to let Bobby touch her and that did have a calming effect on her. Then, she turned to him and put her hands on his chest. Bobby thought at first that she might be going to shove him backwards but she just brushed the imaginary ants off of his shirt.

"We might be in a little trouble, Bobby," Kelly told him.

"What kind of trouble, Kelly?" he asked her. "Tell me, it's okay."

"Mo-Mike," Kelly said but Bobby didn't understand.

"Mike, Dan's cousin..." Kelly said, sounding scared. "He's gone on to Buckeye."

"He's coming back, Kelly," he told her. "Why wouldn't he?"

Kelly nodded a few times like she understood that the guy was coming back. That's what worried her.

"Mo-Mike is going to Buckeye on a drug run," Kelly told him. "He's going to come back with drugs, Bobby."

Kelly told Bobby what she knew of Mo-Mike's dealings in the back alleys and dark streets of Inyo. She accused Dan's cousin of drug sales, marijuana and pills to high school kids, everyone in town knew that, she exaggerated, even the police. Kelly claimed to have seen Officer Malloy in uniform with his police car parked nearby, talking with Mo-Mike as if they were just the best of buddies. Betty Rollins had shown her a plastic bag of Ecstasy one time, telling Kelly that Mo-Mike was selling pills for $7 each, if she wanted to get some quick before he sold out.

Bobby could tell that Kelly was telling the truth, as she knew it.

"What are we going to do, Bobby?" Kelly asked him.

"I don't know," Bobby said. "I don't know."

Kelly looked so forlorn to Bobby and she obviously had no answers to this new dilemma.

"We can call my grandfather," Bobby said, hoping Kelly would say no to that.

When Kelly looked at him, he thought he could see a glimmer of hope in her wet eyes.

"He can come get us," Bobby told her.

Kelly didn't have a cell phone, or if she did, she left it at home. No bulges in her blue jeans today anyway. If she had been pocketing coins, Bobby would have been able to tell her exactly how much money she had to spend.

"Peg's got a cell phone," Kelly said to him, "but I don't want to call Uncle, your grandfather."

Their thoughts about who to call in this emergency were instantly forgotten when they heard Peg's scream. Then, she screamed again, louder.

"Let's go," said Bobby.

Bobby grabbed Kelly's hand and they ran to the gas station.

Martin was just stumbling out of the front door when Bobby and Kelly got there.

"What happened?" asked Bobby.

Martin looked scared when he said, "It's Andy, he's hurt."

Bobby put a hand on Martin and pushed him back through the leaning door.

"Go," he said to him.

Kelly squeezed through the doorway after Bobby and Martin.

When the trio hurried into the mechanic's bay, they saw that Andy was lying on his left side with his arms outstretched in front of him. His body was shaking and jerking like he was having a seizure. Bobby got to him first, putting one hand under his head to keep it from bouncing on the floor and the other hand on his shoulder to hold him as still as he could.

"Get me something soft for his head," Bobby shouted at anyone.

Kelly saw a dirty towel hanging on one wall. She took it and quickly rolled it into a makeshift pillow, then handed it to Bobby.

"What's happening?" Andy said in a normal tone of voice.

"Andy, I'm right here, man," Bobby said to him. "Try not to move, okay?"

Andy's body did seem to relax a little but it was still jerking like a person holding onto a live electric wire.

"What's wrong with my arms and... and legs?" Andy asked.

"I don't know, man," Bobby told him. "It's okay, though, you're gonna be okay."

Kelly went over to Pegs who had found her safe zone at the farthest corner of the bay.

"Give me your phone, Pegs."

Pegs ignored Kelly and kept staring at Andy's twitching body with Bobby cradling him. Kelly saw that the girl was in shock, so she took Pegs by the shoulders and gently turned her away from the scene.

"Pegs," she said in a soothing tone but when she didn't respond, Kelly gave her a little shake.

"Pegs, give me your phone," Kelly calmly spoke to the frightened girl. "I need to call 911, okay?"

Pegs nodded and opened her purse to get the phone. Kelly was just about to dial 911 when Bobby said, "wait. Kelly wait."

When Kelly looked back, she saw that Andy was sitting up now and it looked like the seizure was over. Bobby still held onto his shoulders to steady him.

When Andy tried to stand up, Bobby held him down.

"Don't get up yet, Andy," he said to him. "Rest for a few minutes, right?"

"Is he okay, Bobby?" Kelly asked from across the bay.

"Yeah, he's fine. Right, Andy?" Bobby asked him.

"I'm okay now," Andy said. "a little dizzy, maybe but I'm okay now."

It took only another minute for Andy to fully recover from the episode but the others were still worried. He was walking around, shaking his arms like a fighter that was loosening up for the ring and he was laughing like he had just been on the most exciting roller coaster ride of his life.

"Okay, okay, somebody tell me what happened in here," Bobby looked to Martin and Dan for an answer. Pegs was still useless.

"It was Spylgyn," said Dan. "It attacked Andy, did something, shocked him, I don't know."

Kelly left Pegs in her safe zone and went to Dan who backed up quickly, scared. He didn't like the look on her face as she was coming toward him.

"What did Andy do to Spylgyn?" Kelly asked, taking the amphibian's side.

"He was just trying to stop it," Dan said to her.

That wasn't enough for Kelly and she told Dan that in the way she spoke to him. "You need to clear you mind, start from go and tell me what happened, Danny," Kelly said in controlled anger.

"I wanted to stop Spylgyn from wiping away the pictograph," said Andy.

Apparently, Andy was his normal self again and went on saying, "he was trying to erase it and I tried to stop him."

Martin jumped in, thinking Andy might not have seen what he saw.

"Spylgyn took some wet moss from the ice chest and he ran to the wall and was trying to wipe the symbols off, like on a chalkboard."

"He stung me," Andy said to them. "Like a wasp, that's what it felt like. My muscles started jerking like, I dunno, like an electric shock, maybe?"

"Where is he?" Kelly asked. "Where's Spylgyn?"

"He ran off," said Dan and pointed to the door of the lobby.

"I didn't lose consciousness," Andy told Bobby. "I heard Pegs scream, twice. And, I heard what you said," saying that last to Martin who appeared guilty of something.

Bobby watched Kelly go away to look for Spylgyn but he wanted to hear what Andy was saying, so he stayed.

"It wasn't unpleasant," Andy told them. "I know that sounds crazy and I was bothered by the shaking but it was like I was dreaming while I was still awake. Does that sound bonkers?"

Martin and Dan nodded to him 'yep, crazy.' Bobby saw movement out of the corner of his eye. He looked over to see Pegs slinking away from her safe spot.

Pegs stood at the doorway to the lobby only a moment, then ran past Kelly who was on her knees looking beneath a sales counter. Pegs jumped through the outer door like something had just bitten her on the ass and she shrieked a few sharp yelps as she darted across the station front.

Pegs didn't stop in the shady spot beneath the roof either. She ran all the way across the road and stood on the far side, waiting for a bus that would take her back to town.

37 The Orb Knows All

Kelly searched all over the gas station front area but could find no sign of Spylgyn. There was a door at the very back of the main lobby. It had been locked at one time but someone had broken the hasp away with a sledgehammer or other destructive tool. Kelly had to shove the door open with her shoulder because it was blocked on the other side by some obstacle. Once Kelly stepped inside the dimly lit space, she could see that it had been used as a stock room with corridors formed by massive shelf units, some of which were still standing but others leaning or fallen over as if shaken and dislodged by an earth tremor. There were boxes and other supplies that had fallen from the shelves and were strewn all over the floor. The entire space was quite a huge mess that would be difficult to search. It must have been ransacked by vandals or thieves, Kelly thought with dismay. She noticed that many of the cardboard boxes and crates were still unopened with who-knows-what inside but others seemed to have been searched through with some of the contents missing or tossed on the floor as if discarded. Not worthwhile to steal, she supposed. Stepping awkwardly around the debris, Kelly moved down one corridor, then another but knew it was hopeless to keep looking without a flashlight. She was about to give it up and go get one from Dan or Martin, when she saw a vagrant ray of sunlight at the darkest corner of the back room.

Kelly crouched down to see that a section of the back wall was broken away leaving a ragged hole big enough for a small creature to go through. Kelly flattened out on her stomach to look out the opening, certain that she had found Spylgyn's escape route. The amphibian had gone into the desert.

When the bus didn't come for her, Pegs went back to sit in the shade under the triangular roof. That's where the others found her when they came out of the gas station. Pegs was sitting on the oblong concrete island where the gas pumps once stood. She was idly scratching in the dirt with a stick, moving small rocks into a pile.

"Where's Kelly?" Bobby asked her.

Pegs used the stick to point into the desert.

"Around back?" Bobby asked.

"She ran off, Bobby, okay?" snapped Pegs. "Out in the desert somewhere."

"She ran off!" Bobby said to Pegs. "Why didn't you stop her?"

Pegs looked at Bobby like that was the dumbest question anyone had ever asked her.

"Did anyone bring binoculars?" Bobby asked.

"Yeah," Andy said.

"Get 'em," Bobby told him.

Kelly went northeast toward the cliffs on the horizon. The sun was at its peak and the temperature must have been over 100 degrees, she thought. Kelly wasn't worried so much about herself but Spylgyn being a water creature would lose moisture fast in this heat. Kelly had to find him but just didn't know which way to go. She didn't look for tracks in the sand knowing that would be wasting time.

Kelly had started out at a fast trot hoping to overtake Spylgyn. When that didn't happen, she just walked at a brisk pace. The desert was so bleak and barren, Kelly knew that it was very unlikely that she would find him. Spylgyn really was gone but she kept on walking deeper into the desert, hoping for a miracle.

Bobby was holding the ladder for Dan to climb up to the roof of the gas station.

"That ladder doesn't look safe," Dan said.

"Martin?" Bobby asked him but the boy just shook his head 'no'.

Bobby let go of the ladder and said, "give me the binoculars then."

Bobby took the binoculars from Andy, putting the leather strap around his neck. He climbed the ladder with no assistance from the guys.

Kelly did find some tracks in the dirt. She couldn't be sure they were Spylgyn's but she followed them anyway.

Using the binoculars, Bobby scanned the desert to the north, then made a panning move to the left, then back to the right. He remembered that Kelly only had the white undershirt on that would not stand out like Alice's red shirt. The flesh tones of her skin would blend with the sand color, too. So, he was looking for blue, the color of her denim jeans.

The tracks Kelly had been following bled out to nothing. But, she found other disturbances that were curious. One imprint was a curving trail in the sand that could have been made by a snake. Kelly veered away from that track, changing her general direction to the northwest. She knew the hot sun was blistering her shoulders and regretted tossing the cover shirt away but she wasn't going to give up and go back for it, not yet.

It was the other imprint in the sand that caused Kelly to stop in her tracks. It was a perfect circular depression about two feet in diameter with a center depth lower than the outlying ridges. The oval depression looked to Kelly like it had been made by something round and heavy that had fallen out of the sky. She knelt down at the edge of the pan, looking at the unnatural smoothness of the sand. Kelly was about to reach into the odd depression when the sand was disturbed by a sudden rushing wind.

Bobby came down from the roof fast, gave the binoculars to Andy.

"Get your camera. Take photos," Bobby said to him, then ran off.

When Bobby ran around to the front, Pegs jumped up, thinking he might be coming after her but he wasn't. Bobby shoved his way into the leaning door and went inside the gas station.

Dan and Andy came around to the front and Pegs hurried over to be with them.

"Did he see her?" Pegs asked them.

Dan nodded but neither of them said anything.

Bobby came out of the gas station carrying the ice chest still in a rush but he stopped to look at Andy.

"Get your camera," Bobby told him again. "You need to take photos."

Without waiting to explain Bobby ran to Kelly's angry spot and grabbed the poplin shirt that she had thrown away.

"Photos of what?" Andy shouted at him.

"Photos of the UFO," Bobby yelled at him, "get photos of the flying saucer." Then, he ran into the desert after Kelly.

Kelly didn't scream like Pegs would have when the 'UFO' floated down in front of her. She just dropped back from her squat until her butt hit the ground. Kelly sat like that, stunned, while the orb settled peacefully into its nest. It was a shiny globe without features, like a huge ball bearing or steel marble. When Kelly looked closer, she saw that the orb hadn't actually touched the ground but was hovering just above the pan, still in the air.

It made no sound as it lifted in the air to the same height as Kelly's head. A tiny dark spot appeared on the surface of the globe and grew until it was the size and shape of a football. Kelly stared into that dark void that very much resembled a pit on the darkest night of the year, no moon, no stars, just black. But, it had no depth; it was a surface shadow only.

Then, lights began blinking in the dark space – red, red, yellow, green, red.

Kelly was stupefied and remained motionless, not sure what to do.

The blinks from the orb were more rapid the second time – yellow, red, red, yellow, red.

And, she realized that it must be trying to 'talk' to her.

"I don't understand. I don't know what you're trying to tell me," Kelly said, waving a hand for emphasis.

The orb blinked one final red light then the shadow window gradually began to reduce until it disappeared into nothing.

Desperate, Kelly held out the palms of both her hands to the orb and said in a friendly way, "Spylgyn, Spylgyn."

The orb shadow suddenly reappeared and flashed three rapid blue blinks, then slowly floated upwards until it reached a hovering level of 49.2 inches off ground. When Kelly kept sitting on the ground, the orb dropped back down to the nest, then went quickly back to its upper hovering site.

When Kelly stood up, she was face to face with the orb. Then the 'UFO' flew a short distance away, hovered, and waited for the girl. When Kelly took a step, the orb took a step and that was how it led her to Spylgyn, one step at a time.

Kelly stumbled and almost fell when the orb led her across the desert. She kept her eyes on the strange alien device, not where she was walking and the orb did not dip when it flew over a dry creek bed. The basin was almost four feet deep and eight feet wide. Kelly had to hard step down the sharp incline to keep from falling.

The orb was now above her and Kelly looked up at it.

"You could have warned me," she said to the orb.

The orb dropped down slowly as if to say "sorry but you should look where you're going." The orb floated to her right and Kelly went after it.

Spylgyn was lying on his side, curled into a fetal position when Kelly found him. The amphibian's wet skin looked dry and hot. Kelly thought she saw a red tinge to the spots on his shoulder and back as if he had been sunburnt but maybe that was just her imagination. Spylgyn looked like he was dead or on his way.

Kelly knelt down in the dirt near Spylgyn but was careful not to touch him. After what happened to Andy, Kelly knew that Spylgyn had a defense stinger but didn't know where it was. If the amphibian stung her, there wouldn't be time to save him before she could recover, if he was still alive.

Kelly looked for the orb and was going to plead for help but it was gone. She looked up and then in all directions but nothing, just empty air. A noise from behind her startled Kelly and she turned swiftly to see what it was. Bobby was sliding down the incline on his ass. He had the ice chest in his lap. He brought it to her and set it beside the still unmoving amphibian.

"Is he dead?" Bobby asked her.

"No," Kelly said defiantly. "Spylgyn's not dead."

Kelly reached one hand and carefully slid it up under Spylgyn's head and shoulders. With her other hand, she lifted his back and upper legs. The amphibian made no move to stop her but his lower legs dangled from her hand as though they were lifeless.

"Open the lid," Kelly said to Bobby but he had already done that. She turned on her knees and lowered Spylgyn into the ice chest. Kelly placed him on a bed of moss making sure that most of his body was immersed in the swamp water. She cupped a hand of source water and poured it over his chest and arms. The last few drops fell on his face and the amphibian blinked his closed eyes but didn't open them.

Spylgyn raised one arm and let it rest over his face, the way a child would do when they're crying and doesn't want anyone to see.

38 Cavanah

Craig Cavanah was dressed for a journey into the desert. Most of his clothing was the color of sand with only a white cotton shirt under his camera vest. His pants were the kind with cargo pockets at the side to hold gear or findings. He had desert boots that had gone with him around the globe. They were comfortable and stable for sand, rock or water.

Cavanah was standing on the hood of his jeep. He would have been on the roof if it had been the hard shell but he was equipped with only the canvas top today. Cavanah had turned around on the road about a half-mile past the abandoned gas station, then parked on an embankment. It was only a small rise in the flat land but he wanted to get as high as possible for the best view he could and that was the closest location that he found within of range of the event.

Cavanah had passed G2 on the side of the road about twenty minutes ago. He thought about stopping but she didn't flag him down or make any motion that she needed help, so he decided not to interfere. G2 didn't seem to be in any real trouble. He was curious why she was standing out in the blistering sun at the side of the road but later saw her move under the canopy of the old gas station where it was shade.

He knew all the involved team members by name but preferred to think of them as subjects at this stage rather than six boys and girls with different personalities and traits. It made the task easier for notes on their actions and interplay as they worked together as a group.

Cavanah had designated the tallest boy as team leader because he seemed to take charge most of the time. His designation for this phase of the operation would be A1. The energetic girl with the blonde hair, he had tagged as G1 since she also appeared to exert some control over the other teenagers. This team leader dynamic could alter if circumstances or situations changed in some way but the identifiers would remain the same, locked and unchanging. The rest of the gang were given tags based on their demeanor and involvement in the short time that Cavanah had been observing them. Andy was B2 because he was the most energetic of them all except for G1. Dan was K3 and Martin K4 since their involvement seemed to be minimal at best and there were no clear modifiers to differentiate the two subjects yet. The pretty girl who had been standing at the side of the road was G2.

The binoculars that Cavanah was using were far superior to the pair that A1 perched on the roof had. Those simple viewers looked to him like the standard issue for bird watchers and other civilians. His own SRX-7000 binocs allowed him to see much farther, so that he could go close-up to see each kid's expressions or focus back to get a panoramic look at what was happening out there.

Cavanah could not even guess at why G1 stomped off into the desert to argue with cactus and other inanimate forms. A1 eventually was able to calm her down but then something happened inside the station, something that obviously caused concern for A1 and G1. 14 minutes passed with all of them inside, away from view and Cavanah, unable to observe, became so frustrated that he got into the jeep and seriously considered intervention into the event. He actually started the engine and was putting it into gear when he saw a figure come out of the building and run NE like a person being chased. Cavanah quick jumped back on the jeep's hood and focused the binocs on G1 as she fled into the desert.

7 minutes later, the four boys came out of the gas station and briefly talked with G2. As a result, the roof surveillance was initiated by A1.

While watching A1 on the roof, Cavanah confirmed that the subject was looking for G1, because when he sighted her, A1 left the roof, grabbed a container from inside the gas station and the shirt that G1 threw away, then ran into the desert after her.

Cavanah scanned the desert where he last saw G1 but was unable to find her again even with the high-powered binoculars. She was just gone. He watched A1 a little longer, then took the binoculars away from his face and let them fall to his chest.

Cavanah didn't want to go on a rescue mission if he could avoid it but what G1 was doing might make it necessary. If she kept going far enough out, the heat would eventually cause dehydration and exhaustion. G1 was at risk of death and Cavanah could not let that happen. A1 seemed to have good sense taking the ice chest with water and supplies and the shirt when he went after the girl. But, even that might not be enough to keep them alive if they continued to act irrationally like they were doing.

Cavanah took up the binoculars again to see what was happening. The other kids were not under the canopy anymore. B2 and K3 were now on the roof of the gas station. One of them had the binoculars and was looking out into the desert. The other boy had a camera but seemed to be unaware of what needed to be photographed. K4 and G2 were still on the ground at the base of the ladder.

Cavanah zoomed in to get a better look at the boys on the roof. B2 was now focusing the camera on something in the desert and was clicking off one shot after another. Cavanah pivoted his focus to see what the kid was filming but saw nothing.

A1 had disappeared just like G1 and Cavanah reasoned that they must be in a depression or gully of some kind. There were no rock outcroppings or plant life that could be concealing both of them. Cavanah worried that they might be hurt. He couldn't recall any occurrences of sand pits like the traps in the Sahara. Although Cavanah had never seen one, he knew that a sand pit could swallow up a camel in seconds. Sand pits were like dry quicksand that could pull an animal or person under without any warning and it would not be a good death, suffocating like that.

His satellite phone was in his carry bag but he didn't reach for it yet. If the kids did get sucked into a sand pit, it was already too late for anyone to save them anyway. Cavanah returned his attention to the kids at the gas station. K3 was laying flat on the roof with his head over the edge, looking down at K4 and G2. What they were saying to each other was aggravating to Cavanah. He needed to hear what was going on.

Cavanah jumped off the hood of the jeep and quickly went to the back cargo opening. He removed a shotgun microphone from its canvas case and returned to his place on the jeep hood. He held the barrel like he would a rifle and sighted in on the kids but it was no use. The mike couldn't pick up any words or phrases from that distance, just an irritating wind noise. Cavanah knew it wouldn't work but he had to try anyway.

He laid the shotgun mike down on the jeep hood and took up the binoculars again just in time to see B2 and K3 coming down from the roof. When they reached ground, there was some discussion with two of the boys pointing northeast. Cavanah swung the binoculars in that direction, panning out for a wide view. The binoculars auto-focused on the figures in the desert. A1 and G1 were coming back to the gas station.

Cavanah breathed a sigh of relief. His cover was not blown and the kids appeared to be okay. He kept watching the scene under the canopy but nothing else eventful happened. A1 went back into the building and was out of view for 7 minutes. When A1 came out again, he was wiping his hand on a towel or rag as if he had just washed his hands.

The dark red truck picked them up at 1:17 pm and took them back to Inyo. Cavanah didn't chase after them. He wanted time to investigate the gas station.

Cavanah found the location that held interest for the kids in less than a minute once he was inside. He just had to follow the fumes that were stinking up the place. A1 had used a solvent or diesel fuel in an attempt to destroy the drawing. It hadn't been set on fire but the chemical compound was adequate enough to confuse the markings so that now it was just a mass of black smears on the wall.

"Why would Bobby do that?" he wondered, "destroy physical evidence that absolutely needed scientific analysis and study?"

Cavanah returned to his jeep that was parked under the canopy and took his backpack from the rear cargo. Once he had it settled comfortably on his shoulders, he started walking out into the Inyo desert, taking the same path as A1 and G1 had.

39 Signals and Thought Clouds

The police hadn't surrounded the Inyo Spa when the UFObians got back into town. No DEA agents were there to arrest anyone for transporting drugs. The street was quiet and normal just like it always was.

Bobby and Kelly had mutually decided back at the 'Lost Station' to keep their mouths shut about Mo-Mike's illegal drug run, reasoning that the cops wouldn't lock all of them up but there would be consequences if they admitted complicity to a crime.

Kelly wanted to get Spylgyn back to the swamp as fast as possible, hoping that would make the amphibian perk up, so they all took the ride back with Mo-Mike.

Kelly said a peculiar thing to Bobby on the drive back to town. For most of the trip Kelly was morose and not very talkative. She only lifted the lid of the ice chest twice to look at Spylgn, making sure that he was still there as if he might have disappeared.

"How's he look?" Bobby asked her.

"He wants to go beyond," Kelly said to him.

"Beyond? What is that, Kelly?" Bobby asked her.

"He's giving up, Bobby," she said. "Spylgyn is trying to die."

Kelly scooped some more water in her hand and let it run over the amphibian's body as if that might revive Spylgyn.

"I'm not going to let that happen," Kelly said, talking to Spylgyn. "Not going beyond, Spylgyn. No."

Once the gang was all back at the spa, Andy was energetic and enthusiastic, as if his spastic seizure in the desert was just a minor flip in his life, one that could be easily forgotten. He wanted to transfer the camera images to computer, so that photos of the 'UFO' could be blown up and enhanced for study.

Dan had made a few rough sketches of the orb device while they were waiting for Mo-Mike to pick them up. He went directly to the scanner and began making transfers into his own computer.

Pegs took a position between Dan and Andy, waiting to see which one would call her over to look at their presentation.

Kelly went straight back to the pool arena and Bobby went with her. He held the ice chest while Kelly climbed down the ladder. They didn't talk to each other as if each one understood that this was a solemn task and needed quiet dignity.

At the edge of the swamp, Bobby opened the lid of the ice chest. Kelly reached in with both hands to lift the amphibian out. She gently laid Spylgyn in a shallow spot in the swamp where there was reed grass, lily pads and soft spongy moss for comfort.

Kelly sat back beside Bobby and they waited to see what would happen now.

Spylgyn remained still too long for Kelly and she was just about to reach over and check to see if he was breathing. Before she could do that, Spylgyn turned onto his side and fluffed the moss to make a better pillow for his head, like one would do during sleep.

Kelly took Bobby's hand and squeezed it for reassurance or hope.

"He's not going beyond anymore, Bobby," she whispered to him. "I can feel it."

Bobby didn't answer Kelly right away as they quietly watched Spylgyn resting but his question needed an answer.

"What does that mean Kelly, going beyond?" Bobby asked her.

Kelly looked at him as if she was unsure if she could confide in him, telling him about thoughts and feelings that still confused and upset her. She stood up, still holding his hand. Bobby got up and followed her to the pool steps.

Kelly went out first and Bobby after her. When she sat down on the deck at the pool edge, Bobby sat down right beside her. Their feet dangled over the edge of the pool like they were soaking their tired feet in cool water. Kelly had chosen seats where they could still watch over Spylgyn but not too close. Kelly didn't want to disturb the amphibian with the noises of human voices.

"Spylgn talks to me," Kelly said to Bobby.

Kelly could see by his expression that Bobby was skeptical or just didn't understand what she was trying to say.

"Talks to you," Bobby repeated.

"Not like this," Kelly said, "like you and me talking."

"How then?" Bobby asked her.

"Spylgyn wanted me to let him go out in the desert," Kelly said. "He told me that he was ready to go beyond. That's how he expresses death."

When Bobby still looked confused, Kelly added, "but it's not really like death to Inglings. It's... well, it's like heaven for humans, a good place that we go to when we die."

"What is an Ingling?" Bobby asked her.

"That's what Spylgyn is, an Ingling," Kelly said but she also seemed confused about that statement, even though she said it.

"I'm lost, Kelly," Bobby said.

"So am I, Bobby," Kelly admitted. "Remember I was telling you about the Albino Man in my dream."

Bobby remembered, so he nodded.

"I think Albino Man is Spylgyn," Kelly said.

Before Bobby could start laughing at her outrageous fantasy, Kelly let it all out.

"The first dream I had of Albino Man, he was in the desert and he was drowning and he wanted me to help but I didn't know how. I had three dreams about Albino Man last night. How often does that happen to somebody when they dream? A weird character just appearing in a dream over and over?"

Bobby didn't remember many of his dreams. But then, he wasn't as vigilant as Kelly was with her unconscious thoughts.

"Albino Man is trying to guide me in my dreams, tell me what to do. Albino Man is Spylgyn," Kelly said to him, knowing that it sounded odd.

"Kelly. Kelly, how is that possible?" Bobby said.

"Telepathy," Kelly said. "How do I know about this beyond thing? Really, I don't know where that came from Bobby. I just said it like I knew. And, how do I know that his tribe is called Inglings?"

Brain tumor or bleeding in her brain from the fall, that's what Bobby was thinking but didn't tell her.

"I know you don't believe me but that's what's happening. Spylgyn can't talk to us with his language. And we're too ignorant to understand his hand signals and vocal tonations. Have you watched him when we talk at him? He doesn't like it, especially when we're loud. We probably sound like a freight train to him, noisy and... well, savage."

Kelly put her hand in front of Bobby, palm up like offering him another rock. "That means safe." Then, she curled her two middle fingers up until they touched the tip of her thumb. Twice she made that simple gesture.

"That means careful, be careful," Kelly said to Bobby.

"How do I know that, Bobby. Huh? How do I know that?" she said, frustrated with him.

Kelly got up and went to be with Spylgyn. Bobby didn't go after her.

40 U.F.O.B.I.A.

That afternoon when he went home, Bobby thought he was in for a scolding from his mother about missing lunch and his frequent absences from family activities but that didn't happen.

Jenny was in the kitchen when he cautiously entered ready to be properly censured and punished. He just hoped that his mother had forgotten the word 'grounded' in her vocabulary. Of course, she could say 'stay closer to home' or 'you need to help me or your grandfather more'. But, 'grounded' had a certain finality to it. Bobby thought of that word like another person would think 'guilty as charged, jail term to follow'.

Alice was at the kitchen table with coloring books and crayons taking up way too much space, in Bobby's opinion. She ignored Bobby because she was too busy coloring a fairy sitting on a unicorn and that was much more important to her than any person.

"You missed lunch," his mother said to him. "I can make you a sandwich."

"I can do it," Bobby said, although he wasn't really hungry.

"Reprieved," Bobby thought as he searched the fridge for something to eat. He made a bologna and cheese sandwich, then as an afterthought, he selected some fresh snow peas as a side dish.

"What are those, Bobby?" his mother asked him when he set his plate on the table.

"Green things," Bobby said. "Green things are supposed to be good for you."

Alice gave him a look but didn't say anything about Spylgyn.

"I can make you a salad," his mother told him.

"No, they're good like this," Bobby said as he crunched into a pod like a potato chip.

Bobby almost laughed when he saw his mother's expression at his food choice.

"M'kay," she said, "whatever," and left that alone.

They had a little chit-chat about his activities because that was supposed to happen, checking in with the parent who wanted to make sure you're not getting into any trouble. Bobby made light of the conversation, saying that he and Kelly were almost but not quite, boyfriend+girlfriend yet.

"She was cool, yeah but I don't know," he told her.

Bobby assured his mother that "no, they had not kissed yet."

The lies were becoming easier to fabricate and Bobby wasn't feeling all that guilty about deceiving his mother anymore.

'White lies,' he kept telling himself. 'They are just white lies and of no consequence.'

Alice said, "I want to have long legs and boobs like Kelly when I grow up," then went back to coloring her fairies.

His mother did laugh at that bold statement, while giving Bobby a 'where did that come from?' look. Bobby smiled back at his mother but didn't laugh.

Bobby managed to slip away after a few more minutes of idle talk, saying that he needed to talk about something with Grampa.

Bobby could imagine the gears working in his mother's head.

"He wants to talk about sex and he can't do it with me," he thought she was thinking. And he was right.

"About the club," Bobby added quickly.

"Oh," his mother said, changing gears. "The UFO Club."

"You know about that?" Bobby asked her.

"Know about it?" she said with an expression that was somewhat prideful. "I'm a member. Well, alumnus I guess you would say."

Bobby wasn't in such a hurry to find his grandfather anymore.

"It was your grandfather that actually started The UFO Club when he was just about your age," Jenny informed her son.

"What?" Bobby said as though shocked. "What?"

She could see by the enthralled look on his face that Bobby wanted to know more.

"You didn't know?" Jenny said. "Kelly didn't tell you?"

"No," Bobby said but he was certainly going to ask her 'why not?' the next time he saw her.

"You are a member, aren't you?" his mother asked him in a suspicious way, playing a role for him, having some fun. "Show me," his mother said in a serious way. Jenny held out her hand like expecting him to show a membership card or something.

Bobby was confused for a moment at her odd request but then remembered the black rock that Kelly had given him on that first day. He reached into his watch pocket and removed the two stones. Bobby handed his mother the black rock with the three red spots. He kept Spylgyn's stone in his hand and didn't show that one to her.

Jenny examined the rock briefly, then placed it in the center of the table between her and her son. She watched the stone for a while as if expecting it to levitate or do something remarkable. When it didn't, Jenny picked the black rock up and handed it back to Bobby.

"A black rock," Jenny said almost wistfully. "A black rock is good."

"It means something, doesn't it?" Bobby asked his mother. "Kelly wouldn't tell me."

"She doesn't trust you yet," his mother said.

Bobby put the rocks back in his pocket.

"Do you still have yours?" Bobby asked his mother.

"I do. It's in my jewelry box," she told him. "It was a gift from your grandfather. I wouldn't lose something as important as that."

His mother wasn't lying to Bobby about that. Her stone was still in the jewelry box that held all her other precious keepsakes. Her rock was pink and it was shaped like a valentines heart, almost.

Bobby didn't want to ask his mother what Spylgyn's rock could mean. He was too afraid that she wouldn't know, or that she might tell him something that he didn't want to know. The rock that Spylgyn had given him was not quite white but was a duller shade like ivory with tiny dark spots, and its shape was triangular, flat. Bobby thought it looked almost like a tiger's fang but not as sharp.

As he was leaving Bobby turned back to his mother. "It's called the Bureau now, the UFO Bureau."

"Well, that's odd. It's always been the Club," she remarked.

"Spell it out,"said Bobby.

He ended her confusion by pointing out that 'The UFO Bureau of Inyo, Arizona' had an acronym that seemed appropriate. "UFOBIA," he said, smiling, then stepped out.

"Bureau, my butt," Jenny said to herself. "It's 'The Club'. It's always been 'The Club.'"

41 Who's Who? What's What?

Bobby didn't go directly to his grandfather after the revealing talk with his mother in the kitchen. He wanted to look at the old photo album again, look at it with fresh eyes now that he was formulating a plan. Actually, Bobby still thought it was a ridiculous plan, too far from reality to be true. Or maybe, just maybe, Spylgyn was attempting to talk to him too, just like the amphibian was talking to Kelly, through thoughts, implanting images and ideas through some form of telepathy.

Bobby went through each page of the photo album but this time he was looking for something different or unusual. He was searching for phenomenon and he found it. It was a simple photo of a young boy standing next to a water tank on a metal platform, probably at the sinkhole out in the desert.

Bobby guessed that his grandfather was about 11 or 12 years old when the photo had been taken. He was dressed in overalls without a shirt underneath, just leaning against an iron pylon looking like a worker who was taking a break at a construction site. But there was something else in the photo that Bobby found more interesting than his grandfather and the water tank.

There was a circle in the upper left corner of the photo, only a shade lighter than the sky. Most people would ignore that flaw thinking it was a sunspot caused by the camera lens. Bobby didn't. He thought it could be an orb similar to the one that Kelly had described to him, or just maybe, it was the same one.

Bobby only got a brief glimpse of the orb; he had stopped in his tracks when he saw the thing so close to Kelly in the trench and the orb either saw him or sensed his presence and shot up into the sky faster than Bobby could follow it with his eyes.

When he had questioned Kelly about it while they were under the canopy waiting for Mo-Mike to arrive, she didn't go into any fine details except to say the orb led her to Spylgyn. She mentioned the light flashes but her focus was on Spylgyn then, so Bobby didn't probe for more information, thinking that might upset her even more than she already was. There would be time enough for that later, after whatever was going to happen happened.

Bobby didn't go through all the photo albums with such scrutiny – weddings, portraits and ordinary photos were of no interest to him. He had the evidence he needed and was ready to talk to his grandfather.

It was getting late in the afternoon when he went into the backyard to find his grandfather. Uncle was sitting in an Adirondack chair under the big shade tree like he was waiting for nothing to happen. His grandfather raised an arm to swat away a fly or mosquito and, at first, Bobby thought he was telling him to go away.

"They always come out when it's getting on dusk," Uncle said to Bobby. "I really don't know why God made 'em."

"What?" Bobby asked him.

"Mosquitos," Uncle said. "You look like you got something on your mind."

To answer, Bobby held out his hand to his grandfather, showing him the black rock.

Uncle leaned forward to look at the rock, then settled back again.

"What do you want to know?" Uncle said.

"You started The UFO Club," Bobby accused him.

"I did. Me and Jimmy Nickles," his grandfather confessed. "Long time ago."

"Why didn't you tell me?" Bobby asked him.

"I didn't think it was important," Uncle said.

"Kelly knows but she didn't tell me," said Bobby, disappointed.

"She doesn't know that much, Bobby," Uncle said. "She heard me tell a story one time, that's all. I was just talking to some people at a picnic, I think it was. Fourth of July, maybe. She was just a child then, maybe 11 or 12 years old. She didn't hear about the club from me. I don't know where she got that from."

"What story were you telling?" asked Bobby.

"That old one about Pete Selby and his digging machine."

"Digging machine? I thought it was a UFO," Bobby said, confused.

"May have been, I don't know, I wasn't there," Uncle said to him.

"Kelly said that she was told the real truth from Pete Selby. And he was there," Bobby told his grandfather.

"Did she?" Uncle said. "Well, maybe she went to him after she heard me talk about it. You'd have to ask Kelly about that."

"He's still alive?" Bobby asked.

"Far as I know. I don't check regular on the obituaries," Uncle said. "Him and his boys still got that junkyard a couple of miles out of town. Last I heard, he was in a wheelchair. Had a stroke or something just as bad. It's a terrible thing gettin' old. I'm not looking forward to it."

Bobby looked away from his grandfather as if thinking, planning.

"I wouldn't go out there and bother that man, Bobby," Uncle cautioned.

"So, Pete told you the story about the UFO," Bobby said to him, "and you told Kelly."

His grandfather didn't respond to that, just lowered his head a bit that could have been interpreted as a silent nod.

"I need to know the truth, Grampa," Bobby told him.

Uncle seemed reluctant to go past this point but he asked Bobby the right question anyway.

"Why?" Uncle said, already knowing the answer.

"There's been an occurrence," Bobby told him.

"When?" Uncle asked.

"This morning," Bobby said quietly, knowing that he was about to spill the beans.

"Where?" Uncle asked him.

"The gas station where Alice got lost," Bobby said.

"Damn, Bobby, you went back out there?" his grandfather said, sounding upset.

"Mom doesn't know, please don't tell her," Bobby pleaded.

"Lord, I should've torn that place down years ago," Uncle said. "Don't know why I didn't. Damn."

Bobby sat back in the chair and waited to hear what his grandfather was going to do. Uncle took some time to settle down. He fidgeted in his chair, cleared his throat a time or two. He had quit smoking close on to seven years now but he had a sudden urge to go get a cigarette. There was an old pack still in the work shed, another thing that he was reluctant to throw away.

"What exactly did you see, Bobby?" asked his grandfather.

And Bobby told him everything.

42 Overnight, Sleep Tight

Kelly was going to spend the night with Spylgyn at the swamp, no matter what she had to do. She didn't want to leave and go home but knew that she had to or her mother would call the cops again.

Spylgyn finally got up from the resting place where Kelly had put him. The amphibian didn't acknowledge her presence, just wandered off to find some food. After eating, Spylgyn swam lazily through the swamp as if he was checking for any disturbance or evidence of change that may have happened while he had been gone. He wasn't as energetic as usual but Kelly did not sense that he was still willing to go beyond anymore.

So maybe if Kelly left him alone for a while, that would be a good thing. But, she was going to stay the night, even if Spylgyn ignored her.

All the others had gone home already when she came out to get her bicycle and Kelly liked that. She didn't really want to get in a long conversation with anyone. She didn't even look at the photos Andy left for her on her desktop.

Kelly got back to the trailer just in time to eat pizza with her mother and 'the mechanic'. The pizza was probably offered as an apology to his mother for some slight that the man had done to upset her. Apparently, candy and flowers don't exist for mechanics. Neither does engagement rings, she hoped. Kelly took the last two slices of pizza, said hello-goodbye and went to her room. There was only one beer left from a six-pack on the table, so they would probably settle in for the night and watch some tv before heading to their bedroom to 'sleep'.

Kelly waited for noise to go quiet, then gave it another hour before she felt that it was okay to make her escape. She left her bed rumpled like she had slept in it, then crept out through the living room to the front door. Since Kelly usually left on her adventures before dawn, her mother wouldn't be concerned if she didn't make an appearance for breakfast.

There was no rush to get back to the spa, so Kelly took a leisurely route but kept her eye out for any police cars that might be cruising looking for burglars and vagrants. She couldn't think of a good reason for a night bike ride and didn't want to have to explain to the 'Police' what she was doing out this late. No matter what excuse Kelly could come up with, she knew that whoever was the cop that night would call her mother and report a violation, even though there wasn't a curfew for young girls out after dark.

Kelly brought her blankets and pillow from her secret room and dropped them into the swimming pool. She remembered where there was some foam masseuse pads in a storage area and took two that were still sealed by plastic and hadn't been used.

Kelly built a makeshift mattress out of the foam layers and laid out her blankets on top. While she was doing all that, she kept a watchful eye on the swamp but Spylgyn was either underwater or had left and gone somewhere else. She wasn't afraid that the amphibian had run away but she couldn't say why. Anyway, if Spylgyn wanted to escape captivity, how could she stop such a clever and elusive creature?

"Why would I want to?" Kelly asked herself.

She lay looking up at the stars through the skylights for just a short time, then rolled over on her side and went to sleep without saying 'good night' to anyone.

If Kelly dreamed that night, she didn't remember any when she woke up. If she had a clock, it would have shown that it was 5:57am. If that clock had an alarm, it wouldn't go off for another 3 minutes.

Kelly usually could remember at least one dream when she woke up but not this morning. Albino Man hadn't come to her asking for help. There were no fairies, no giraffes and no pink clouds that she could recall. But, Kelly felt completely refreshed even though she had only slept for five and a half hours.

Kelly sat up and hugged her knees like it was too cold to get out of bed but it wasn't. The air was cool but she didn't feel like getting dressed yet. There was no sign of Spylgyn who was still hiding from her.

"I need coffee," Kelly said aloud, then quickly held a hand to her mouth for quiet. She didn't want to wake any mermaids that were sleeping late.

In bare feet, Kelly tip-toed up the steps and quietly left the pool arena. She hurried into the tactical room where the coffee machine was. "Enough for me, not for you," she said in a rhythmic way.

While the coffee was brewing, Kelly noticed that the tactical room had a visitor while she slept. Spylgyn had been busy during the night. There were papers and photos strewn all over the floor.

"Spylgyn, Spylgyn," she said like a mother would say to a small child. "Naughty, naughty boy."

"But, was he a boy?" Kelly thought to herself. It's possible that Spylgyn was a girl. She hadn't seen any evidence one way or the other. Albino Man was without any sex organs visible. Kelly knew because she had looked when she ran to him in the desert dream. So, if Albino Man was a male, that made Spylgyn a male.

"Do you have a girlfriend, Spylgyn?" Kelly said as she poured a cup of coffee. "Is that why you're so desperate to get back?"

She took a sip of black coffee and looked around the room one more time, shaking her head at the disarray and wondering who was going to clean it up.

"Not me," Kelly said and went back to the pool arena.

Kelly sat at the middle of the shallow end on the deck overlooking the pool to drink her morning breakfast. She was wiggling her legs inviting any of the sharks to take a big bite of her toes when she noticed Spylgyn sitting in the swamp watching her. He was sitting in the bottom near the center of the swamp, almost a mirror image of Kelly. Only his head, shoulders and chest were visible. Kelly thought the amphibian looked like a petulant child sitting in a bathtub, one that was unhappy about getting bathed.

Kelly paid no attention to the amphibian. She could ignore people and Inglings if she wanted to.

"So there," Kelly thought as she concentrated her attention on the ocean to her right. The sharks were not coming off the wall to eat her. Not thinking about it, Kelly raised her arm and made an eating movement with her hand, imitating a shark's jaws as it gobbled up all the little fish.

Spylgyn chirped at Kelly, a loud noise that echoed around the arena.

"Be quiet, Spylgyn, the mermaids are still sleeping," Kelly said to the amphibian.

Kelly used her hand to wave at Spylgyn, a gesture that said 'yes, I see you but I'm busy ignoring you.'

Spylgyn chirped again as if saying 'you can't tell me to be quiet. I'll chirp when I want to'. The amphibian dove underwater but came back up quickly. Spylgyn jumped out of the swamp and spring-hopped toward Kelly like he was suddenly excited. It only took one leap from the floor of the pool up to the deck where Kelly was and Spylgyn was there with a pea pod for her.

Very matter-of-fact, the Ingling placed the tasty edible in Kelly's lap. Then, he stood upright and made the shark eating hand signal to her.

Kelly got it immediately. That gesture means 'food' or 'I want food' or 'I'm hungry'.

Kelly took the offering from Spylgyn, put it in her mouth and ate it. Then, Kelly gave the amphibian the 'safe' gesture with her palm up because she didn't know the movement for 'thank you'. Spylgyn showed her how to do that. It was a simple motion of his right hand brushing across his face. When Kelly gave Spylgyn that hand signal, Splgyn made the bubble sound with his voice. Kelly tried to do that but it sounded more like a kitten purring but maybe that was the right sound, after all. Spylgyn did a modest happy dance for Kelly.

Then, Spylgyn did something really extraordinary. The amphibian stood upright, placed his hands on his hips and cocked his head at her. It was a familiar stance that Kelly would use when she was annoyed or pre-angry.

"I don't look like that at all, Spylgyn," but she smiled when she said it, knowing that he had imitated her as good as he could do it.

It was a busy morning after that. The amphibian taught Kelly more hand signals, simple and easy lessons, like a child would be taught about letters and how they can become words and sentences. And, she was almost very sure that they were exchanging thoughts and emotions between them. That was how communication began between two very different species, one Ingling and one Oolong.

43 Preparations and Logistics

Morning breakfast was a typical event at Uncle's house the day it all happened. Jenny made eggs, bacon and hash browns. Uncle didn't make flapjacks but his frying pan biscuits were hot, mouth-watering and delicious. So good that Bobby asked his grandfather to make another batch for the day outing to the Hulamar Cliffs.

Bobby didn't know how many of the UFObians would actually go. They needed to get permission from a parent or guardian before Uncle would agree to taking them out there. That was a big stumbling block for the expedition but Bobby only wanted to make sure that Kelly could go. If any of the others were left behind, well, that's how life is sometimes, he reasoned – disappointing and unfair.

Uncle was going to meet with the teenagers at the spa at 10am. That didn't give Bobby a lot of time for preparation and logistics. All of it could fall apart depending on what happened with Kelly and his grandfather. Uncle wanted to have a talk with Kelly about the pool arena violation but he didn't seem all that angry when Bobby told him about that. It was almost like he knew it would happen sooner or later. After all, Kelly was the adventurous type who could break a few rules if they happened to disagree with her and consider it 'no harm done'. A forbidden area at the spa would be like 'a pony at a fence', his grandfather told Bobby.

"That neighboring field would be too inviting for the pony not to jump," he told Bobby. "If he wasn't big enough to jump, that pony would just bust right through to get over there. That's what ponies do."

That's just what Kelly did, Bobby thought. She didn't go over the fence or bust through, though. Kelly went around the obstruction and found a convenient opening to get into the pool arena.

And, because he was a curious man, Uncle wanted to see Spylgyn. Bobby knew that his grandfather was skeptical about the amphibian and its origin. He probably thought it was just some lizard or other creature that lives in a desert environment. It was when Bobby told him about the orb that appeared out there with Kelly that really got his grandfather's attention.

It was at that moment that Grampa jumped over the fence, thought Bobby.

Bobby knew that the door would be locked at the spa but he tried it anyway just to be sure. He climbed in through the burglar window. When he passed the door to the pool arena, Bobby knew that Kelly was in there but he didn't want to go in yet. He quietly pushed at the door to see if it was locked. It was.

In the tactical room, Bobby made a large sign with a magic marker on poster board and left it taped to the entry door for the other UFObians. They couldn't help but see it when they came in.

The sign read, "If you want to go on a day trip to Hulamar Cliffs, you must get your parents' permission. The bus leaves at 11:30 am. Don't be late."

Bobby went back to the pool arena door and knocked. Softly at first, then when she didn't open up, louder. During the long wait, Bobby went through all the things that he was going to say again. He had worked on the dialog well into the night before he went to sleep. Words and phrases changed in his thought process until he was satisfied about how to tell Kelly about his betrayal.

When Kelly did open the door for him, all those prepared statements just vanished from his mind. Bobby didn't know what to say to her.

Kelly grabbed his arm and pulled him inside the pool arena.

"Bobby! You've got to see this. Come on," she said pulling at him.

"No, Kelly wait," Bobby said, resisting her efforts to take him. Kelly let him go but kept going toward the pool steps. His next words stopped her cold in her tracks.

"I told my grandfather everything," Bobby said

Kelly turned back to face him and said, "What?"

"I told him about this," Bobby said, waving at the pool arena. "All of it, I told him all of it."

The shock on Kelly's face was hurtful to Bobby. Like Kelly's broken promise, Bobby had broken a vow.

"Tell no one about what we do here," Kelly had cautioned him at the start. "Why would you do that, Bobby? Why?" Kelly asked him.

"We need his help, Kelly," he said.

"No!" Kelly was defiant when she said that.

She turned away from the traitor and walked over to the far corner of the arena. Kelly stood in that corner facing the wall like a child that was being punished for bad behavior. She clunked her head a couple of times on the wall but softly, not hard enough to hurt.

"No, no, no, no," she whispered. "This place is mine just as much as it is his."

Kelly spun around and came back at Bobby.

"Uncle may own the property but I am a paying tenant. I've got rights!" Kelly said angrily. "I've got a written contract. It doesn't say anything, not one thing, about a restricted area."

Bobby stood as still as he could during Kelly's tirade. He wanted to give her time to calm down before he said anything else.

"He can't evict me. I'll take him to court!" Kelly exclaimed as she began to pace. "Violation of landlord tenant agreement. I'll sue Uncle, that's just what I'll do."

Kelly walked over to Bobby. He didn't flinch when she came at him. Bobby was ready to take a slap or fist from Kelly.

"I want you to leave now," Kelly said in a tense voice.

"I told him about Spylgyn and what happened..." Bobby started, trying to justify his reasoning but Kelly was adamant.

"Leave now! Leave now, leave now!" Kelly warned Bobby.

When he didn't move, Kelly put both of her hands on Bobby's chest and shoved him hard. Bobby stumbled backwards but quickly regained his stance.

Enough was enough for Bobby. He stood his ground against Kelly.

"You need to listen to me, Kelly," Bobby said sternly. "My grandfather is coming over here at 10 o'clock. Yes, he wants to talk to you about breaking the rules but he's not as angry as you seem to think he is. And, we need his help."

"Leave now," Kelly ordered him.

"I've arranged with my grandfather to take all of us on a field trip to the Hulamar Cliffs. That's where Spylgyn was going when you found him in the creek bed. He was going to the grotto."

"Will you leave now?" insisted Kelly, her voice normal now.

"Yeah, I will," Bobby told her. "You need to decide what you're going to do. Spylgyn is coming with us."

Bobby turned away and left her standing there, alone in the forbidden zone. He went into the tactical room to wait for his grandfather's arrival. Bobby had seen all the papers and photos strewn around the room but hadn't given it much thought before. Bobby needed something to do, so he began to straighten the room up. While he was doing that, Martin came in.

"Whoa, what happened in here?" he asked.

Bobby looked up to see Martin standing on the poster message that had been taped to the door.

"Read that," Bobby said to him, pointing at Martin's feet.

Martin stepped back and read the message.

"We're going on a picnic?" he asked Bobby.

"You need to get your parents' permission if you want to go," Bobby told him.

"That might be a problem," Martin said.

"Why is that?" Bobby asked him but didn't really care.

"My father is in Utah and my mother went to Yuma for the day," he said.

"Call them," Bobby said.

"I can get my aunt to do it. Is that okay?" Martin asked him.

Bobby wasn't really listening to him anymore. One of the photos on the floor was the pictograph. That piece of evidence lying at his feet was now warranting Bobby's full attention.

"Is that okay, Bobby?" Martin asked again.

"Yeah, okay," Bobby replied.

"Is it really a field trip or… it's about Spylgyn?" Martin asked.

When Bobby heard that, he looked at Martin like he was just noticing him for the first time.

"Yeah," Bobby said, "it's about Spylgyn. We're taking him home."

When Martin left, Bobby reached down, picked up the photo and took it to a table. He wanted to look at it again with fresh eyes, attempting to decipher the strange drawing by sheer will.

Dan came in a few minutes later and walked right past the message on the floor without reading it. He stood looking over Bobby's shoulder at the image of the pictograph. Dan pointed to the lone triangle that was isolated from the other symbols.

"That's Spylgyn," Dan said to Bobby.

Then, Dan put his finger in the shed structure with the other two triangles.

"That's his rescue team," Dan said.

"How can you know that?" Bobby asked him. "They could be directional pointers or art like the cavemen did."

"No, don't think so," Dan said as if his translation was fact.

"What's that?" Bobby asked him, pointing to the thick curvy line.

"That's Big Black Joe," Dan said. "You got that one right."

Bobby pointed to the jagged line above the snake saying, "that?"

"That's the northeast face of the Hulamar Cliffs, if you're looking from the 'Lost Station'," Dan told Bobby.

Bobby rotated his chair so that he was facing Dan.

"There's a cavern there," Dan said as he went to grab a chair. "A deep cavern."

"The grotto," replied Bobby. "How deep is it, do you know?" asked Bobby.

Dan moved in to sit catty-corner to Bobby at the table.

"I don't know," Dan admitted. "No pictures on the internet that I could find and not a whole lot of information either. Private property, wouldn't you know? Now, the circles, here, there – not the sun and moon, no balloons and not spaceships – they're all orbs." Dan let that sink in, then said with certainty, "there's more than one."

When Pegs and Andy came in a few minutes later, Bobby told them all the details about the trip out to the Hulamar Cliffs. Both of them managed to get permission over the phone. When Martin came back he gave all of them a thumbs up. Everyone was good to go except Kelly and Spylgyn.

44   The Rules Change

Kelly was standing at the center of the beach mural when Uncle entered the pool arena. He thought she might be in a protective stance, or maybe trying to blend in to the scene so that she wouldn't be noticed.

"She sees me as an invader," Uncle realized.

"Are you going to evict me?" Kelly asked him.

Uncle didn't say anything, just kept walking over to where she was. He looked at the mostly empty pool, then at the swamp at the deep end.

"How long has that been there?" Uncle asked.

"What?" said Kelly.

"That filth in the pool," Uncle said.

"It's not filth," Kelly said to him. "It's a swamp."

Uncle stopped walking at the shallow end steps. Kelly had not moved.

"There used to be chairs in here," Uncle said, "lots of chairs for mothers to watch out for their kids when they were swimming."

"Are you going to evict me?" Kelly asked again.

"I don't know," Uncle said to her.

"This place is mine, just as much as it is yours," Kelly said defiantly.

"Is that so?" Uncle said but without anger.

"Please don't make me leave, Uncle," said Kelly, "please," not begging but very close to it.

"Well, we need to talk about that, Kelly," Uncle said to her.

"I know you're angry at me. I'm sorry," Kelly said.

"You see that blonde woman in the yellow bikini right there," pointing to the mural behind Kelly.

Kelly stood away from the wall and turned around to see but she knew who Uncle meant without looking.

"That's my mother," Uncle told her. "All these tiles, they were custom made, painted by a very talented young man, D.L. Grainger. He became quite the celebrity later in his life."

Uncle didn't say anything more, about the young man's death. Even though many years had passed, it was still too painful to remember. And, not something that he wanted to share with this young girl.

"What are you going to do?" Kelly asked, without turning to face her tormentor.

"First, I am going to sit down. Can you get me something to sit on?" asked Uncle.

Without looking at him, Kelly walked away toward the diving platform and went out the wide opening that led to the showers. She went past the shower room and into the locker room where people used to change clothing before and after swimming at the pool. Kelly took two of the canvas folding chairs that looked decent and went back to the pool arena.

When Kelly came back, Uncle was standing where she had been at the beach mural. It bothered her that he was doing that, looking at her wall. She took the chairs all the way to the shallow end of the pool and set them up on the deck, facing each other. There was no chess board between the beach chairs but it was going to be like that, Kelly thought – a battle of wits.

And she wanted to win this game.

Kelly sat in her chair and waited while Uncle circled the pool, like he was inspecting the place. Once or twice, Uncle looked into the swamp from above but didn't make any remarks about that again.

Kelly sat in her chair, first crossing her arms in defense, then dropped them to her sides, then crossed them again. She was unsure if she should be confrontational or apologetic to the landlord.

Uncle admired the ocean mural in passing, then unhurriedly went to his designated spot for the contest.

"In answer to your question, Kelly, no, I am not going to evict you," Uncle said to her.

Kelly uncrossed her arms.

"I knew you would get in here eventually," Uncle told her. "It's not you that I was concerned about."

"I... I don't understand," Kelly admitted.

"Anytime kids get together for an extended time, there's bound to be horseplay," Uncle explained to Kelly. "I didn't want any one of you to fall in this empty pool and get hurt."

"Nobody comes in here except me," Kelly told Uncle, then added, "and Bobby."

"Okay," Uncle said, "let's just keep it that way. Nobody else, agreed?"

Kelly nodded and wanted to hug him at that moment but didn't.

"I always meant to fix this place up," Uncle said looking around at the arena. "Don't know why I didn't." But, he did. He couldn't tell Kelly the reason, though. It was too personal. Kelly was too young to know the odd and stupid things that some grown-up people do when they're unhappy.

"My wife, she loved this place," Uncle said wistfully.

"So do I, Uncle," Kelly told him.

"Do you?" Uncle asked her.

Kelly just nodded.

"Good answer. So, are we all settled about that then?" Uncle asked.

Again, Kelly just nodded, not wanting to say the wrong thing when she was about to get everything that she wanted.

"Well, the other kids are waiting, Kelly," Uncle said to her.

"What?" asked Kelly.

Uncle looked at the swamp and said, "is the, uh, creature in there?"

"Yes," Kelly squeaked, remembering that Bobby had said that he told Uncle all of it.

"I didn't see it," Uncle said.

"He's good at hiding," Kelly told him.

"But, he comes to you," Uncle said to her.

"Sometimes, not always," Kelly admitted because it was true. "I don't think Spylgyn will come out while you're here."

"Why is that?" Uncle asked her.

"He's frightened of you," Kelly told him. "Your voice..."

Uncle looked away from the swamp and focused on Kelly.

"Tell me," Uncle said.

"Your voice is gruff sometimes and, well, it sometimes sounds like you're growling when you talk," Kelly said.

"I growl?" Uncle said.

"I think Spylgyn's ears are more sensitive than ours," Kelly explained. "Loud noises disturb him. I've seen him close his earholes when there is a sound that he doesn't like, or maybe it hurts."

"I've seen dogs that will cower like that, yeah," Uncle said to her.

Kelly wanted to tell Uncle that Spylgyn was not an animal like a dog or cat. He was something more. But, she didn't want to alienate Uncle when things seemed to be going so well.

"I want you to do something for me, Uncle. Don't ask me why. Just do it, okay?" Kelly asked him.

Without waiting for an answer, Kelly turned her chair until it was facing the swamp. Uncle did the same with his chair. Then Kelly leaned forward in her seat, laid her arms on her knees and opened her hands until both were flat with the palms up. Uncle didn't ask why. He just did it.

There were silent for a few moments, waiting, each one looking into the swamp to see if the amphibian made an appearance.

Very quietly Kelly said, "don't make any sudden moves but look at the right side of the swamp, all the way to the back corner, in the shadows."

"Kelly," Uncle said quietly.

"He's right there, Uncle. Can't you see him?" Kelly asked him.

"I don't have my glasses on. They're in my pocket," Uncle said to her.

"Which one?" Kelly asked. "Let me do it. Keep your hands out. Don't move."

"Inside pocket of my jacket, right side," Uncle said.

Kelly scooted her chair back and leaned over Uncle to get his glasses. After she put them on him, she sat back down and put her hands out like before.

"Do you see him?" Kelly asked Uncle.

"It's larger than I thought it would be," Uncle said to Kelly.

Kelly didn't correct Uncle by saying, "he's not an it, Uncle. He's an intelligent being... like us."

Both of them sat like that for a few minutes, watching Spylgyn, hoping the creature would make some kind of movement but Spylgyn remained still, staring at them as if wary or uncertain if there was danger.

Kelly took a chance and wiggled her hand at the amphibian.

"Spylgyn, Spylgyn," she sang to him.

Uncle took his hands back and stood up.

"Uncle, what are you doing? Sit down," Kelly said to him.

"I just want to try something, Kelly," Uncle said. "Just want to see what happens."

Uncle took a gold pocket watch out of his pants pocket, then sat back down. He showed Kelly the watch by dangling it by the gold chain that was attached to it. Then, Uncle showed the watch to Spylgyn. He opened the pocket watch as though he was going to tell everyone what time it was.

Kelly could see that the inner workings of the watch had been removed and replaced with a soft cloth. Uncle unfolded the cloth to reveal a small stone. It was a smooth rock with a color like ivory but it had very small black stripes on it. It reminded Kelly of zebra stripes, irregular, like someone had purposely painted them on the rock with a tiny brush. The rock was not unlike a flattened ice cream cone, rounded on the two bottom corners and bluntly curved on the third edge of the triangle.

Uncle plucked the rock out of the case and held it between his thumb and forefinger. He presented it to Kelly for her to get a good look, then he showed it to Spylgyn. Uncle put the stone in his hand and presented it to the creature.

Spylgyn chirped once and came out of the swamp. He sprang across the mermaid lagoon and disappeared from their view at the shallow end of the pool below the deck where Uncle and Kelly sat.

Then, Spylgyn sprang up and landed between Kelly and Uncle on the blue floor tiles. Uncle slowly moved his left hand with the stone into his lap, leaving his knee available. Spylgyn didn't hesitate when he jumped up and landed on Uncle's leg to confront the man.

"Not sure what I'm supposed to do here, Kelly," Uncle said softly, trying to quiet his gruff voice.

"Show him the stone," Kelly said.

Uncle moved his hand across so that Spylgyn could examine the rock. The amphibian looked at it closely, then cupped his webbed hands to pick up the stone. The Ingling could feel the energy emanating from the relic as he rubbed it between his hands and was certain that this was an ancestral stone from long ago years. Spylgyn put the stone back in the Oolong's hand and began to talk with chirps, pops and the bubbling noises, also using hand and arm movements that were expressive, excited.

"Can you whistle, Uncle?" Kelly asked him. "Sometimes he responds or seems interested when I do that."

Feeling a little foolish, Uncle began to whistle a tune for Spylgyn and, surprisingly, the amphibian did seem to show a genuine interest in the sounds that the Oolong made.

45 The Jump

Uncle drove his loaded truck to the north on county road 41. That road was not used by many people because it didn't really go anywhere except the desert. It went away from all the major routes to Yuma, Phoenix and Tucson. It was only a short ride of about 3 miles until they reached the junction where an access road went further into the desert. There were no barriers or signs to identify that road except a 3 foot post with the legend 'Private Road – No Access'. That access road took them deep into the desert and toward the Hulamar Cliffs.

There was a barrier across the access road at the 2.7 mile mark. It was a locked pipe gate with a sign hanging from the crossbar that read 'Private Property – No Trespassing'. Uncle stopped the truck but left the engine running. He handed a key to Bobby who was sitting in the back seat.

"Bobby, unlock that gate and swing it open," Uncle said to him.

Bobby jumped out and ran to the gate. After the lock was opened, Bobby swung the gate wide and waited for the truck to come through. Then, he locked the gate back to prevent anyone else from entering after them.

It was another 2 miles in to reach the base camp. Uncle drove past an outbuilding that looked like a concrete bunker of some sort but there was no attending guard to stop them from going in to the site. Uncle went past another concrete building and pulled into an open shed with a corrugated tin roof not far from a 2-level bunker.

Before anyone could get out of the truck, Uncle said, "listen up. No one wanders off-site without permission from me. And, if you do go off, you go with a buddy. Nobody goes anywhere alone. Is that understood?"

All of the UFObians agreed in their own way, even though Uncle had already made them promise that back at the spa before the trip even began.

"We'll get settled in first up on Level Two in this building. Take the food baskets and whatever equipment you've got and put it there. That will be our base camp. I'll go over any final details when you all are ready," Uncle instructed them.

Everyone climbed out of the truck and went directly into the bunker. There was no hi-jinks or whooping like at a picnic, as though every one of them understood that this was a serious event and not a time for fun and play.

Pegs and Martin carried the food baskets while Dan and Andy took their equipment bags. Kelly didn't take anything except Spylgyn's ice chest. Bobby and Uncle took the other two containers with the drinks and perishables.

The first floor of the bunker had been used as a storage area. That room was crammed full of all kinds of stuff that was left when the station was closed. There were boxes, crates and gym lockers in there. The staircase to the second level had open grid metal steps like those used at power plants and oil refineries.

Level Two might have been used as an observation deck or maybe just a break room for the onsite workers. It was furnished with three industrial tables that could have been used in an office as equipment tables. There were metal folding chairs, two office chairs and a lounge chair that was probably someone's personal seat at one time. The floor was concrete without any homey rugs or carpet. It was strictly a functional work space. There were open air windows on all sides, large rectangular shaped openings with no glass, although there may have been at one time.

"Crikes," Dan said when he looked around the room while the others filed in after him. "It looks like an observation bunker, the kind they used to watch the nuclear explosions from in old movies."

Everyone took a little time to get settled, all of the guys looking out the windows to see what was and wasn't there, while Pegs went around the room looking forlorn because of all the dust and debris that needed to be cleaned up. Kelly put Spylgyn's ice chest on a small table in a corner of the room but didn't open the lid and let him out yet.

No one had thought to bring any cleaning supplies but Uncle got a pail of water and towels from the equipment room and everyone pitched in to get Level Two squared away enough for the place to be somewhat tidy. Once that was done, all the UFObians sat at the large table and waited for more instructions from Uncle.

"Okay," Uncle said to them, "what's the plan?"

No one seemed to know until Bobby said, "I think we need to defer to Kelly about that. After all, this is her project."

Even as he said it, Kelly didn't want to do it but knew that she had to.

"We need to let Spylgyn go," Kelly said.

"Just like that," Andy said, "we're just going to let him go?"

"Why did you think we were coming here, Andy?" Kelly asked him, sounding angry.

"He's going to run away, just like at the gas station," Andy said.

"If that's what he wants to do..." Bobby said.

"It's the right thing to do," Pegs said. "He wants to go home."

Kelly looked at Pegs with surprise. Kelly hadn't expected Pegs to be so caring considering her past behavior with the 'rat' or maybe Pegs just wanted the amphibian gone so that she wouldn't have to climb on tables anymore.

"Not here, though," said Bobby. "At the grotto. Spylgyn can find his way from there."

"Where is the grotto?" Martin asked Uncle. "I didn't see it on the way in."

"It's up the cliff a ways. We have to climb," he told them.

Pegs was the only one that hadn't considered the proper foot gear to wear for an expedition into the hills. She had on stylish black pumps that were fine for sidewalks and carpet but not for craggy rocks and sand.

"There might be some sneakers or boots in one of the lockers downstairs. You can look," Uncle told Pegs.

Pegs grabbed Andy to be her buddy while she went down to Level One to find some climbing shoes.

While the rest of them waited, Bobby popped open a soda because it gave him something to do.

"Are you ready for this?" Bobby asked Kelly when he sat back down.

"Yes," Kelly answered.

"Still mad at me?" Bobby asked.

Kelly nodded.

Bobby let that lay for the time being. He noticed his grandfather looking out the east window where there was a good view of the cliffs. Bobby went over to stand next to him.

"There's a lot you haven't told me, isn't there?" Bobby said to him.

"Tell you what, I'll tell you everything when this is all over," Uncle said.

Bobby took a drink of the soda and waited, hoping his grandfather would say something now.

"I didn't see the creature. Jimmy Nickles did. He didn't describe it like..." his grandfather stammered.

Uncle looked over at the ice chest in the corner.

"Spylgyn," Bobby said to his grandfather.

"Jimmy said it looked like a dragon, with scales and a snout like a crocodile," Uncle told Bobby.

"But, you saw something," Bobby told him.

"I saw the orb," Uncle said. "It looked like a bubble, just floating across the desert, like it was being blown by the wind."

"Alice thought it was a balloon," Bobby said.

"Lots of people see weather balloons," said Uncle, "thinking they're UFOs. But, maybe some are not."

"Kelly calls them phenomenon," Bobby said. "Orbs, UFOs, petroglyphs, anything that can't be explained or is strange, that's a phenomenon."

"Yeah, Kelly," Uncle said.

"Got 'em," Pegs said loudly when she came back in.

She was wearing someone's old work boots that were in their last stages of use. The boots were scuffed and worn out but they still had enough bottom soles that could probably handle the cliff hazards.

When Kelly went to get Spylgyn's camper, Andy followed her over there.

"Kelly," Andy said to her, "this is my last chance to take pictures. Please."

"Yes, Andy, take pictures," and she brushed past him as if she was in a hurry to get it over with.

46 The Lair

All the UFObians were gathered around Uncle at the trail head leading into Big Black Joe's lair. There were two large boulders at the opening, standing like entrance statues, big stone orb guardians.

Uncle stood facing the group as he told them, "a few more rules before we get going." .

There were a few groans and comments from the hikers, just kids tired of being told stuff that they thought they already knew but probably didn't.

"I'll take the lead," Uncle said. "Bobby, you bring up the rear. Kelly, you're behind me. If anyone falls behind, everyone waits for them until they're ready. Always keep the person in front of you within sight. Just say 'wait' if you can't keep up. If anyone turns back, Bobby will take you down and we'll wait for him to return before going on.

Anyone who goes back stays at the station, no wandering off until all of us get back. Any questions?"

No questions from anyone. Everybody was ready to go.

It was an easy trek for the first leg. The path was well trodden or maybe it had been a path for Big Black Joe when the snake came down from the cliff. Bobby could see thick shards of black rubber along the trail. The flexible water hose had been eaten away by the unrelenting sun over the years and only those tattered bits of its skin remained.

There were very few words spoken during the climb. Each person kept a safe distance from front buddies and concentrated on their footing and handholds. When they came to the first obstacle, Uncle waited for all of them to get there before he went on.

"This is the blind dog crevice," Uncle said to them, not explaining why it was called that.

The pit was not wide and if you were a person who was willing to take a risk, it could be jumped over. There was a wooden bridge for anyone who was not that foolhardy. The footbridge looked sturdy and had obviously not been there forever. It was constructed of two 2x12 planks with a generous sub-structure for stability.

After everyone had looked at the hazard, Uncle said, "it's not deep but if you fall into it, you could get hurt. I don't want to have to tell your people about any broken legs or cracked ribs when we get back. Does anyone want to go back?"

Bobby was standing next to Pegs, waiting for her to speak up.

"What?" said Pegs when she saw Bobby giving her the look. "I take ballet."

Then Bobby noticed Martin nervously fidgeting but he didn't raise his hand or say anything.

Uncle stepped onto the bridge to show them that his weight didn't even bend the boards. There were no handrails or ropes, just the boards across the chasm.

Some of them went slow, others fast as they could. Pegs went across with her arms out like a tightrope walker.

The second leg of the trail was at a more steep incline so that everyone had to use the cliffside or boulders for balance and there were high step-ups where the girls had to be helped. All the guys were like rock apes and didn't ask for any help at any of the obstacles.

Eventually the expedition reached a wide level pan where Uncle wanted another pause before continuing.

"We're at the sinkhole now," Uncle said to all of them. "Don't get too close to the edge, even if there are solid rocks to stand on. Except for the shallows, the pit is over a hundred feet deep. Fall in there and you're done for."

It took a moment for that very real danger to be realized by each of them.

"Death was close if you took the wrong step," Martin might have said, if he wasn't so scared..

"It's dry," Kelly said to Uncle, "there's no water."

"There hasn't been any water here for over 40 years, Kelly, except all the way to the bottom. I told you that," Uncle said to her.

"What happened to it?" Pegs asked.

"Just dried up, went another direction, sunk," Uncle said with some sorrow.

At the western side of the sinkhole was where the swamp pond would have been if there had been any water to fill it. It had a shallow depth of maybe three feet, enough for a person to wade or stand like Bobby's great-grandmother had done years ago. but the shelf drop off to grotto bottom was severe. One wrong stumble and you would disappear into the sinkhole.

"Even when you're looking down from above, you can't see bottom," Uncle said.

"What's down there?" Andy asked.

"Rocks, boulders and a few tunnel shafts that go deep into the cliff, some big enough for a man to climb through. But no water," Uncle told them.

"Did you go down?" Bobby asked his grandfather.

"No, my father hired a geologist to go down to see if there was any way to get to the water," Uncle said. "He didn't find anything. It was mostly dry, just a few pools of water that didn't get swallowed up."

Everyone took some time to look around before Uncle said, "Well, that's it. What happens now?"

"This can't be the source," Kelly said.

"There's nothing else here, Kelly," Uncle answered. "The geologist called the sinkhole an aquifer. That means it was a temporary lake caused by underground water punching through the rocks. He couldn't say what caused it."

"An underground ocean like Jules Verne wrote about in Journey to the Center of the Earth," Dan suggested. "Or Pellucidar!"

Nobody seemed to like that idea so they paid little attention to that theory.

"So, we just let him go?" Pegs asked. "Here?"

Everyone looked at Kelly who was still holding the ice chest. Andy got his camera ready for the release but Kelly was stalling. She put the ice chest down, then sat down next to it.

"It doesn't feel right," Kelly said. "It's too dry here. There's no water."

Bobby went over to Kelly and sat down next to her.

"What do you want to do, Kelly?" He asked her.

"Take him back. I want to take Spylgyn back to the swamp," said Kelly but she didn't get up. She didn't take the ice chest and go back down the cliff.

Everyone waited on Kelly to make a decision but nobody wanted to force the situation. It was her decision to make.

Then, there was a noise that got everyone's attention. Andy was rapidly clicking photos with his camera. He was focusing at Kelly and Bobby sitting at the ice chest.

"Andy, come on, man, not now," Bobby said to him.

Andy lowered the camera but only to switch the operation to video, then he raised the camera again to film.

"There's an orb behind you," Andy said quietly.

The orb was stationary in the air, floating about 15 feet behind Kelly and Bobby. It wasn't high in the sky but right there with them hovering about 5 feet from the earth. It was still and silent like a wild animal would be if it were stalking prey. The orb was twice as large as a beach ball with a silver shell that reflected its surroundings like a mirror. The orb slowly floated toward Kelly and Bobby who had to move aside as it passed close by them. The orb was not diverting for obstacles on this day, it seemed. When it reached center of the sinkhole it hovered for a few seconds, then dropped so fast that it became a blur, faster than a speeding bullet, one could say.

"I haven't seen one of those in 40 years," said Uncle. There was quiet then, a silence that seemed to remove all noise in the area around the sinkhole. It was like Uncle and the UFObians were suddenly inside a vacuum where noise didn't exist.

Then, the earth shuddered. There was a sudden explosive whoosh of air that came up from the bottom of the grotto. It was like rain that was falling up from down below.

Bobby grabbed Kelly's arm and pulled her behind a boulder. The others found similar cover. Only Uncle stood where he was as if he knew what was happening.

After that first burst of air, the sinkhole went silent again.

"What the hell just happened?" asked Dan.

Nobody could answer that, not even Uncle.

In the unnatural silence that followed, Spylgyn began to sing from inside the ice chest. In the rocks behind Uncle, there was an answering call. They all heard it but none could see what creature made the peculiar whistling noises.

Bobby put his hand on Kelly's shoulder to make her look at him.

"We have to let him go, Kelly," he said to her.

Kelly nodded and they both crawled over to the ice chest. Kelly released the fastening clasp. Bobby lifted the lid.

Spylgyn jumped out and landed several feet away. The amphibian quickly took in its surroundings, then looked at Bobby and Kelly. He chirped once at them, maybe to acknowledge them, then ran to the sinkhole and jumped in.

"No, Spylgyn!" Kelly screamed.

Kelly scrambled after Spylgyn and got all the way to the edge of the sinkhole before Bobby was able to grab her legs to stop her from falling in.

"Kelly, get back here!" Bobby yelled at her.

Kelly tried to get away from him but Bobby held onto her as she struggled.

The silence was fading. Now, there was a noise like that of a waterfall but it was coming from the bottom of the grotto and it was getting louder by the second. Another blowing wind came from below, much stronger than before, like it was being forced upward out of the grotto by a mighty geyser.

"Let me go, Bobby!" Kelly yelled.

"No!" Bobby yelled back.

Kelly was laying flat on the ground with her head out over the edge of the pit. She was looking down into the abyss. Her long blonde hair was being blown upwards by the powerful wind that came from below.

"It's coming!" she said loudly. "The water is coming up!"

Kelly was twisting and kicking at Bobby. He grabbed her pants at the waist band and tried to pull her back but she was strong. He needed help to hold Kelly or she was going into the sinkhole after Spylgyn. The powerful noise of the geyser drowned out his call for help.

47 Into The Abyss

Craig Cavanah had arrived at the sinkhole well in advance of the UFObian expedition. He had walked in past the security gate while it was still morning dark. Cavanah would have liked to bring the jeep in closer to Station One but it would have been too visible there even if he parked under the shed. So, he left it in a culvert near the access road where it was hidden from view.

Cavanah knew he was trespassing on private land but that didn't bother him. He had done it before in China, Thailand and Africa where people carried guns and there was the threat of prison if he had been caught. Here at Inyo, he might be cautioned but there would be no jail time. He would get off with a warning, maybe a fine if Huncle was really pissed off at him.

Cavanah was dressed in the same fatigues as he had been at the gas station but he was carrying more equipment with him this time. His backpack was loaded with all the tools that would be necessary for going up the cliff and for going down in the hole. He had been in the pit before three years ago but he couldn't get all the way to the bottom. This time he had enough rope to get him down there.

Cavanah found a comfortable spot on the cliff to drink the last of his coffee before he went down. He watched the shadows recede on the desert below when the sun began its slow rise into the morning sky. From that distance, it looked like the wind was blowing the dark shadows back into the cliff below him, he thought.

When it was light enough, Cavanah went to the sinkhole. He retro-bolted one end of the rope at the same boulder that he had used on the previous drop. Then, he threw the remaining coil of rope into the sinkhole.

There were step-down rocks on a shelf at the western side of the sinkhole. It was almost like someone had built a shallow end at that side of the abyss like at a swimming pool but the drop-off from shallow to deep was strange, curved like the inside of a football. Cavanah used rocks and crevices on his way down, so that he didn't have to hang from the rope all the time. When he reached the point where he had turned back three years ago, Cavanah checked the depth finder. As he thought, he was now 120 feet down.

There was a safe rock ledge where he could rest and search for a niche for an anchor. Cavanah hammered a pinion into a crack until he felt it was secure, then found another place for a secondary belay. He removed the second rope from his shoulder and attached one end to both of the metal rings and let the rest of the rope fall down into the deeper part of the sinkhole.

He didn't have to go very far to reach the bottom, only another 75 feet. The base of the pit was not flat but was structured with rocks and boulders like those that could be found in almost any grotto or cavern. He didn't pay much attention to the many pools of still water that he passed over as he explored the floor of the grotto. He realized much later that he should have taken samples.

He found three not large openings on base east that were interesting to him. He could fit an arm and shoulder through two of them but felt no water in these recesses when he did that. The last opening was a smooth tunnel on the north-east floor that was large enough for a person to get through. It was shaped like a gourd, fat at one end and tapered off to a smaller cylindrical tube.

Cavanah lay flat and crawled into the opening. He didn't go all the way in but left his legs out in the grotto. Going any further would be dangerous without a skilled team of cavers and scuba divers with proven backgrounds of knowledge and experience. He used a flashlight to examine the walls and ceiling of the tube and was quite certain that this was a corrasional pipe, the primary faucet for the water to flow into the grotto.

He lay on the floor for several minutes just listening for sounds but heard nothing. The underground water source was too far deep to hear any noise but Cavanah could smell it. It was a pungent odor, not bitter or stinking but aromatic like the underground grotto at Koh Tao.

Cavanah backed out of the tunnel and sat on the floor of the grotto, giving him some time to think about the assembly and logistics for such an arduous undertaking. He knew that he would need to assemble a rugged group of individuals to go any farther down the cavern. That was the only way to know for certain if there was anything beyond. There was water down there somewhere, an underground river or lake and Cavanah wanted to be the one to discover it.

For the next hour, maybe longer, he roamed around the grotto bottom taking photos of any fissure or outcropping that could prove advantageous to the next phase of exploration. If he had delayed his departure any longer, Cavanah would have been caught by Hunkle and his team as they approached the sinkhole.

There was no way down the cliff without being seen, so he chose to go higher and remain out of sight until they left. Cavanah remained hidden until he was forced to reveal himself when G1 was trying to jump into the sinkhole.

48 The Flood

Cavanah grabbed Kelly around the waist and jerked her up, away from the sinkhole. He held onto her tight as she fought to get back to the pit.

When Bobby realized what was happening, he jumped up ready to fight the intruder that had taken Kelly. The man was yelling at him but the words were lost in the storm caused by the sinkhole geyser. It was raining, water falling from the plume that had erupted from below.

Bobby stepped in closer to hear what the man was shouting. Kelly was just hanging from Cavanah's arms. The big man had lifted her off the ground so that she couldn't get a footing to escape.

"If the water comes over ground, it will be a flood," shouted Cavanah. "Can't go down the trail, it will flash flood! Got to get to higher ground!" he shouted, pointing up.

Bobby looked over at Uncle and the others. They were already climbing the rocks to get to safety from the deluge. Cavanah couldn't wait any longer. He went to the escarpment where he had gone up to his hiding place. Bobby ran after him.

Cavanah handed the girl off to Bobby and climbed up the cliff. Kelly wasn't struggling anymore. She allowed the two of them to lift and pull her up into the rocks above the sinkhole. Cavanah tossed the girl onto the flat ground near his backpack and turned to help Bobby scramble up the cliff.

Cavanah's hiding place was like a balcony that looked over the sinkhole. Kelly stood up to confront the man who had manhandled her. Cavanah was thankful that she didn't have a knife because it certainly looked like she would have used it on him.

When she moved, both Cavanah and Bobby stood ready to block Kelly if she tried to go back down. But, she calmly walked to the balcony railing where she could observe the unnatural and devastating deluge coming out of the earth. Cavanah and Bobby gave each other a look that said 'be ready if she decides to jump off'.

Each one took a side to box Kelly in and they stood with her to see what was happening below.

From above, they could see that the water level was now about seven feet from the rim of the sinkhole. The water was still in turmoil, with the surface showing froth and waves like an ocean would have but it was calming down. Cavanah could see that there were things bobbing up and floating on the surface water. It was plant life that had been taken away by the upheaval from below. Kelly paid no attention to that. She was looking for Spylgyn.

When the water was a few inches from ground level, someone or something turned off the spigot on the faucet. The sinkhole was full, its level completed.

The silence returned after that but they all continued to watch to see if anything else would happen.

"Who are you?" Bobby asked Cavanah.

"Cavanah," he said to him. "I was just wandering by and saw what was happening."

"Bullshit," said Bobby and Cavanah laughed.

"Is it okay if I go down now?" Kelly asked but didn't look at either one of her captors.

"I think it's safe now," said Cavanah.

Cavanah grabbed his backpack and slung it over his shoulders. Bobby helped Kelly descend from the balcony.

When they reached the level ground around the sinkhole, neither one of the guys expected Kelly to do what she did. She ran to the sinkhole and dived in.

Bobby was stunned and stood where he was.

Cavanah came up beside him and said, "are you going in after her, or am I?"

Before either one could jump in to save her, Kelly came up for air. She came up facing away from Bobby and Cavanah. Kelly saw Uncle and the others at the far end of the pool but she didn't wave at them. She twisted in the water to face Cavanah and Bobby.

"Abductors!" she accused. Kelly glared at them with a 'got away from you good that time' look, then she went under again.

The water wasn't as clear as it would be later on because the silt and earthy matter was still disturbed by the recent turmoil. Kelly could feel the plant life swirling around her as she swam beneath the surface. There were leaves, vines and other green things that Spylgyn might have liked for lunch.

Kelly came up for air when she needed to but she didn't want to get out of the pool yet. She saw that Cavanah and Bobby had joined Uncle and the others near the trail that led down from the sinkhole. They were making plans that would probably include her but she wasn't interested in hearing what was being said. Kelly was having too much fun right now and didn't want it to end quickly.

Eventually though, Kelly swam to the edge of the pool and let Bobby help her out. She was soaking wet but there weren't any towels or blankets to wrap her in. No one had thought to bring any.

"That was a stupid thing to do, Kelly," Bobby said to her.

"We go down now," Uncle said, "we're done here."

Back at Station One, Andy and Pegs found some towels and old clothes in the lockers and brought them up to the second floor for Kelly. There was no privacy for Kelly to get out of the wet things she had on, so she went downstairs to change. When she had been gone for too long, Bobby went down to check on her thinking that she might have gone back to the grotto for one last try to find Spylgyn.

Kelly wasn't in the downstairs storage area. Bobby found her wet clothes piled up on a crate but she was gone. He found her outside not far away from the building. Kelly was looking up at the cliff when he came up from behind her.

Kelly looked like a ragamuffin in the worker's clothes. They were baggy and way too large for her small body but it was somehow endearing to him, not funny.

"It was like a warm bath, Bobby," she said in a quiet way. "The water wasn't cold; it was pleasant and comforting."

"My grandfather is going to close it off," Bobby told her. "No admittance to anyone."

Kelly smiled and said, "he'll change his mind about that."

"I wouldn't be so sure, Kelly," Bobby said. "He's not real happy about what you did up there."

"Oh well," Kelly said. "I guess that's that, huh?" she said, not expecting an answer.

"Don't you want to know who that guy is?" Bobby asked her.

Kelly shrugged. "Not important to me," was all she said.

"Everyone's hungry, so we're having a feast up on level 2 where it's cool," Bobby told her.

Kelly followed him back to the bunker but only to get her wet clothes from the storage unit. She didn't follow him up for food. She returned to the base of the cliff where there were some boulders large enough to lay out her shirt and pants, socks and sneakers. The sun was high in the sky and hopefully the clothes would dry out quickly as they baked on the rocks. She didn't want to go back to town dressed like she was.

As she was smoothing a pant leg out, Kelly heard a gruff grunt. At first, she thought it was Uncle who had come out to talk with her but it wasn't unless he had climbed the cliff while she wasn't looking. The grunt came from above her. Kelly looked up and saw a rock ape, or something like that but only as large as a very big housecat with much less fur, all white just sprinkled in patches on its body, most on the shoulders.

The ape was squatted down on a protruding rock about seven feet above her but it wasn't looking at Kelly. It seemed to have an interest in some other thing than the girl watching him. There was a casual indifferent attitude about the ape. It was almost like he wanted Kelly to get a good look at him.

Although Kelly was amazed and startled, she did the one thing that seemed natural for her to do. She raised her arms and showed that her hands were empty. The ape pretended to not notice what she was doing. Then, of a sudden, it looked directly at her and grunted again. G'Thorpe laid one hand, palm up, on the boulder that he was sitting on, Spylgyn's hand movement for safe.

G'Thorpe only gave her one hand, not both as she was doing. Kelly wasn't sure what a single hand meant but it was enough to satisfy her.

The ape let its open hand lay there for only a few seconds, then took it back to scratch his chest.

Kelly turned her right hand over and wiggled it at the ape and, after a short hesitation, the gorilla did the same thing to her. Then G'Thorpe raised his arms above him and stretched like one would do when sitting too long in the same position. The white ape moved off the rock and climbed up the cliff rapidly, leaving Kelly standing alone.

Kelly went back to Level Two to be with the others. Of course, they were enthused and animated about their experience at the sinkhole, talking over each other like at a junior high dialogue in a class that had become unreasonably agitated. Uncle and the tall man who dragged her away from the sinkhole were at another table and appeared to be involved in a somewhat friendly conversation but Kelly couldn't hear what was going on with them. Bobby engaged Kelly once or twice, trying to get back in her good graces but she all but ignored him and he finally gave up.

Kelly was considering how her life was changed by the events and just didn't want to be bothered with ordinary things today, not even a boyfriend. She noticed that Uncle would occasionally look at her from across the table but didn't say anything to her. Cavanah looked at her once but she didn't smile back at him.

While the others were packing up to leave, Kelly went to get her clothes. The sneakers were still moist but dry enough to wear. The shirt and pants were warm from the sun's heat but not wet anymore. Since no one could see her from the bunker, Kelly changed clothes there. She kept looking at the cliffside to see if any more creatures might appear but if any were watching they were very good at hiding.

When Kelly was dressed, she left the old clothing in a pile behind a rock. She also left a plastic baggie with slices of apple and grapes and a half-eaten can of mixed nuts. Kelly didn't know if simians liked those particular edibles but she wanted to leave something for the ape to find if he came back.

As Kelly was walking back to the building, she saw Cavanah in the far off distance. The man was just walking away into the desert. Kelly stopped and stared at him. Shortly, he turned around to get a last look or maybe he sensed that he was being watched. Cavanah raised an arm to her, his way of saying good-bye. Kelly did the same to him.

49 Nothing Is Normal Anymore

The alarm clock woke Kelly up at 6:01 am. She had overslept. Kelly reached over and stopped the ringing but didn't get out of bed. A dream was still fresh in her memory and she went over the details before the images disappeared.

Kelly was standing at a building with large Greek columns and a pair of lions guarding the entrance. It could have been a library but it was not the local Inyo library that she was familiar with. Kelly had the distinct feeling that it was at a college or university.

Kelly didn't want to go inside with the other people there, so she walked across the street to a vacant lot that was overgrown with weeds and grass. There were wooden benches there like those found at a public park or zoo. One bench was very small, miniature like one that could be found in a child's doll house. Then, there was a medium sized bench and a very large bench. Kelly wanted to sit on the middle bench but there was a gaggle of baby ducks in front of it. The ducks were very tiny, about the size of ping pong balls and Kelly didn't want to step on any.

A bigger duck flew out from under the bench and attacked Kelly, flapping its wings and making duck noises to keep her away from the middle bench. That yellow duck was an odd fellow, not like a real duck at all. It was a cartoon duck with a red knit cap on it's head and it talked to her.

"Get away," the duck squawked at her. "Look out what you're doing!"

Although Kelly backed away from the bench, the duck kept on coming at her. So, she kicked it. The duck landed a few feet away and when it righted itself, looked at Kelly in shock.

"Why did you do that?" the duck asked her.

"You were attacking me," Kelly said.

"I wasn't doing any such thing," the duck explained. "I was going after the wasp on your head."

Kelly swatted at the wasp that was now flying near her face.

"Use your hat," the duck yelled at her while jumping up and down like it was skipping rope.

"I don't have a hat!" Kelly shouted back while still using both hands to keep the wasp away.

The cartoon duck picked up it's red cap and put it back on its head.

"You should get a hat," said the duck. "A hat is good for swatting at wasps that are trying to sting you."

Then, the duck waddled away on other business, leaving Kelly to fend for herself and that's all she could remember about that.

Kelly didn't bother to write that dream down in her journal. It was just too silly and nonsensical.

There were no scribbles on her note pad by the bed and Kelly couldn't recall any other dreams that might have happened during the night.

Kelly went through her regular morning duties as she would have done on any other normal day. She stopped for coffee at the diner on the outskirts of town and took it away with her to Pete's Overlook.

Kelly was not considering time this morning, so she didn't feel rushed to do anything in particular. She sat at the picnic table and just enjoyed watching the desert come to life. The darkness and shadows receded as if the Inyo desert was slowly waking up from a deep slumber.

She couldn't see the Hulamar Cliffs from the Overlook but she knew that the buttes and the sinkhole mesa were out there. So was the 'Lost Gas Station' and 'Recovery', parts of a puzzle that could not be completed because there were too many missing pieces.

Kelly stopped at the police station where Officer Posen gave her the logs for last night and the other days that she had not seen yet. There was nothing of interest for her, just routine calls of loud noises at a party, a broken window at the drug store and other stuff like that. Inyo was a quiet town without a lot of crime or curious phenomena. "Unfortunate," Kelly thought. It might be time to give up this stop on her route, it was just so boring to her now.

As she got up to leave Posen spoke, "I didn't make a report about Missus Marchen's dog. That's something for animal control, not a police action. You know, she's going into her 70's, maybe experiencing a bit of dementia, makin' things up."

"Go on, Officer Posen," Kelly said as she sat back down, "tell me."

Well, must've been about 3am, I guess it was," he began, giving the girl his best Columbo impersonation. "She called up and said something was attacking her dog in the yard," Posen laughed thinking about it. The old lady had been in a baby doll nightgown that hid nothing, not that he wanted to look.

"When I got there, the animal was fine," said Posen. "She claimed the dog had a fit or a seizure, something that scared her. And the thing that she saw, the way she described it, well, c'mon."

"How did she describe it?" Kelly asked.

"She said it was a monkey, jumping around and making hooting noises." Posen laughed again remembering how Missus Marchen had tried to imitate what she thought she saw.

"Missus Marchen, she lives over on Preston Lane?" Kelly asked him.

Posen nodded, still chuckling about the peculiar incident.

The door to the spa was unlocked, so Kelly parked her bike inside the entry room where it would be safe from thugs and vagrants. The door to the tactical room was locked and when she tried to open it with her key, it didn't work. The lock had been changed.

Like any other visitor would do, Kelly knocked on the door, wondering if anybody would open it for her.

As Kelly feared, it was Uncle who unlocked and opened the door. He stood there blocking her from coming in. He didn't seem angry at her but he looked tired, like he didn't have a good sleep last night.

"Come on in, Kelly," Uncle said and stepped to one side. "Take a seat at that table over there."

Martin was inside already but none of the others, not even Bobby. Martin was at his computer working on a project and didn't say anything to her when Kelly came in.

The table was empty except for a few papers and a pen.

"Read that document and if you agree, sign it," he said bluntly.

Then, Uncle went over to Martin to watch what he was doing on the computer.

Kelly sat down at the table, picked up her noted file and began to read. It was a non-disclosure agreement, a legal document like a lawyer would write up with too many words when one sentence could have said the same thing.

"I will not make public the location of the 'Lost Station' or the Hulamar Grotto, nor will I disclose the recent events that have happened there."

After Kelly had read the entirety of the legal document, she looked at the separate files on the table. Martin, Bobby and Dan had already signed agreements. Pegs, Andy and Kelly still had outstanding warrants. Kelly didn't sign the document. She wanted to talk things over with Uncle before she proceeded one way or the other.

"Finally," Martin said, "all done."

"That's everything?" Uncle asked him.

"Yes sir," Martin replied, "All gone, everything relevant."

Uncle stepped back when Martin got up from the chair.

"I'll see you later, maybe," Martin said to Kelly as he walked away and left the building.

Uncle sat down at the document table with Kelly, ready for a discussion with her.

"He took down everything?" asked Kelly. "From the website, Facebook and... everything?"

"Only recent events," Uncle nodded and said, "what's out there is out there; there's nothing I can do about that. But it stops now. The 'Hulamar Event' never happened."

"We don't need your permission to keep quiet about this," Kelly said to him.

"You do if you want to stay here, at the spa," Uncle said. "You can keep the club going but I don't want a lot of UFO hunters and tourists coming around. I can't let that happen."

Kelly held up the document and said, "this won't hold up in any court. We're all minors. It's not any good."

"Is that your argument? asked Uncle.

"I'm not arguing, Uncle," Kelly told him. "I'm just saying."

"You're not signing that for any court of law. You're signing that for me," Uncle said. "Have you ever been to Roswell?" Uncle asked her.

"No," Kelly admitted.

"I don't want to see Inyo become like Roswell. This is my home, Kelly," Uncle said. "And, I like it the way it is. Peaceful, quiet and natural."

"I can stay in the spa? You're not going to kick us out?" asked Kelly.

"The spa is yours. And, I'm not going to stop your research either but it has to be done in secret, like it is supposed to be done. Nothing more posted on social media about the 'Hulamar Event', that's what you're calling it, right? And, I want to be informed of any other developments if that should ever happen. I am now Acting Director of The UFO Bureau, self-appointed. Anything of importance goes through me first. Understood? All you have to do is agree to those terms."

Kelly signed the document.

"Craig Cavanah is coming over to the house for lunch," said Uncle after Kelly handed him the signed non-disclosure agreement.

Kelly didn't know his name but she knew who Uncle was talking about.

"Before we got there yesterday, Cavanah went down into the grotto, while it was still empty," Uncle told her.

"He didn't," Kelly said, astonished.

"He did," Uncle said. "And he told me some very interesting things about what he found down there."

"What?" asked Kelly.

"Well, you should hear that from him, I think," said Uncle. "Do you want to come over for lunch, say around 11? That will give us time to talk before we eat."

"Yes, I would like to do that," Kelly told him.

"Are you still mad at Bobby?" Uncle asked her.

"Not so much now," Kelly answered.

Okay, then," Uncle said as he stood up. "The spa is on lock down until Pegs and...uh..."

"Andy," Kelly informed him.

"Yeah, Andy. Both of them have to sign on before anything goes forward," Uncle told her.

Kelly stood up because she knew she was meant to leave now but before she went, Kelly reached over and hugged Uncle, really hard to show him that she was being sincere.

"Thank you, Uncle," Kelly whispered, "thank you so much, for everything."

Kelly didn't rush over to Uncle's house right away although that's what she wanted to do. She hung around outside to catch Pegs and Andy before they went in to see Uncle. Kelly wanted them to understand how important it was for them to sign their documents without any delays.

50 The Worth of Stones

Kelly got to Uncle's house for lunch at 11 o'clock on the dot. Cavanah wasn't there yet and Uncle seemed to be enjoying private time under the shade tree in the backyard. As she approached Uncle, Kelly got the odd impression that she was not welcome, like an uninvited neighbor who just showed up too much, a bother.

Without any small talk Kelly jumped right in, asking about Cavanah, worried that he had changed his mind and was not coming. Uncle said that he was going to be late, something about his work had delayed him. All the UFObians had signed the non-disclosure agreement, so she was confused by Uncle's seeming lack of emotion. He was somehow different from the affable and social person that she knew and respected. And, Kelly thought that she could be the cause of it.

"I'm sorry for causing so much trouble, Uncle," she said quietly.

"Kelly, hon, if you were not in my life, I would go looking for you," Uncle told her. "You are that needful to me."

They both could understand that their relationship would be the same in most ways, friendly and casual – Uncle as the sage counselor and Kelly, wild as a pony looking at all the high fences. Some changes would be necessary, however, considering the complications and uncertainty that they now faced and whatever was going to happen next.

There was a comfortable silence then, each lost in self thoughts and wonderings, until Jenny called out from the kitchen door.

"Kelly, could you give me a hand in here?" Jenny asked.

Kelly was put to work as a salad and side dish chef as well as the toaster of buns in the oven. Jenny was busy with meat, fries and other pot boilers on the stove. At least Bobby's mother seemed to be in a pleasant mood today. She was talkative and animated and that cheered Kelly up a little bit.

Kelly had to really concentrate on the food preparation. She wasn't used to delivering food for a crowd, never having done that before. Jenny had to teach her how to properly melt cheese on buns in the oven, not a frying pan.

When they were taking the food out to the picnic table in the backyard, Kelly saw that Cavanah was with Uncle now. Kelly really wanted to know what they were talking about but felt that she couldn't just walk away from her waitress duties.

Bobby came through the kitchen, saw Kelly and said, "hey, how's it going?"

He had an old scrapbook in his hand and he held it up for her to see like it was the 'Book of All Secret Things That You Want To Know'. Then, Bobby waved a hand at her to come with him.

"Kelly, can you get the banana pudding from the fridge and take it out?" Jenny asked.

Kelly shrugged at Bobby and did as she was told. Bobby just left her there and went outside. Alice rushed by Kelly without saying anything to her.

"Don't run, Alice!" Jenny said sternly. "You'll trip and fall."

Alice paid no attention to her mother and pushed the screen door open, still going fast. Kelly watched Alice run across the lawn and join Uncle, Bobby and Cavanah. Now, everyone was where Kelly wanted to be and she was still stuck on kitchen duty.

Dropping dessert on the picnic table was going to be Kelly's last scullery job but before she could get away, Jenny called out, "food's ready, let's go guys!"

Kelly was able to get some information about Cavanah during lunch. He was a geologist and engineer that had worked on bridges and excavations in Asia, South America and other foreign countries. Cavanah explained that he was taking a short leave from a project that he was doing in China but he didn't say what that work was, like maybe it was a secret operation that he couldn't talk about.

Too soon, the conversation shifted to Cavanah's family and how they were doing. His mother was still in Utah, he told them but she was having thoughts about moving back to Inyo now that all her children were out in the world. It had been seven years since the plane crash that killed Cavanah's father and his mother didn't like living so isolated in the wilderness anymore.

"What happened to your finger?" Alice asked him.

"Alice," Jenny scolded her, "that's not a nice thing to ask."

"That's okay," Cavanah laughed, "kids want to know about things like that."

Cavanah held up his left hand to show them his injury.

"I lost that finger in Gili Motag, that's in Indonesia," Cavanah told her. "Dangerous place to be, I found out. I got in a fight with a lizard and he bit it right off."

"A lizard?" asked Alice incredulously.

Cavanah explained, "big lizard, mean lizard...it came..."

"How big?" the little girl asked before he could go on.

"Oh yeah, real big, 8 maybe 9 feet long," he exaggerated.

"Yes, that's big," Alice admitted.

Uncle turned the conversation again when he said, "there's good property around if Beth is really considering coming back here."

"Well, I'll let her know about that," Cavanah said to him. "Mom's been looking at some real estate online, so she could be serious about it, I guess."

Once lunch was over, Uncle and Cavanah went back to the shade tree to talk some more but Kelly didn't want it to be a private conversation, so she went with them, ignoring any dish washing chores. Bobby helped his mother clear away a few plates but then he went after the others.

Uncle and Cavanah had taken the chairs, so Kelly was sitting on the grass. Bobby took a seat beside her.

Coming late as she was, Kelly had to catch up to the conversation that was going on.

Cavanah was saying, "... Dad's stone wasn't recovered from the plane crash or if it was nobody ever admitted to finding it."

"A stone?" Bobby asked.

"Yeah, you know about the rocks, right?" Uncle asked him. "You have a rock, don't you?"

"Yeah, I've got a black rock," Bobby said looking at Kelly.

"Oh," said Uncle, as if he understood what a black rock meant.

Kelly didn't look at Bobby but he could see that she had a definite smirk on her face.

"That was a tradition that me and Jimmy Nickles started when we decided to have the club," Uncle said. "Well, yeah," he went on, "his real name was James Cavanah but everybody called him Jimmy Nickles because of the rock."

"He was my father," Cavanah explained.

"My dad's rock had some very peculiar properties," Cavanah told them. "It could float coins. Dimes and nickles but nothing larger than that. It wouldn't do pennies at all."

"That's no lie," Uncle said. "I thought it was a magic trick until he showed me how it worked. Damnedest thing."

"Where did he get the stone?" Kelly asked.

"Just found it in the desert, he said," Uncle told them.

"It was shaped like an ice cream cone," Cavanah said. "My dad kept it in a hollowed out pocket watch. He never went anywhere without it."

Kelly looked at Uncle and almost blurted out, "just like yours," but didn't when she saw the look on Uncle's face, like a 'don't say nuthin' stern warning.

And, that was okay with Kelly. She would just add that to the list of secrets that Uncle would tell her when he was ready to reveal everything that needed to be disclosed to his top level agent.

"What color was it," Bobby asked Cavanah.

"Ivory, off-white but with a little tinge of yellow at one end," Cavanah told him.

"I've got a rock like that," Bobby said. "Spylgyn gave it to me."

Now Kelly looked at him, like saying "What! When did that happen?"

"Can I see it?" Cavanah asked him.

Bobby dug it out of his pocket and handed it to him.

"Who's got a nickel?" Cavanah asked.

Uncle went through his pocket and found some coins. He gave a nickel to Cavanah who held it between his thumb and forefinger just above the table. Then with his other hand he placed the rock directly underneath the coin. Once he let go, the nickle hovered almost an inch in the air above the stone.

"How can it do that?" Kelly asked.

"I don't know, it just does," Cavanah said.

He did the trick again with a dime to prove that it wasn't a magician's illusion.

"Okay, okay, that's just, like really weird," Bobby said.

"Magnetic?" Kelly asked.

"No, as far as I know, it only works on those coins, nothing else," Cavanah told her. "I don't know that my father ever tried any foreign coins or other metals."

"It does something else," Cavanah told them.

Cavanah set the rock down and took his hand away. Nothing happened and all the while Cavanah was smiling as if he was satisfied with a well-played joke. Everyone was quietly waiting in anticipation.

"If you leave the rock where it is, undisturbed, it could take five minutes or an hour but it will slowly turn," Cavanah claimed, "to point in that direction." He used a good finger to show them where north-east was.

The geologist had everyone's attention.

"Oh, oh," Kelly asked, "can I hold it?" She took it before anyone could say 'no'.

"I didn't know it could do that," Uncle said.

"It doesn't always move that way," said Cavanah.

Kelly was admiring the shape, hue and color of the stone like another person would handle a rare and precious jewel of enormous value.

"It's a compass. It turns in the direction of the grotto," ventured Kelly looking oddly at Bobby's stone as if she could will it to move faster.

"Yes," Cavanah responded, "very clever, Kelly."

Bobby reached his hand to Kelly, kindly asking for his rock back. Surprisingly, she gave it to him willingly but he knew that it would be a shared artifact between the two of them from now on.

"So, what happens now?" Kelly asked.

"Nothing," Cavanah said as he stood up. "I've got a plane to catch and I'm late."

Cavanah shook hands with Uncle and Bobby, then offered a final one for Kelly. She took his hand and squeezed it as hard as she could, hoping that he would understand the not so subtle meaning.

51 Zoom!

Cavanah was leaning against the fender of his jeep when Kelly ran around from the back of Uncle's house. He had waited for her.

"Okay, what?" Cavanah asked Kelly.

"When you go back down, in the grotto, I want to go with you," Kelly said to him.

"Hunkle won't let me go back down. He's flat out against any exploration," Cavanah said to her.

"That won't stop you," Kelly argued. "You'll find another way down. There has to be other entrances."

"How old are you, Kelly?" Cavanah asked her.

"16," Kelly lied.

"Even if I could find another way down to the grotto, you're too young," Cavanah said. "I couldn't take you with me."

"So, what happens if I get there first, before you?" Kelly asked.

"If... if I was considering going back down there, it wouldn't happen for at least a year," Cavanah told her, "maybe longer."

"I'll be 17, almost 18," Kelly said.

"How much influence do you have with Hunkle?" Cavanah asked.

Kelly didn't respond to that question, just looked at him with her twinkle eyes and a crooked smile.

"How long can you hold your breath?" Cavanah asked.

"Longer than you, I'll bet," she replied.

Cavanah let out a big sigh and said, "you need to start training. Rock climbing with bare hands, rappel and scuba diving. Can you do all that?"

Kelly nodded, knowing that she would find a way.

Cavanah reached into his jacket pocket and produced a plastic card that was, conveniently, right there.

"This is my private phone number, SAT phone and my email," Cavanah said to her. "Don't give it out to anyone else." He handed it to Kelly.

Kelly took the card and put it in her back pocket without looking at it.

"Anything else?" Cavanah asked.

"I saw another creature at the cliffs," Kelly said. "It wasn't like Spylgyn, he's amphibian. It was something different."

"What was it?" Cavanah asked her.

"I don't know," Kelly told him, "Maybe a monkey?"

Cavanah looked at her like she had just made that up to keep him interested.

"I'm not lying. It was an ape, or something like that," Kelly insisted.

"I'll be back next summer, Kelly," Cavanah said. "You need to be ready."

After Cavanah had driven away, Kelly went back to say a quick goodbye to Uncle, Bobby and Jenny. Alice was chasing butterflies or some other flying insect and could not be bothered with farewells at the moment, it seemed. Uncle gave her a new set of keys to the spa when she asked. He didn't say anything about the pool arena but she had a feeling that the door to that area wasn't entry restricted anymore.

Martin was absent when Kelly entered the tactical room but Dan, Andy and Pegs were there and all of them were busy on assignments. Apparently, there was still much to do concerning strange events and phenomenon at Inyo, even without mentioning the Hulamar Cliffs and the Ingling subterranean enclave. Kelly went past the other UFObians without so much as a 'how do you do' and hurried to the pool arena. The door was locked but one of the new keys opened it easily and entry was granted. Kelly went inside and turned the latch so that no one could follow her. She walked calmly all the way around to the diving platform, climbed the ladder and stood as if ready to plunge into the empty pool.

Kelly raised her arms as high as she could and shouted, "Zoom!"

52   No Truth At All

This is not a true story – well, almost not.

As Uncle would tell it, "why, that's just a made up story for little children who want to believe in fairies and uni-corns. No truth to it at all." Then he'd smile at you, maybe even wink if you're the right person to do that to.

There is no massive cavern beneath the Inyo Desert in Arizona. There is no underground ocean deep below the Hulamar Creek Basin. So, don't go there looking for any. There are camp sites near those cliffs for day strolls and hikes, picnics. After dark, you can watch the stars amble across the night sky and listen to the quiet, mysterious sounds that the desert whispers. There's even a creek now that comes out of the mountains, even when it hasn't rained for quite a while. Some campers have said that if you soak your tired feet in that surprisingly cool creek water after a long hike, that stimulating water will replenish you and give you enough energy to go even farther on your journey.

There is an Inyo Spa and Health Resort and it's open to tourists and travelers from all over the world. If you ever decide to go there for relaxation and fun at the swimming pool, take a massage from Aaron or a comforting soak in the mud baths, any attendant will tell you that there is no source water that will heal your aches and pains. "That's just a myth," they will say, as if memorized from a written script. That same script would have other phrases and comments to dissuade anyone from asking too many questions of a sensitive nature. "No, there are no secret rooms hidden away for private sessions, no matter what you've heard from a 'friend'." There have been a few who try the wiggling fingers gesture but almost all of them get it wrong.

The 'Lost Gas Station' out in the desert is also open again. You can get gas or oil for your car and there's always plenty of water if your radiator's gone dry. It's called Station 3 by the UFObians. They have a nice selection of postcards, souvenirs and various snacks and soft drinks. There is also a 'quarry' bin near the check-out counter where you can choose stones and rocks that have been gathered from the Inyo Desert. The first stone is free – after that they're only 50¢ each. Buy a few, who knows? You might get lucky. The ice-cold bottled water is special. When customers buy a bottle of 'Blue Grotto Purified Water' on their way out, they often come back in before leaving to get more. It tastes that good and is very refreshing on a hot day trip through the Inyo Desert.

There's no such thing as Inglings, Dorfoos and Nurlings. Just like fairies, these creatures are made up things, not real. Wouldn't it be nice if there were such creatures in the world, though?

One last thing, Pete Selby's 'land submarine' is real but no one who has access to it refers to the device as that. It has been identified by experts to be a IEVUO, or 'EVO', as they call it at Area 51. To date, it is the only Inner Earth Vessel of Unknown Origin in captivity.

a final note for the reader

As the author of this story, it was necessary for me to take certain liberties with the speech patterns, physical signals and telepathic imagery that Spylgyn and the other Inglings use as a multi-level language. Their voice is unlike anything that I have ever heard and so, I had great difficulty about just how to express that for the reader.

Spylgyn's vocal intonations are a combination of chirps, whistles, clicks and the bubble noises. Those familiar sounds were the easy ones to describe but there are so many other sounds that confounded me. Inglings do not speak in a way that can be readily understood by humans, just as we are unable to decipher dolphin and whale conversations.

It wasn't until years later that Spylgyn and I would have a real understanding when we were finally able to talk and communicate with each other on a level that was pleasing for both of us but I'm getting ahead of myself.

The musical quality when hearing the amphibian songs – nothing, I have no way to give anyone a description of the joy when hearing those beautiful sounds performed. Just let's say that a caveman suddenly came across a seashell lying on the white sand of a prehistoric beach and because that prehistoric man heard noises coming from inside the funnel, he put it to his ear and heard Jill's Theme by Morricone or Silvestri's Feather. How would he describe that beautiful music to his tribe? He wouldn't be able to, not so they could understand. Yes, those other cave people could listen to the music and decide for themselves. So, you must listen for yourselves to the Ingling songs to know what I mean. Maybe that will happen one day, I don't know. But, it would be a foolhardy task for me to try to describe Spylgyn's language and music with mere words on a page. I cannot. I can only say that if you could hear the Ingling sounds and songs, it would be one of the most fascinating and wonderful experiences of your life.

The arm and hand gestures used by Spylgyn to convey meanings to the Oolongs is equally complex, so I have made that simpler just for the sake of not complicating the storyline.

I hope you, the reader, will forgive these frailty's used by this author. If not, place a thumb on your chin and a finger on your nose. I'm not going to tell you what that means. I'm pretty sure you can guess.

KCBryant is a pseudonym for the real person

Kenneth Wayne Caldwell

and is being used here solely to
shield the identity of the true author.

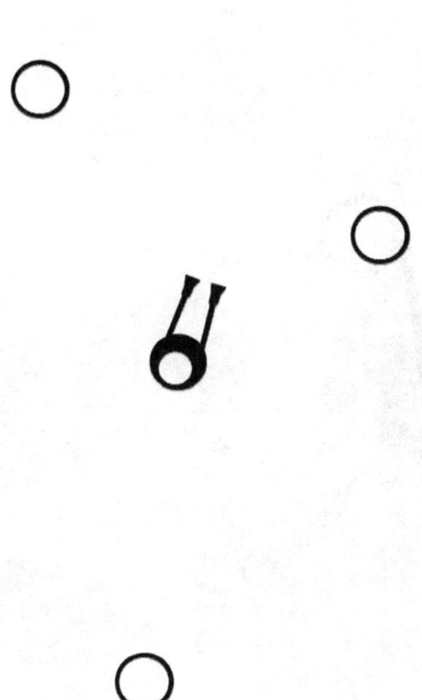

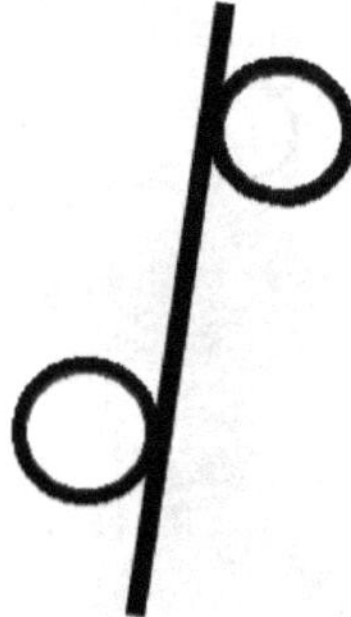

* 9 7 9 8 2 1 8 3 0 9 3 3 6 *